INTO THE LION'S DEN

THE DANIEL FAMILY OF AFRICA

A novel inspired by true events

ANGELA D'EGVILLE

ISBN print: 978-0-620-63189-1
ISBN e-pub: 978-0-620-63190-7

Design and pre-press production: Patricia Crain @ www.empressa.co
Cover design: Patricia Crain @ www.empressa.co
Illustrations: Rob Owen
Digital conversions: MYeBook @ www.myebook.online

In honour of

SAMPSON O'MALIA DANIEL

and

AMELIA MARGARITH D'EGVILLE

This book is dedicated to my daughters – Simone and Danielle.

KEEP IN TOUCH

anjidegville@gmail.com

https://www.facebook.com/groups/1526828904206145

anji_degville

oured to keep dates and facts accurate. Some characters were real people who lived in that era, while others are fictional.

It is a love story. It is a tale of the power of man to overcome adversity and win – sometimes. It is a story of the fight for survival of varied cultures in an unforgiving land – each fighting for the same right to life, land and liberty.

Every culture has different ideals and their own ideas about how best to obtain them. They have differing perceptions of what freedom means. Throughout history we hear various voices crying out to be heard. The Daniel family, like other migrants to southern Africa, experienced these differences first-hand. From necessity, they merged their own culture and identities with that of others, not only for the sake of their survival, but also for the sake of peace and progress. Colonialists came from a different world and culture, and as such, imposed themselves and their ways on the lands they inhabited, in a way which was both foreign and unprecedented to the local people.

To this day, South Africa remains a cultural melting pot, as the immense diversity of peoples who call the land home continue to strive for common ground. In 1996, Former President of South Africa, Nelson Mandela, had the following to say in his speech to re-dedicate the Monument building and Memorial dedicated to the 1820 Settlers, after it was burnt down in 1994. It overlooks present day Makhanda (formerly Grahamstown):

> "*There are monuments which stand as mute pointers to a fixed and ever-receding past. Devoid of life, they have little meaning outside the history books and the minds of learned people. This National Monument is not of that kind … Pawns in a larger game, the 1820 Settlers came to the part of Africa at the behest of an imperial power seeking to use its own poor and unemployed in a bid to advance conquest and imperial ambitions.*
>
> *Though their own impulse to freedom rendered them largely unsuitable for that task, they were nevertheless caught up on the wrong side of history, unable or unwilling to acknowledge as*

equals those into whose homeland they had been implanted. The founders of the monument two decades ago sought to redeem that limitation, without denying it, by dedicating the monument to the universal application of the ideals which the English Settlers cherished for themselves. Today, our country a democracy, and our people masters of their own destiny, we are re-dedicating the monument to the universality of those ideals at a time when we are working together to make them a reality for all." – ***Former President Nelson Mandela***

What follows are the reminiscences of one such 1820 British Settler family – the Daniel family of Africa, who dared to venture into the lion's den.

1

THE IRISH JEWELLER

which, I am famished!"

Recognising his father's suitcase, Sampson collected it from the porter. The two men walked up the cobbled lane past Hillwood House and into Gote Lane, joining up with High Street. There was no mistaking them as brothers. Peter was six foot one, and Sampson was not much shorter. Both had piercing crystal-blue eyes and thick dark eyebrows. Their dark hair was in stark contrast to their fair complexions.

The summer sun warmed their backs as they headed to the Priory for breakfast. Peter chatted about life on the home front and his jewellery business. Some of the passengers from the ferry walked ahead down the street to the Staghead Hotel, to check in to their lodgings. Otherwise, all was quiet.

It was a Sunday after all.

During breakfast at the Priory, the conversation turned to politics and religion.

"Ireland is in turmoil. There's widespread famine and conflict between the churches," said Peter, noisily eating his oats porridge before moving on to his poached eggs.

He reported that the violent outbursts between groups and opposing families were becoming more frequent. The increase in the demand for Irish labour in England, with the constant talk of the coming industrial growth, had undoubtedly caused many Irish citizens to seek better living and working prospects, in Scotland and in England. Agricultural depression, as a result of the Napoleonic Wars, depleted farming opportunities, and Irish labourers were heading for London in their droves.

The vicar nodded in agreement and said it was indeed a sorry state of affairs. He confirmed that many Irish Protestants had taken refuge in England to escape the abusive Catholic rule. The brothers' uncles were Protestant vicars at the parish of Swords, just outside Dublin. Their advice to the boys' father was to send his sons to Scotland due to the iron hand of the current rulers.

"I believe my father made a wise decision sending young Sampson here to complete his jewellery apprenticeship. Once he is qualified, we can go into business together," Peter said.

Sampson looked across the table and smiled back. He never questioned the judgment of either his father or his big brother. He had vowed to himself to excel in his chosen profession. He would make them proud.

Later, Sampson persuaded Peter to take a walk around the village. It was a fine afternoon and they strolled along the High Street. Peter chatted to Sampson about living in Edinburgh. He lectured him about being diligent with his studies and making the most of opportunities.

"Count your blessings, lad. Not everyone has the chance to start working life in another country. You are lucky to study the trade under a master jeweller."

They walked along the twisted, cobbled High Street, and caught glimpses of the seashore between the rows of terraced houses. High-pitched tiled roofs with attic windows spewed smoke from multiple chimney pots.

"You need to learn to turn a penny for yourself, lad," lectured Peter. "Also remember not everyone is trustworthy. Be discerning with whom you make friends – although remember not every stranger is a scoundrel. Some strangers can become close friends."

Sampson soaked up the moments spent with his sibling. He knew Peter would soon be heading back to Ireland. They reached Hawes Inn at the east end of town. Peter placed his arm around Sampson's shoulder and pulled him close.

"Come on my lad, let's go in for a pint," he grinned, showing a set of slightly uneven, but healthy, white teeth.

"Or two…" thought Sampson, raising an eyebrow.

The following morning, the two brothers caught the stagecoach bound for Edinburgh. Peter spent a few days there with Sampson, settling him into Thomas Gladstone's boarding establishment, before heading off to London to meet with a prospective business partner.

Sampson spent the next two years completing his trade in Edinburgh. During this time, he lived at Gladstone's boarding house. The old stone building, built in 1617, had four floors of accommodation

"I wear rubies in everything – pendants, earrings and rings. I would wear one in my belly button if I could!" she quipped, flinging one of the tassels on her outfit negligently over her left shoulder.

Her comment and her mischievous chuckle had made Sampson blush. He felt a red glow rise in his cheeks. Lady Pembroke asked to see some of his latest hatpin designs.

"I've heard a lot about your new fashion items, Mr Daniel," she said, "Do you have any with rubies in them?"

Sampson brought out a black velvet pincushion into which a dozen or so hatpins had been stuck, like bejewelled quills on the back of a porcupine. Lady Pembroke pulled out a silver pin with an intricate design of silver thread and pearls, exclaiming, "Is this one of your new Irish designs, Mr Daniel?"

"Uh, yes, Madam," he replied.

The bright yellow ostrich feather in her bonnet, which swayed from side to side as she moved her head, distracted him.

"I am working on a few others, but I will certainly create one which will include rubies, especially for you."

"Oh, I rather fancy this one with the pearl. I'll take it."

Pleased with this unexpected sale, Sampson brought out her delicate flower-shaped ruby pendant, pointing out the tiny claw he had repaired. Lady Pembroke was delighted. He held the pendant gently in the soft cloth between his thumb and middle fingers and gave it a final polish before placing the pieces of jewellery into separate velvet drawstring bags.

He was distracted yet again. This time it was the ring of the doorbell. Diverting his attention from his customers, he looked towards the shop entrance. He stared at the young girl standing in the doorway, and she stared right back, smiling confidently. The attraction was instant and their eyes locked. Her presence caught him off guard. He was not sure if it was her exquisite youthful beauty or her innocence. She was a classic beauty – nothing like any of the English or Irish girls he knew. He had never seen her before.

The depth of his gaze from those intense blue eyes astounded Amelia d'Egville. She had expected a much older man to be behind the counter. His dense black lashes created the effect of charcoal eyeliner on his eyelids. There were subtle silver streaks at the temples of his dark hair. She dropped her eyes coyly and stepped inside onto the carpeted floor. The heavy wooden door swung closed, and the bell rang for a second time as it clicked shut. Sampson smiled broadly, greeting his new customer warmly.

"I will only be a moment," he said, reluctantly shifting his attention back to the older customers. There was a slight unsteadiness in his hands as adrenalin coursed through him. His body was on fire with feelings he had never experienced before. He desperately hoped Mrs Pembroke would not notice. Amelia waited politely for the two women to complete their business. She observed how dashing the jeweller looked in his dark tailored suit and white cravat. Mrs Pembroke concluded her transaction, paying for the repaired pendant and the pearl hatpin, before popping them into her reticule.

"I look forward to calling in and seeing your newest designs on my next visit to London, Mr Daniel."

Sampson responded with a weak smile, "I look forward to your next visit, ladies."

The two older women nodded to the girl and walked towards the door, stopping to admire some expensive jewellery pieces in the display cabinets. Amelia stepped aside and approached the highly polished counter where Sampson was standing, her long skirt rustling on the thick carpet. She acknowledged the well-dressed women politely as they passed her.

"Good day, Sir," she smiled, looking into Sampson's eyes. She caught herself staring at them again, trying to determine whether the unusual eyeliner was natural or not. "My brother, James d'Egville, has asked me to deliver these theatre tickets to a Mr Sampson Daniel Esquire."

Placing both hands on the counter, more to compose himself than to steady himself, Sampson felt the blood rise in his cheeks. He was trying to keep his rapidly beating heart under control and prevent the hands by way of introduction and Sampson took an immediate liking to the man.

"How is your new business venture coming on, Mr Daniel?" Mulligan asked as he passed him a pint of beer. Sampson leant forward as John Kemp lit his cigar.

"Considering the current state of affairs in the country and the recession, there is still a big demand for quality jewellery pieces. I have had numerous requests from aristocrats for my unique hatpin designs and precious stone teardrop earrings. They are designs my brother, Peter, and I brought them over from Dublin. I also make costume jewellery for the Drury Lane theatre."

"Good news," beamed Mulligan.

"I'll become your best customer one day when I stop sailing long enough to find myself a wife."

The young men laughed, raising their beer tankards in agreement.

"Speaking of wives," Sampson said, "is anyone here acquainted with the French dancing family, the d'Egvilles, from Lyons? Peter d'Egville is the local ballet master and his son, James, is the choreographer at the Drury Lane Theatre."

"I know of them," said Mulligan. "My sister is at the convent with the d'Egville sisters. Amelia and her sister … I cannot think of her name right now. My sister takes dance classes with the ballet master in Broad Street every Saturday morning. Pretty girl, Amelia. Why do you ask?"

"Oh, no particular reason," said Sampson absent-mindedly. The picture of the exquisite Amelia filled his thoughts.

He made up his mind to see her again, and soon.

CHAPTER 3

DRURY LANE THEATRE, 1804

The large theatre foyer was abuzz with excited chatter. Londoners were out in their finery to attend the opening night of James Harvey d'Egville's new pantomime, *Hercules and Deianara.*

Standing at just over six feet, Sampson Daniel was taller than most of the theatregoers. He looked dapper in his dark tails, tailored pin-stripe trousers and white silk cravat. He had an air of calm confidence about him. Recognising a few of his regular customers, he acknowledged them politely with a smile and a nod. Sampson saw Mr St John-Ayre. He was not at all surprised that the lady on his arm was not the same one who had recently accompanied him to the jewellers. He greeted Monsieur d'Egville and his wife. It was the first time Sampson had seen Amelia's mother. She was an elegant woman who carried herself with grace and poise. She, too, was a dancing teacher.

By now, Sampson had settled in London. He felt privileged to be moving in the city's higher echelons. It was good for business. The invitation from James could not have come at a better time. It was his chance to see Amelia again. Her role tonight was minor, but he was determined to see her backstage later.

Amidst the background din and chatter of patrons in the theatre foyer, he found himself staring at the full-colour poster advertising the show. He admired the detail in the artist's rendering of the image. It intrigued him. Draped with a spotted leopard skin over his shoulder, a well-muscled Hercules hoisted a fair Deianara above the ground, safely

II

THE IRISH JEWELLER AND THE FRENCH DANCER

guests and the couple loved to socialise.

One afternoon in the summer of 1806, while in the sunny drawing room, Julia heard their two beagles and three spaniels barking excitedly as they raced up the driveway towards the big house she had inherited. The dogs always ran ahead of her husband, who invariably walked his horse home from a hunt, especially after a long day out. With toddler Benjamin in tow, Julia ambled outside to the stables to meet him. The sounds of dogs barking and the crunching of horses' hooves on the ground excited Benjamin, who always expressed delight at his stepfather's homecoming.

Edward dismounted and the groom took his horse. The exhausted dogs were already lapping up water from the wrought iron bath in front of the stables, panting to cool down. He flashed Julia a wide smile that, as usual, melted her heart.

"How was the hunt, darling?" Julia asked, eyeing the four pheasants hanging from his saddlebags.

"An exhilarating ride today, my dear," he replied, hoisting Ben onto his hip when the toddler held his arms out.

"Lord Barry cornered a fox and managed to shoot it at twenty paces. The dogs went berserk. Mystery took the fox by the throat and shook it like a rag doll. He then stood guard over the animal, convinced it was his kill and his alone. He is still a bit young and definitely needs more training."

He bent down to stroke the young beagle.

"I shot a few pheasants for the pot," he continued, holding up the bundle of colourful birds.

Julia admired him. He might not have a clue about business, but was rugged and passionate about the outdoors. He spent most of his days outside, instructing the gardeners, cleaning the horse tack, oiling his numerous guns or grooming his horses. She could not envisage Edward sitting at a study desk all day.

Oftentimes, when she looked for him, he would be sitting outside on the lawn, sketching trees or buildings. He really was a talented artist and although he was good at many things, he was unable to focus long enough to master any of them.

Edward took Julia's hand and led her to the wooden bench next to the fountain in front of the house. The pretty hedgerow around it was neatly trimmed and the sound of water was soothing. It was Julia's favourite place in the garden. In summer, she would spend hours there, soaking up the sun, watching the boys play in the meadow.

Edward put Ben down and the couple watched as he eagerly dipped his hands into the water.

Julia's husband loudly cleared his throat. The serenity of the moment was broken. Julia knew he had something of importance to tell her. Her instinct told her it would be something to do with money. It was unusual for Edward to break away from his devotion to his horses and make time for his wife.

After a short pause, he broke the silence.

"Lord Aiken was with us on the ride today. You remember, we met him and his wife at a dinner party at the McGrath's house, last week?"

"Mmmm … I do. His wife is the blonde lady who drank too much wine and had to be escorted to bed by the butler."

"The self-same one," answered Edward.

"Well, Aiken and McGrath own a shipping company in Dublin and they are looking for assistance with an investment. I have their proposal. I have agreed to be a sleeping partner and I will be entitled to dividends from the profits of the company."

Edward then went on to explain the details. Julia was sceptical. They had a big, comfortable home on a large property near Dublin with horses, stables and servants, and Julia was aware of the importance of protecting their capital. Nonetheless, she listened intently to her husband's talk of utilising her inheritance for a financial business gamble.

"Edward, you know I support your love of horses and hunting. We have a busy social life. A private governess tutors my sons. I am reluctant to do anything that will jeopardise this way of life. Give me some time to think about this. I will write to Peter and Sampson for advice." How she wished her two brothers were still living in Dublin.

Friday, 24 February 1809

It was closing time at Daniel and Gaubert Jewellers. Business had been slow for most of the day. Sampson kept himself busy working on the selection of costume jewellery for the forthcoming Forty Thieves pantomime at the Drury Lane Theatre. He re-read his sister's letter for the third time. He found it hard to comprehend the enormity of her financial crisis. It distressed him to know that Julia was under duress resulting from Turvey's stupidity. He looked up when the doorbell rang. Pushing his chair back from the workbench, he rose reluctantly to greet his customer. He was in no mood to be pleasant. It was Peter, and he was suddenly pleased for the company. At least he could share the burden of their sister's sad situation with him. Sampson did not recognise the woman on Peter's arm. It certainly was not his wife, Eliza.

"Greetings, brother. I thought you were out of town for a few days." said Sampson, raising an inquisitive eyebrow.

"Good day to you, lad," said Peter in his broad Irish accent, "I was just in the area and I thought I'd come and see how you're doing with the new jewellery order for the Drury Lane Theatre!"

Peter was behaving rather strangely, Sampson thought.

"Oh," Peter added, almost as an afterthought, "may I introduce Ann Mitchley – the new au pair for our children and assistant for Eliza." Knowing Peter's wife to be poorly in health, Sampson understood the need for a family carer.

Sampson stepped forward and extended his hand respectfully to the attractive woman whom he guessed to be about twenty years old – at least thirteen years Peter's junior. She had an open oval-shaped face with large doe eyes and long lashes. He instantly noticed the fullness of her lips. When she greeted him back, her whole face lit up, showing perfectly formed teeth.

"A pleasure to make your acquaintance," he smiled knowingly. Sampson knew his brother well. He could see that this had already gone beyond simply a business relationship. It was most unlike Peter to introduce his brother to his employees, let alone bring them to town with him.

"Um, would you excuse us a minute, Ms Mitchley?" said Sampson clearing his throat. "I have some business to discuss with Mr Daniel."

"Would you mind watching the front of the shop for us, Ann?" Peter asked, the woman's first name slipping off his tongue quite casually. Ann nodded and politely walked away from the brothers.

The two men went into the back room and closed the door.

"Brother!" he exclaimed, "What on earth has gotten into you?"

"Don't say anything, lad. I am in love with the woman and there is nothing I can do about it!" said Peter, putting his finger against his pursed lips. He continued, "I love my Eliza. I do. She is the mother of my children, but as you are aware, she is not a very capable person. This young woman does things for me that makes my heart sing. And, what's more, she wants to do things with me."

"You are treading on dangerous ground, Peter. What about Eliza and your children?"

"Oh, I would never do anything foolish to jeopardise my marriage. I am extremely discreet. You are the only one who knows about this."

Sampson pledged his silence and support to Peter. He knew better than to try to convince his brother otherwise. Besides, he had other more pressing issues on his mind.

He told Peter of their sister's financial woes. Peter immediately agreed to help Julia. It sounded as though this Turvey fellow was a bit of a cad. But if Julia loved him, then they needed to rally together to help. He would introduce Turvey to the Men's Club and the Ale-houses. Sampson had already taken care of the accommodation. Peter agreed to look out for a position for Turvey as a draper or drawing master.

Just then, Ann Mitchley strode boldly into the room.

"Oh, Peter, please come and have a look! I've just seen the most delightful piece."

She openly took him by the hand and pulled him playfully to the front of the shop. Sampson watched as the couple gazed into each other's eyes. Ann giggled as Peter pressed the brooch against her breast, letting his hand linger there for a moment.

CHAPTER 7

1810 – THE STREETS OF LONDON

"Take yer skirt off! Let's see yer booty!"

The crowd of inquisitive bystanders outside 225 Piccadilly egged on the clearly inebriated loudmouth as he waved his big, grimy hands in the air.

"Yeah! Let's see what the women of the Dark Continent look like!" shouted another.

A number of finely groomed aristocrats on business in the city sporting top hats and tails, hung back on the outskirts of the jeering crowd – politely aloof, yet equally curious. Twenty-six-year-old jeweller Sampson Daniel and his wife Amelia stopped to see what was causing all the fuss.

Unable to see over the tall men in top hats, Amelia let go of her husband's arm and pressed through the front of the leering crowd. She stopped dead in her tracks, stunned at the inhumane spectacle before her. The exhibitor displayed a scantily dressed young woman as if she were a wild beast.

"Ladies and Gentlemen," cooed the keeper, "I present to you Saartjie Baartman, the Hottentot Venus from Darkest Africa."

On cue, the honey-skin coloured woman with short, jet-black, wool-like hair, dropped the sheer fabric covering her body and turned around slowly. There was an audible gasp from the audience, as the young Khoikhoi woman from Africa exposed her bulging buttocks and privates for all to see.

"Dance, Saartjie!" Instructed her captor eagerly, oblivious to the woman's obvious discomfort.

The woman stood with her naked back to the crowd and wiggled her oversized backside from side to side, much to the delight of the predominantly male onlookers. There was a collective gasp. Some pointed at the compromised position of the poor woman's private parts. Some men discreetly steered their female companions away from the spectacle.

A smattering of women bystanders peeked over the top of their fans. Amelia was incensed that a woman be debased in this manner. She had been in the theatre and seen naked women before in the dressing rooms, but never had she seen such outrageous exploitation of another human being. She felt exceedingly uncomfortable and the public exposure of the woman's nakedness came as a shock.

For a brief moment, the two women locked eyes.

Some of the crowd threw money into an upturned top hat before the handler lead his live "exhibit" away. Amelia defiantly found her way back through the onlookers to where Sampson stood.

"She doesn't deserve this, it's not right, Sampson," Amelia whispered with tears in her eyes. "She is a woman, not a thing."

Saddened, Amelia followed her husband. The spectacle had rattled her. She had seen something in the other woman's dark eyes. The passionate fervour of innocence that had once burned in those eyes had clearly long since died. What lay behind them was a vacant, unquenchable stare. A fatalistic acceptance of her powerless plight.

"Come, *ma cherie*," he replied, protectively interlocking arms with his distraught wife and leading her away, "this is how things are. There is nothing we can do." They walked on as Sampson's thoughts turned to his appointment with Julia's husband, scheduled for later in the day.

Edward Ford Turvey was late. Sampson waited at least forty-five minutes before he showed up. He was annoyed with the man and he had not even met him yet. Even though the unexpected exhibition had delayed them, Sampson and Amelia were in time to meet Turvey at 32 Southampton Road. Julia had warned him about Edward's tardiness.

CHAPTER 8

THE SETTLER APPLICATION AND FORMING OF THE PARTY

Colonel Richard Collins had proposed the introduction of British settlers on the south bank of the Fish River on the eastern frontier of Southern Africa, believing this would reduce the expense of additional soldiers to the area and ultimately, gain additional colonial ground for the British government. He proposed that the newcomers would form a human buffer between the indigenous cattle herders and the greater colonised Cape.

In 1814 the Cape Colony was officially ceded to the British under the treaty of Versailles, which ended the Napoleonic Wars in Europe. Britain formally purchased the Cape from the Dutch for six million pounds. Lord Charles Somerset was appointed the Governor of the Cape Colony.

In the final months of 1817, the last of the Dutch *trekboers* who were earlier occupiers of the land, abandoned their holdings bordering the Fish River, unable to withstand the frequent Xhosa attacks on their homesteads and the theft of their livestock. The unwillingness of the Xhosa chieftains to allow them to settle on the land drove them inland, to places like Uitenhage and beyond.

The power struggle on the Eastern Cape frontier raged on between the sovereign government, hell-bent on staking an additional claim on these foreign shores and the indigenous Xhosa tribe who retaliated to prevent this from happening. Ongoing negotiations between the British troops stationed in the Zuurveld and local Xhosa chiefs to secure the area, failed.

In the summer of 1819, Xhosa warriors, under the leadership of a Christian convert named Makhanda, advanced across the Great Fish River into the Zuurveld. Their intention, to drive out a small settlement of people occupying around thirty dwellings in Grahamstown. The tribesmen wanted their land and their livestock back from the invaders. They were angered that the troops had crossed the river and confiscated thousands of their cattle. The locals had once moved their herds about freely, until the colonialists put up imaginary boundaries and pushed them back across the river by force.

Makhanda, a self-professed prophet, believed he had a chance to defeat the land invaders.

"The God's will be on our side and the British bullets will turn to water," he confidently told his Chief, Ndlambe.

The day before the attack, the British commander Lieutenant Colonel Thomas Willshire received a message from Makhanda declaring an act of war with the backing of Chief Ndlambe.

"I will breakfast with you on Wednesday," the Xhosa leader warned. The message was simple but precise. The threat was sinister, but Makhanda underestimated the fire power of the British soldiers.

"Everything will be ready for you," Willshire replied.

In broad daylight on Wednesday, 22 April 1819, Makhanda led an attack on Grahamstown with a mass of more than six thousand Xhosa warriors, armed with assegais and spears. The battle for control of the small settlement broiled under the African sky.

Willshire organised his three hundred and fifty soldiers into a military formation on the parade ground and waited. Amongst them were members of the Royal African Rifles and Khoikhoi trained marksmen. Scores of seething locals poured over the tops of the slopes and descended on the town, spears and assegais raised in ferocious attack. As the screaming, animal-skin clad warriors ran at the square formation of uniformed soldiers, the trained military men waited. Then, on command, they opened fire, rapidly killing over 1000 Xhosa evening to solicit names of other interested applicants. Through Julia, Edward finally convinced the brothers to join the scheme. Julia still had an uneasy feeling about his hair-brained idea. First, Edward did not have two pennies to rub together. Secondly, he was not making ends meet as a draper, and he only dabbled in architectural drawing. One of his only customers, Lady Louisa Ford, paid for two of his paintings, saying she hoped it would contribute to his trip to Africa. Julia rather wished Edward's uncle, the Baronet Sir Edward Ford, would talk some sense into the man.

Edinburgh, SCOTLAND

Sampson and Amelia loved the Edinburgh lifestyle. On weekends, they walked to the market through Cowgate, just as Sampson had done when he was apprenticed there, almost fifteen years before. Edinburgh was a vibrant, bustling city and the New Town area had grown considerably. The couple and their children were regulars at St Andrews parish and often picnicked in the town square after church on Sundays.

In April, the couple received an urgent letter from Julia regarding the proposed Settler scheme. Sampson had caught wind of the British Government's idea through the local newspaper. He had not given it another thought until receiving Julia's pleading letter.

Mrs J. Turvey
32 Southampton Street
London, England

Mr S Daniel
New Town
Edinburgh, Scotland

25 April 1819

My dearest Sampson and Amelia

It has been a long, cold winter in London and we are all looking forward to the coming sunshine.

We are all well here. Mary, Eliza, Edward, Louisa and our latest addition, George, are all fine and growing up far too quickly. Mary is almost ten years old. She gets on very well with my Benjamin, who is growing into a handsome lad.

The main purpose of my letter is to tell you Edward has decided to make application to join the new emigration scheme proposed by the Government. He has applied through Catharine, the Dowager Countess of Liverpool, for approval as a Party Head. He has already sent in his forms and wondered whether you, Sampson and Amelia, would be interested in joining us to make up the Party. Edward has already approached Peter, who is considering the proposal.

I have enclosed some newspaper cuttings and information. Read through it and let me know whether you will be interested.

There is great excitement here in London about the possibility of sailing to Africa early next year. Edward feels there will be opportunities to make good money. You know how Edward loves the outdoors and adventure, although he is not very clever when it comes to money matters. He despises city life. He is not doing very well in his position as a draper.

CHAPTER 9

THE 1820 BRITISH SETTLER SCHEME

The British Government received over 90 000 applications for the settler scheme, approving only 4 000 of these. Edward Ford Turvey's group was among those accepted. It included Sampson and Amelia Daniel, Peter Daniel and his wife Eliza, their half-brother John Nivens and Peter's mistress, Ann Mitchley, who had her own children fathered by Peter.

It was an emotional time for Sampson and Amelia. With mixed feelings, they wrapped up their life in Edinburgh to move back to London where they were to join other prospective settlers. Sampson sold his jewellery business and home, Glen Lyons. He left the task of selecting personal belongings and furniture to Amelia. He held his tongue when Amelia chose her piano, but he knew it brought her much joy.

On their last Sunday in Edinburgh, the family went to St Andrews. The melodious sounds of the pipe organ played as the congregation sang Sampson's favourite hymn, *Rock of Ages.* At thirty-three-years old, his throat constricted and he fought back tears, as he looked around at the familiar faces. He was overwhelmed with emotion. He glanced at Amelia as she sang the words, '…let me hide myself in thee.' Sensing his discomfort, she smiled and squeezed his hand.

"Trust … such utter trust," he thought.

"God, grant me the strength and the fortitude to endure whatever lies ahead, that I may stand strong and not let my family down. God help me," he implored, looking up at the exquisitely moulded ceilings of the church.

There were emotional goodbyes as the family left the Church. Sampson turned for one last look at the place, which since his arrival as a boy starting out his life's journey from Ireland, had been his rock, his place of comfort, stability and refuge.

The family wandered around town, visiting their favourite places for the last time. Edinburgh had become home. He felt the heartbeat of the city and everything was familiar. Sampson O'Malia Daniel, a family man, chose to follow his extended family, and in doing so, he let go of his own dreams.

The Daniel family left Edinburgh at dawn the next day on a stage-coach bound for London.

London, October 1819

Chaos reigned at 32 Southampton Street, Strand. Edward Ford Turvey was in the midst of it. He was uncertain about the names and numbers of people on his list which kept changing. His applications were submitted late and government officials were getting twitchy. At one stage they threatened to refuse his application, but it was too late. They decided to allocate the Turvey party to one of the last ships to sail, to give Edward enough time to sort it out.

"John, it's so good to see you again," said Sampson, heartily shaking Burgis' hand. The last time I saw you was in London, with John Kemp and old Mulligan at the Hare and Hound alehouse, back in 1801."

"Daniel – how the devil are you and what are you doing here?" Burgis asked, equally pleased to see his old acquaintance. Before Sampson could answer, he rattled on, "I am here to collect a letter from the Government about the scheme. Edward Turvey's party has accepted my application. This is my wife, Ellen, and my children – John, William, Mary, Francis, Josiah and little Eliza," he said, proudly touching the crown of each child's head.

Sampson greeted each one in turn, and noticed that the petite Ellen was pregnant – again.

"Come in, John," he said, stepping aside to allow the guests through, "We are staying here with my sister, Julia, and her husband Edward Turvey, who is the leader of the party, until we set sail for Africa."

Sampson ushered the family into the parlour and introduced the Burgis family to his children, Jane Sophia, Eliza, Amelia and Frederick.

"My wife will be with us shortly. She has made us some tea and her delicious lavender shortbread."

As the group settled down to tea, there was a knock at the door. An excited party leader, Mr Mills, arrived with an official government letter in hand.

"The authorities have sent me this letter confirming the ship to which our respective parties have been assigned. The Turvey and Mills' parties will set sail on the *Sir George Osborn*, probably around mid-December 1819, and will be sailing from Gravesend, Deptford Port here in London."

There was a loud cheer as the group stood up and excitedly began hugging one another. It was the first official confirmation of their migration to Africa. The men discussed how they had made the final decision to emigrate, and what they had sacrificed because of their decision. This included the financial and emotional implications.

"Turvey must have some kind of hypnotic powers to have been able to convince us all to join him on this outlandish scheme," Mills said jokingly. The others agreed.

"I am still not fully convinced as to why I gave up my comfortable life in Edinburgh, only to find myself awaiting embarkation on a ship bound for unexplored Africa. It is sheer madness," said Sampson, who still had huge doubts about whether the decision he had made was indeed the right one for his family.

Others smiled and nodded. Each one secretly harboured the same doubts and feelings of trepidation about the trip. On hearing the commotion, the man of the house, Edward Ford Turvey, walked into the crowded parlour. As Mills shared the good news with him, Turvey went over to the drinks cabinet. "Ladies and Gentlemen, I do declare that this calls for a celebratory drink. To Africa!" he raised his glass and promptly downed a shot of neat cognac.

Despite the great excitement and the electric air of expectancy amongst the prospective settlers, there was also a tangible anxiety amongst them. Unbeknown to the intrepid adventurers, the people of the Xhosa tribe in South Africa were aggressively attempting to capture the *Kaffir Drift Post* near the outpost of Grahamstown in the Colony. Things were difficult for the British soldiers, who had engaged in a battle to ward off a horde of two thousand Xhosa. Lord Charles Somerset was exceedingly careful not to spread this news as it would have caused panic, and many prospective settlers might withdraw their applications.

Regardless, Somerset pressed on with his campaign to bring out British settlers and, on 22 November 1819, he advised Colonel Jacob Cuyler to instruct the Land Surveyor Johan Knobel to proceed with the process of surveying locations for the project. To finalise applications, there was frequent correspondence between the various party leaders and government officials regarding the emigration. Edward Turvey sent the following letter to the government officials in London.

[Undated, 1820]

Sir,

Nothing pains me more than being forced to give trouble, but in the situation I have been placed, it becomes my duty to do everything in my power for the Party going out under me. A Dilemma occurs in the following manner:

*John **KEMP**, Sawyer and five children are going out with me. His eldest daughter Nancy **KEMP** aged fifteen has married within the last 2 months to John **SUTTON** aged 17 years and Mr **KEMP** is in much trouble fearing his daughter will not go without her husband. Mrs **WILLIE** aged 26 wife of Mr **WILLIE** Carpenter has offered to remain at home for the present and join our party in*

6 months, if the Colonial office will have the goodness to permit John ***SUTTON*** *to go in her place. I have been most particularly requested by overseers of the Parish of Burwash in Sussex to make known this Circumstance and their Earnest Entreaty that this may be complied with – this will compleat our Party and make no difference in the number going out or in the amount of our deposit as it now stands having paid £185-0-0 and our party now making only the amount of £182-10-0.*

I have the honour to be, Sir
Your most obedient and most humble svt
Edward TURVEY

For the prospect of owning 100 acres of land and the promise of economic opportunity in the south of Africa, the prospective settlers had sold properties and possessions, given up businesses and good jobs in England, Ireland and Scotland. Growing fears were aggravated by rumours the European settlers were to form a human buffer against those tribes who had already invaded earlier Dutch settlements. Concerns abounded, as most of the applicants were ill equipped to be soldiers or combatants. Some scoffed at the stories, believing them to be exaggerations by those who were afraid to take a calculated risk. Settlers were, after all, under the protection of the British army stationed at the Cape.

The rumours unsettled the ever-cautious Sampson. He had misgivings when he first heard of the scheme. The man had serious doubts about his decision to relocate his family. It was unlike him to be hasty. He tried to rationalise his decision, wrestling with his thoughts day and night. If it had not been for his brother and sister, he would have chosen to remain in Edinburgh.

Sampson blamed Turvey. The man's gnawing insistence had convinced him to divert from his original goal to settle in Edinburgh. A heavy nagging feeling sat in the pit of his stomach. Although this was not one of his wisest decisions, there was no turning back.

Sampson O'Malia Daniel feared the unknown.

CHAPTER 10

FINAL PREPARATIONS AND GOODBYES

29 January 1820, London

"Death of the King! Read all about it!" yelled the newspaper seller. News of the death of King George III was on the front page of the *London Times*. It was all the citizens of London could talk about and proved a diversion for the settlers. The Prince of Wales succeeded his father as King George IV.

The British navy prepared twenty-one ships to transport the settlers to southern Africa. Constant changes to the Turvey party list postponed the departure of the *Sir George Osborn* to mid-January 1820. In the weeks leading up to embarkation, the Daniel family explored London. Sampson took the children to the site of his first shop, Daniel and Gaubert Jewellers in Drury Lane and the newly-built Drury Lane theatre. He regaled them with tales of theatre life and how their late grandfather, Pierre d'Egville, had been a ballet master together with their uncle, James. Seven-year-old Jane Sophia thought this a grand notion and aspired to be a great ballet dancer.

They took carriage rides around Hyde Park, with the children and their cousins chattering excitedly. Sampson and Peter deliberated how to make money in Africa. Their wives discussed packing, children and which personal belongings to take with them. Of all the children, seven-year-old Robert, Peter and Eliza's son, was the apple of everybody's eye. He had a mop of blonde hair, sparkling blue eyes and a mischievous, adventurous spirit. By comparison, Frederick, his two-year-old cousin, had a sallow complexion and dark hair and he followed Robert – his hero – everywhere.

Ann Mitchley became an integral part of the Daniel household. She openly lived there with her own children by Peter, nine-year-old Thomas, six-year-old Sampson, four-year-old Eliza and two-year-old Ann. Then there were Eliza's other children from Peter, Eliza Jane, sixteen-year-old Peter, fourteen-year-old Isabella and Robert, the youngest. All witnessed arguments between Eliza and their father over Ann Mitchley.

Amelia noticed Eliza becoming increasingly reclusive. She was prone to seizures and she stayed in her bedroom a lot. As a result, Ann Mitchley took over the running of the home. Ann's strong character and bubbly nature brought a positive energy to any situation. Her presence and influence on the family was stabilising. Amelia did not know what to make of Peter's infidelity, but realised that Eliza was mentally unstable and Ann was an empathetic carer.

Early one evening, Amelia knocked on Eliza's door. When there was no reply, she entered. Eliza was sitting on the bed staring vacantly at the wall, wringing her handkerchief in her hands. She seemed edgy and unsure of herself. When she saw Amelia, her eyes widened in panic.

"Eliza," said Amelia, "are you feeling alright?"

Eliza only groaned, rocking backwards and forwards. Amelia sat on the bed beside her, but the other woman seemed not to notice. It was as if she was not there. Amelia could smell alcohol on Eliza's breath. She searched the drawers, finding a bottle of brandy under some clothes in the armoire.

Clutching the half empty bottle in disbelief, Amelia stood for a while with her back to Eliza. The seizures and her sister-in-law's reclusive behaviour, as well as the times she had noticed Eliza's unsteadiness and her stumbling, began to make perfect sense. Numbing her pain with alcohol was Eliza's way of coping with Peter's infidelity and Ann Mitchley's presence in her home. But it seemed more than that. She seemed to be losing her mind.

The Strand, LONDON

Idle chatter and talk about business filled Turvey's Southampton Street house at the Strand, in the months leading up to the departure of the *Sir George Osborn*. Various settlers popped in to sign documents or discuss the imminent voyage. The Daniel and Turvey cousins and other children created a continuous ruckus, until an adult told them to be quiet. The excitable cousins were difficult to control when they were all in the same house. Julia's two older boys, William and Benjamin, and her children from Edward, added to the mix.

Sampson took Amelia on an outing to the new Burlington Arcade shopping mall close to Piccadilly. There were fifty-one shops in all, including eight milliners, eight hosiers, glovers, five linen shops, four shoemakers, three hairdressers, three jewellers and watchmakers and two lace shops – Amelia's favourite. There was also a shawl seller, an optician, a wine merchant, a pastry cook, a bookseller and a stationer. The contemporary, covered arcade was two hundred yards long.

Playfully, Amelia tugged Sampson's hand, pulling him into a lace shop. She felt the crisp linen and admired the intricate, colourful embroidery on the various pieces. A delicate lace handkerchief with a lavender design caught her eye. Knowing it to be her favourite flower, Sampson took the handkerchief from her and handed it to the shopkeeper.

"Please wrap this for my sweetheart," he said, knowing how pleased Amelia would be.

His wife stood just behind him and discreetly put her chin against his shoulder, placing her hand in the small of his back. He turned and looked lovingly into her eyes. The response on her face was gratitude enough for him. She was so easy to please. He gently touched Amelia's porcelain-like cheek with affection.

"They say it gets swelteringly hot in Africa. You will need to keep your pretty face shaded from the sun at all times," he said, adding a bonnet to his purchase.

Not knowing what supplies and services would be available to them in South Africa, they made the most of their shopping day, including a visit to the optician, the shoe shop and the bookseller. They bought a few children's books for Julia to read on the ship to occupy the children during the long days at sea. The couple left the Burlington Arcade. London was so vibrant, colourful, organised and civilised.

Africa, on the other hand, was so far away and there were so many unknowns.

CHAPTER 11

THE SIR GEORGE OSBORN – JANUARY 1820

"There she is!"

Sampson's excitement was tangible. The wooden sailing ship loomed ahead of them in the harbour. The *Sir George Osborn* was ninety-four feet long and had a twenty-eight-foot beam. Captured from the French during the Napoleonic wars, the British renamed the ship and registered it as weighing 313 tons.

It was a bitterly cold day at Gravesend at Deptford on the Thames. The Daniel clan gathered at the harbour, joining the other members of the Turvey and Mills parties, all preparing to embark. A frosty wind blew snow particles around their ankles and an icy draft crept up under trouser legs and skirts like frozen fingers. Wearing their thick winter coats, gloves and fur caps, the young Daniel family walked hand in hand, forming a human chain up the gangplank and onto the wooden deck.

"Stay close to *Maman*," Amelia told her children as they jostled between the other passengers heading in the same direction.

Their household belongings – cutlery, crockery, clothes, linen and spare blankets – were neatly packed in wooden trunks lined with wallpaper and sheeting to prevent dust from getting in. Sampson had securely locked and covered each one with a thick-tarred canvas for extra protection. The porters loaded their larger trunks and possessions, clearly labelled for identification, into the storage hold.

Amelia interlocked her leather-gloved hands over her stomach. She felt the slight feathery movement of their unborn child. She was six months pregnant and had huge reservations about this epic adventure across the ocean.

"This way Ma'am," said the deck steward, as he led them to the cabin.

Bewildered by the numbers of people and the festive atmosphere, Jane Sophia, Amelia and Eliza clung to their mother's full skirt. Toddler Frederick sat snugly on his father's hip, while his cousin Robert held tightly onto Uncle Sampson's hand. Sampson's nephew adored him. In turn, the doting uncle treated Robert as one of his own.

Amelia took one look at the confined space allocated to her family and groaned. There was no privacy and their sleeping bunk had a mattress that looked hard and uncomfortable. A curtain hung over the bunk, to be drawn only when privacy from other passengers was required. Large communal wooden tables and benches were fastened to the floor in the living quarters.

"I know it's small, *ma cherie*," Sampson said, gently kissing Amelia on the cheek, "but it's only for a couple of months and then we will have all the space in the world!"

Once they had placed their suitcases and personal goods under the allocated bunk beds, the passengers of each party congregated on the deck. The deckhand announced the house rules, which he read from a sheet of paper.

"All passengers allocated spaces between the decks will be awake by seven o'clock in the morning and are required to take their bedding up onto the deck for airing by seven-thirty. Bunk curtains are to be rolled up. Passengers are to dress in the cabin. Only those passengers who are feeling unwell can stay below deck in the bunks. Otherwise, all passengers are to remain on deck for the duration of the day, except for mealtimes, which will be taken in the cabin."

On deck, the Daniels met the head of another party, Edward Gardner. They were surprised at his presence, as only the Turvey and Mills parties had been assigned to the *Sir George Osborn*. On further discussion, Gardner informed them he had read his government communication incorrectly. His party should have embarked at Liverpool. He, however, thought they were supposed to embark from the Thames. Therefore, after spending all their money on transport to get to London and realising they were actually meant to be in Liverpool, they appealed to the authorities to allow them to change their plans. Fortunately, the officials gave the Gardner party permission to board the *Sir George Osborn*, as there was sufficient space available.

Back in the cabin, Amelia sat down on the hard, uncomfortable bunk. She secretly hoped the family would be at home in Africa before her baby was born. She did not want to give birth out at sea. Fingering the intricately designed wedding ring Sampson had made for her, she determined in her heart to make the very most of her situation. It was too late to start complaining. The wheels of adventure were in motion – there was no turning back. Amelia set about making her small living space as comfortable as possible for her family. She pulled a white crocheted cotton bedspread over her bunk to bring a sense of home to the bleak surroundings.

Being one of the coldest recorded winters in London's history, one morning, whilst waiting to sail, the Thames River froze over.

The ships with their cargo of settlers became icebound. There was no telling when the first ships would be able to set sail for Africa. After months of preparation and planning, the waiting passengers became despondent as they realised they had no choice but to wait. They resigned themselves to making the most of the cold and miserable living conditions.

"Oh, well, at least the children will have time to adjust to their new surroundings before we set sail," said Amelia to the other disgruntled mothers on board. She tried to look for the good.

"The party leaders had a formal meeting with the Captain. He announced we will be setting sail within the week. However, all passengers are to respect the house rules set out by the Captain. Anyone not complying will receive reduced rations during the voyage," reported Amelia.

According to reports, *The Nautilus* had, on 5 December 1819, broken through the barrier of ice with loud cracking noises that sounded like gunshots. It was exciting for the passengers, who had already been on board for two weeks, to be the first ship to sail. People heard frightening ripping sounds, as chunks of solid ice split apart with the movement of the ship. Settlers amongst the Mandy, Owen, Rowles, Crause and Scott parties on board that ship, had grown weary and agitated at having to wait so long for the departure of their vessel.

Passengers on the *Sir George Osborn* watched the other ships slowly crunching their way out of the ice-encrusted harbour, one by one. There were renewed feelings of hope.

Amidst the loud cheers of celebration from other passengers, Sampson and Amelia hugged each other, sighing with relief as they watched another ship depart. The sooner they could escape the bone-aching cold weather and head for the sunny African shores, the better. They had heard the weather in southern Africa was warm most of the year. The thought of this lifted their spirits.

The first few ships to depart moved heavily down the Thames and out into the open seas.

Late in the afternoon of Monday 10 January 1820, a strange calm filled the air. Dark ominous storm clouds banked up on the horizon. Amelia felt an uneasiness creep in and settle deep in her belly. At first, she thought it had something to do with her pregnancy. The nagging discomfort persisted into the evening and she mentioned it to Sampson.

"Something's not right, Sampson. I have a strange feeling in my stomach and I can't put my finger on it," she said.

Sampson shrugged it off. He did not have an answer for Amelia. He knew she sometimes had these strange premonitions. Nothing he could do about it. That day had been particularly bleak, and the passengers had permission to turn in early. Despite the news about setting sail within the week, the mood on board was sombre. However, their meal of bread with beef and potato stew did warm their stomachs and the ship's cook prepared a special treat of hot custard for pudding.

At around 9 o'clock that evening, the last of the children had just settled down to sleep. A howling, gale-force wind rocked the ship violently from side to side. Amelia sat up fearfully, tightly grasping the sides of her bunk to stop herself from falling. Instinctively, she thought of the children. She felt her way to the bunks beside hers. As the ship swayed roughly from side to side, she lost her balance and bumped her head against something sharp. Cursing the pain and ignoring the warm trickle of blood down her forehead, she steadied herself and located her anxious children, who were screaming out for their mother. She gathered them to her and sat on the lower bunk with them.

"Hold on tightly to *Maman*!" she instructed.

The children wrapped their arms around her as she clung to the sides of the bunk for dear life. It was pitch dark in the sleeping quarters. Crew had extinguished all the candles and lamps for the night.

"Hold tight," she screamed at the girls. She grabbed little Frederick. His tiny hands clutched the fabric of her cotton nightdress in the dark. The three girls started to cry and scream in unison. Other passengers were also up and seeking sturdy props to hold onto.

The fierce gale raged outside, swirling around the hull of the ship and its deck, threatening to sweep away everything in its path. The ship listed and rolled wildly. Passengers shouted and called out for their family members. Some began to pray aloud. Frightened children, woken from their sleep, cried in distress as mothers and fathers tried to console them and prevent them from bashing themselves against the bunk beds and wooden furniture. Loose belongings hurtled wildly around the cabin.

Suddenly, there was a loud crack. The ship wrenched violently from its moorings. The wind shoved the large vessel like a cork along the water, rocking it back and forth. Some passengers fell out of their bunks. Others were hit by flying objects. Water gushed in through the cabin windows and one little boy was washed off his bunk and onto the floor. Amelia clung to her own children for dear life. Passengers were soaked through as water spilled into the cabin. Their clothes and bedding were drenched.

The violent ripping and tearing continued until the ship finally ran aground opposite the Greenwich hospital with a forceful jolt. The intense rocking motion ceased, but the gale-force winds continued unabated for another hour and a half.

The screaming finally subsided and, for a moment, deathly silence descended on the cabin. Then pandemonium broke out again when the passengers realised their ship was no longer moving. People scrambled to get to the safety of the deck for fear the ship was sinking. Amelia huddled her children around her like a protective mother hen as panic set in. They clambered up the stairs to the upper deck, rudely jostled by other passengers.

Crew members and deckhands tried to calm everyone. They lit lanterns, urging them to stay below deck. No one listened. The ship had run aground and was severely damaged.

"Women and children, stay calm. Get back to your sleeping quarters and try to settle down. At first light, we will inform you of the damage," instructed the First Mate, giving his assurance that the ship was not going to sink.

The male passengers joined the crew on deck to see if they could assist, awaiting instruction from the commander of the vessel, Captain Taplin. What a traumatic start for the distraught travellers. First, the extraordinarily below-freezing winter conditions, then the long wait for the ice on the Thames to crack and soften, and now this.

"This is a bad omen," thought Amelia, trying to console the frightened children as she coerced them back onto their bunks in the shadowy flickering of the lantern light. The worried look on the faces of the other mothers did not help. Their faces were ashen, drained of blood. Some of them looked grey and ghoulish in the false light. She busied herself with her own children, picking up their possessions which had been strewn all over the floor. Sampson helped the sailors on deck, but not before lovingly reassuring her all would be well.

Mother and children squeezed onto one bunk. Amelia pulled the blankets up over them and softly began to sing a French lullaby. The beauty and sweetness of her voice brought a sense of peace and calm to the wet, confined space below deck. They could hear heavy footsteps and the sound of displaced articles being dragged to their rightful place on the deck above.

Somehow, amidst the chaos and in the early hours of morning, she managed to fall asleep in an awkward sitting position; her little ones huddled around her. At first light, Sampson woke her, offering a hot cup of tea he had begged from the chef in the galley kitchen, saying it was for his pregnant wife.

"Amelia, *ma cherie*," he whispered, "wake up. Get the children ready, we are going ashore."

All one hundred and eleven passengers disembarked, whilst the crew members stayed on board to clean the decks and cabins, clearing them of debris.

The *Sir George Osborn* was in need of intensive repair.

"Sampson, do you think it is wise to continue with this trip?" Amelia asked wearily as they made their way down the gangplank and back to shore.

"We don't have much choice, *ma cherie*," he said shaking his head. "We have sold up everything. We gave up our life in Edinburgh for this." He cursed, "That damned Turvey! Damn him to hell! It's his fault. I should have realised when he caused trouble with Thomas Mahoney things were not right. We were included just to make up the numbers Turvey needed to form his own party. I can see that now. We should have stayed at home in Edinburgh. It's too damn late to change our minds now."

Amelia had never seen her husband so angry.

For over two hours, Amelia tried to calm him down. The couple sat together and chatted about their predicament. They weighed up the pros and cons of withdrawing their application. Their other option was to stick to the plan and emigrate. After intense deliberations, the pair reached a stalemate. They had given up everything. There was nothing more to lose by sailing to Africa.

If things did not work out, they could always return to England and start again.

The brave couple made a pact to stick together, no matter what the future held. To remain faithful and positive to their commitment, no matter how tough things became.

Sampson held his wife tightly reassuring her of his love. His eyes could not hide the anxiety he was experiencing. There was no turning back. They clasped hands and Sampson fervently prayed for God's protection, guidance and wisdom in the months to follow.

CHAPTER 12

THE OCEAN CROSSING

For two months the passengers of the *Sir George Osborn* watched other settler ships leave the harbour during the repair work to the damaged hull of theirs. The passengers on board found various ways to wile their time away. The leader of the Turvey party, Edward Ford Turvey, took the opportunity to pursue one of his favourite pastimes – art. He delighted in painting a portrait of Ann Mitchley, commissioned by Peter Daniel.

One of the last ships to depart, the *Sir George Osborn* finally set sail on 16 March 1820 after being made seaworthy again.

As they sailed out of the harbour and into the English Channel, Sampson watched the coastline fade away. He felt emptiness and remorse. As the English coastline grew more and more distant, his thoughts turned once again to the beautiful city of Edinburgh. He remembered his thriving jewellery business with pride, his friends in the congregation at St Andrew's and their comfortable home. Those memories would soon grow dim.

Seeking a secluded spot on deck, Sampson put his head in his hands and wept like a child. After a long time, he looked out over the ocean again and saw the sun's rays twinkling over the vast expanse of water like diamonds. He stood up abruptly, checking to see if anyone had seen him cry.

"Pull yourself together, man. For the sake of family. With the help of the Lord, I will make this African adventure a success." He spoke to himself sternly.

The emigrants soon settled into a regular routine. The excitement of reaching their destination kept them in high spirits. On calm, clear days, they enjoyed soaking up the sun and socialising on deck. The First Mate divided the passengers into groups of twenty-four. He allocated each person a daily task depending on age and capabilities. These included serving meals, cleaning up after meals, collecting rations and issuing them, scrubbing the decks and airing bed linen. The women sanitised the bed boards. Captain Taplin was a stickler for on-board hygiene. The lack of it could lead to all kinds of diseases breaking out. Crew members sprinkled the decks with chloride of lime for sanitation. The Captain allowed the women to bath in wooden tubs filled with seawater. The men, however, had to douse themselves with water from buckets. The ship's surgeon was in charge of all alcohol, vinegar, hops, malt and soap rations. It was forbidden for men to light matches or smoke their pipes anywhere between the decks.

On calmer days, the party leader Edward Ford Turvey spent his days sketching.

Downstairs in the cabin, Amelia noted the date in her diary. It was 18 April, 1820. They had been at sea for just over a month. The weight of the child in her womb was almost unbearable. She had not walked much in the last few days and was at full term. The skin on her stomach felt stretched and tight and she experienced some unusual twitches in her abdomen. Amelia left the cabin and went in search of company and fresh air. She needed something to distract her from her discomfort. As she emerged from below, into the bright sunshine, the main deck was a hive of activity.

Looking relaxed and tanned, Edward Turvey, the party leader, was puffing on a cigar and chatting to one of the deck hands. He kept a watchful eye on his plate of salted beef and mashed potato, balanced on top of the canvas cover of a life raft. He was in the habit of leaving plates of his food in the sun to heat up his meal.

"You sure are an unusual fellow, Mr Turvey," she thought as she walked past the two men, who greeted her politely.

Little parties of women huddled together, making soap and candles. Amelia's sister-in-law, Julia, sat on a deck chair nearby and at least a dozen children gathered around her, concentrating on her expressive face as she read them a story. Julia had become a mother figure and friend to all. She always had a listening ear and a kind word. The little ones loved her kind heart. Her son, nine-year-old Edward Mortimer Turvey, and Amelia's seven-year-old Jane Sophia, were hovering around a group of children. Julia had 'put them in charge'. The two of them were inseparable. Jane Sophia adored Eddie, as she called him, and they did everything together. Eddie was her self-appointed protector and best friend. Amelia knew that Julia encouraged the children to play games and do group activities with them to keep them active and healthy. It prevented them from getting bored with one another and from getting up to mischief.

Amelia smiled happily. How content everyone looked. Even her little Frederick was sitting happily with his older sister, Jane Sophia, engrossed in story time. His cousin Robert was climbing in and out of the life rafts with Henry Dugmore and a few other boys.

"It is going to be difficult to keep the boys entertained for the entire voyage," thought Amelia.

She sat down in a sunny spot next to Ellen Burgis, John's wife. She looked around the deck for Sampson and spotted him deep in conversation with his brothers. The three men, Peter, Sampson and their half-brother John, sat on benches on one side of the ship, looking out to sea. Sampson was looking more relaxed than she had seen him in a long time. The sun had already touched his fair Irish complexion even though she had put balm on his cheeks and neck to protect his skin. Poor Sampson's skin went bright red, blistered and then the skin peeled. She, on the other hand, was more fortunate. Her skin absorbed the sun more easily and it turned a healthy, tanned colour after just a few hours on deck.

It warmed her heart to see her husband conversing so freely and animatedly with his brothers. It gave her confidence that everything would be all right in the end.

"We'll adapt to our new life...," she thought positively.

Amelia took out the white linen tray cloth she had begun embroidering a few days ago, placing a silver thimble on her finger. She had hemmed the edges of the cloth and had already embroidered the stem of a lavender flower on the fabric. Threading her needle with a length of purple cotton, she continued to work on the pattern.

"How are you feeling today, Ellen?" asked Amelia, knowing she had been complaining of diarrhoea and stomach cramps.

"Oh, not much better, Amelia," replied Ellen, "but I thought I would just come on deck to get a bit of sun on my back. I shall not be able to sit here for long, though. The stomach cramps are quite severe." The severity of the pain showed on her face. "My stomach runs like tea from a kettle. I have lost my appetite and whenever I do try to eat something, it comes straight out."

Amelia looked at Ellen's weary features, her cheeks devoid of colour. Her heart went out to this woman. She had lost a lot of weight since boarding the ship and she noticed that Ellen ate very little at mealtimes.

"Have you been to the ship's doctor?"

"Oh, aye. He has given me medicine to ease the cramps and the vomiting, but the stuff tastes so vile I am loathe to take it. I really have no energy. John and William take care of Mary. Mrs Cartwright has been very gracious in looking after the smaller ones. Francis is only four and little Josiah who is two, still clings to me. He doesn't understand why his Mummy can't pick him up anymore."

Amelia looked up from her work and saw the worry in Ellen's eyes. She reached out and held the woman's limp hand. The two stared out towards the horizon, absently pondering their futures. The ocean was unpredictable and temperamental.

Two days later, angry waves battered the *Sir George Osborn*. The large ship bobbed like a cork on the rough seas. The thunder of the raging storm was deafening. Amelia could not believe just a couple of days previously she had been chatting to Ellen and enjoying the sunshine on deck. She lay cooped up in the sick bay, in full labour, in the middle of the severe storm. She held tightly to the edges of the wooden cot as a contraction gripped her already exhausted frame. The young mother panted heavily and laid her head back on the hard pillow.

Only one month at sea, but tonight it felt like a lifetime. The cabin closed in on her and the wooden bunk was hard and unforgiving. There was no respite from the rough pounding and rocking motion of the ship. Sapped of energy, she was not sure how much longer she could endure the excruciating pain.

Julia Turvey anxiously watched over her. She mopped Amelia's clammy brow with a cool, wet cloth and shouted, above the noise of the thunder, "Push, Amelia. Push! Once more!"

The ship's doctor had hurriedly ushered Amelia and her sister-in-law into the sick bay cabin and instructed Julia to stay with the expectant mother. He had rushed off to attend to other sick patients on board, promising to return shortly. It had been twelve hours since her waters broke.

Julia knew there were children on board with whooping cough, and two adults had already died at sea from dysentery. She prayed for the doctor's return, as she was not a midwife.

"*Mon Dieu*! *A l'aide*! *Au secours*!" Amelia cried out, as the next contraction clamped her exhausted body.

With one last heart-wrenching scream, she bore down, forcing the child from her. One final concerted effort and her fifth child slid from her womb. The agony of childbirth was over. She let out a massive sigh. Her relieved body went limp. Above the noise of the tumultuous ocean, Julia excitedly mouthed, "It's a girl!"

Amelia silently welcomed the little girl into the world. Exhausted, she lay back on the pillow.

The ship's doctor arrived in time to sever the umbilical cord. Amelia let herself drift off for a few minutes, while Julia and the doctor washed and wrapped the baby. After placing the tiny infant back in her arms, the doctor left the room, instructing Julia to call Amelia's husband.

Sampson peeped around the cabin door, smiling broadly. Holding

Amelia's face between his large hands, he kissed her gently. He then kissed the sleeping infant on the forehead, welcoming her into the Daniel family.

"Let's call her Isabella," she said, and Sampson nodded his agreement.

After a time of contented silence, Sampson spoke in a whisper, as if that would soften the words he needed to say. "Amelia, my love. Poor Ellen...," his voice trailed off and he found it difficult to finish the sentence.

"What? What, Sampson?" quizzed his wife.

"Your friend died this morning."

Amelia closed her eyes, picturing Ellen's kind, wan face. Pain filled her heart as she laid her head on Sampson's shoulder and sobbed for her friend. Clinging tightly to tiny Isabella, the couple prayed for God's mercy. They realised just getting to the end of this sea voyage safely would be a miracle.

That afternoon, the ship's chaplain held a simple funeral service for Ellen Burgis. The sea was calm and the sun peeked through a gap in the cloudy grey skies. It was a dull day, and the mood on board was sombre. Before the service, the chaplain asked the congregation to join him in giving thanks to God for the safe delivery of the Daniel's baby girl, born that day.

"For every birth there is a death. Today we also gather to say goodbye to a dear friend and fellow settler, Ellen Burgis. We lay her to rest here at sea."

The passengers sang a hymn after which the Reverend said the ship's prayer for the deceased. John Burgis struggled to contain his emotions as he gave the eulogy.

As was the custom for those who died at sea, the ship's doctor sewed Ellen's tiny, inert body into her featherbed. He fastened the final stitch tightly through her nose to ensure first that she was dead, and secondly, to hold the covering in place. A crew member fastened a piece of lead shot to the foot of the bedclothes for added weight. When Captain Taplin consigned the canvas cocoon of her body to the depths, it hardly made a splash as it hit the ocean swells, bobbing briefly with the shifting seas before sinking slowly. John Burgis held his youngest baby in his arms. His other five children stood in a row on top of a wooden bench, forlornly watching the sea swallow their mother's body. The passengers and crew dwindled away. Some wondered how the poor man would cope in a foreign land with all those children and without a wife at his side.

As the *Sir George Osborn* sailed closer to the Tropic of Cancer, the days became warmer. With good trade winds, the ship sailed at an average of six to seven miles an hour. Passengers saw whales and shoals of flying fish and schools of dolphin. When they anchored off Madeira, small vessels rowed by dark-skinned men swarmed around the ship, much to the delight of the children. It was an opportunity to stock up on much needed fresh fruit such as grapes and oranges, vegetables and water.

When the ship's cook threw old food or the remains of slaughtered and butchered animals such as sheep or chickens overboard, sharks would hungrily circle the ship. Whale sightings were a delight, especially to the children. Schools of dolphin often playfully led the ship. In a display of frivolity, they leapt through the clear water, smooth bodies glistening as the sun's rays caught the water on their backs. At times like this, the mood on board was playful. Nevertheless, after three long months at sea, the passengers were unsettled and irritable. Everyone needed space and they were all eager to walk on dry land again. They tried to keep out of one another's way, as they awaited their arrival at Simon's Town in the Cape.

On 17 June 1820, a golden sun rose, spreading its glow over the ocean. A misty white cloud draped Table Mountain. This iconic mountain rose up as the symbolic landmark of the Cape. Sampson pulled his coat collar up around his ears. He had heard so much about it that he rose early, to be the first of the passengers to see the landmark.

With the other passengers still asleep, all was still on deck. Savouring the moment, Sampson lifted his arms and stretched them out, greeting the day with praise. The fine sea spray lightly tickled his face as it splashed up, before the chilly breeze carried it away. The silver streaks in Sampson's hair shone stark white in the early morning sunlight. A few of the ship's crew appeared and they prepared to drop anchor.

Sampson was glad that he had not joined the men the previous evening. Edward, Peter, John Burgis and a few others had a night celebrating the journey's end. They had sat up until the wee hours playing poker, drinking whiskey and smoking cigars, speculating what life in Africa would be like. The more whiskey they drank, the prettier the picture they painted.

Sampson's body moved to the rhythm of the gentle sea swell. It was a welcome change from the rocking and rolling on the open sea. He caught sight of hills in the distance. They would soon be nearing Simons Town. His first proper view of the imposing mountain was everything he had expected. As he leaned forward to get a better view, his gold wedding band knocked against the wooden railing.

"Africa – our new home," he said aloud.

He hoped the British Government would keep their promises.

He heard movement and low murmuring, as a group of sailors gathered near one of the life rafts, removing the canvas and untying some of the ropes. Sampson walked over and greeted them.

"Morning to you," he called, "what might you be doing?"

"Oh aye, we're preparing the raft to row the Captain and your party leaders ashore," replied one of the sailors. "Captain Taplin needs to report to the British officials we have arrived in port, and we have to replenish supplies for the final leg to Algoa Bay."

There was a flurry of excitement as passengers began emerging on deck. Party leaders Edward Gardner and Daniel Mills appeared, on schedule as requested by the captain, both men fresh and ready for their crossing by rowboat to the mainland. Gardner carried a small leather briefcase containing official documents and details of his party list, as did Mills. The two men chatted with the captain while they waited for Turvey to arrive. After some time, Captain Taplin sent one of the crew to locate Turvey. He was found in the dining hall, casually finishing his breakfast.

"Mr Turvey, the Captain is waiting for you. He is ready to disembark for Simons Town with the other leaders. Please follow me immediately, Sir!" The man turned and smartly left the room to report to the Captain of Edward's whereabouts.

Gardner and Mills shook their heads as Turvey finally emerged from below deck and sauntered over to them – a half-eaten boiled egg sandwich in one hand, and his mug of hot tea in the other. His dishevelled, unbrushed blonde hair stuck out from beneath his straw hat. His bag containing the vital passenger list documents was nowhere in sight.

A breathless Julia came running up behind her husband. "Here, Edward, you forgot these!" she said handing him his document case.

"Hard night, Mr Turvey?" sneered the Captain, as he gave the order for the boat to be lowered into the sea below. The men clung on tightly as the small vessel hit the swelling water.

"A great white shark has been sighted on numerous occasions by the naval officers based at Simons Town. It is called the Dark Prowler and must be at least twenty feet in length," he warned.

Much to the disappointment of the rest of the passengers, the Captain only allowed the leaders of the three settler parties ashore. The ship anchored offshore for ten days while the men went about their business on land. Their mission was to meet with the military command and to replenish their food and water supplies. It was also an opportunity to find out how the other settler groups had fared on their sea voyages. They wanted to hear news of developments at the camp at Algoa Bay, as well as their allotments in the Albany District, further up the east coast.

The authorities instructed all other passengers be quarantined for a period of at least ten days as a precaution against outbreaks of dysentery, measles and whooping cough which had been experienced by some during the passage from England.

As the days passed, the temperature dropped. The air was icy and the wind howled through the portholes. It was like being back in England. The sun made a brief appearance at about nine o'clock each morning, and it was dark again before five o'clock each afternoon. The days were damp and cold and a south-easterly wind blew. The women and children had to stay in the cabins to keep warm.

Ten days later, seventeen-year-old Benjamin Wright saw a small boat headed in the direction of the *Sir George Osborn*. "Mother, come quickly! Father is coming back!" he said excitedly.

Despite his stepfather's eccentricity, Turvey was still Benjamin's hero and he had been at his stepfather's side for most of the three-month journey. He watched excitedly as the small craft drew closer. He hung over the side, eagerly looking out for Turvey. Much to Benjamin's disappointment, his stepfather was nowhere to be seen.

"I'm afraid, Mrs Turvey, we had to leave Simons Town without your husband," the Captain informed a stunned Julia. "He disappeared over the last two days. He was last seen in the company of a group of off-duty soldiers. We had no option but to depart without him."

Julia's cheeks flushed red with embarrassment, as the other passengers murmured their disapproval.

"Typical Turvey,' she heard one man say under his breath.

"That man does nothing by the book," said another.

Julia walked away quickly to avoid hearing any further negative comments. Benjamin put his hand on her shoulder, trying to prevent her from leaving.

"Mother, where's Father? Why isn't he back? What if something bad has happened to him?" he demanded.

Julia was too distressed to respond.

"We can't just leave him there!" cried Benjamin, looking in the direction of the mainland.

She knew her husband was tired of the confinement of the ship the past three months, and he had been desperate to go ashore, but she never dreamed he would not return.

"Arrangements have been made to have him escorted to Grahamstown with the next military dispatch to the area," explained the Captain, "that could be anything from a few days to a couple of weeks – even months. I am afraid your party will have to elect a new leader for the final leg of this journey. We have about a hundred miles to sail until we reach the port of Algoa Bay. I need to know of your decision in the morning."

He walked off to the Captain's quarters, closing the door firmly behind him. He was quietly pleased to rid himself of that scatterbrain, Turvey. In fact, he would be glad when this voyage was over.

Back in the cabin, Julia sifted through Edward's belongings and found his paintbrushes and paper were gone and she realised he had planned to abscond. Sampson was unmoved when she told him what she suspected as Edward was not prone to conforming to rules and regulations. Sampson and Peter called a meeting of the other men in their party to elect a new leader for the final leg.

Burgis was unavailable for the position as he had his hands full looking after his brood without a wife. Cartwright was too soft-spoken. Henry Holland, John Keevey, John Nivens Daniel, Thomas Pennell, the brothers William and Benjamin Wright and Tom Willy were all too young and inexperienced. Old man Turvey, at eighty-two, was too frail and the sea voyage had taken its toll on him. That left John Mulligan, John Kemp, Robert Cartwright and the two older Daniel brothers, Peter and Sampson. After a brief discussion, the men elected Peter Clarke Daniel as their leader, tasking him with managing disembarkation and settler registration at Algoa Bay. He would also oversee their transport arrangements to the Albany settlement.

After that, it would be every man for himself.

III

INTO THE LION'S DEN

CHAPTER 13

SOUTHERN AFRICA 1820

It was early July in 1820 when the bleak coast of Algoa Bay confronted the newcomers. Their enthusiasm quickly turned to disappointment and the mood on board was decidedly sombre. The British citizens had sailed from England during one of the harshest winters in living memory and arrived during the middle of an African winter.

Added to that, there was no wharf, no jetty, neither dock nor harbour at Algoa Bay. There were no rooftops or chimney pots along the skyline. There was neither city nor town. In fact, nothing except a barren landscape. A vast expanse of wide, white beaches followed the coastline for mile upon mile as far as they eye could see, dotted with a handful of small, insignificant buildings and the tops of rows of Government issue white canvas army tents.

Amelia's heart sank at this sight. There was little sign of civilisation.

The passengers dressed in their Sunday best for disembarkation. The men, all set to boldly step ashore and face their new future, donned their starched collars and cravats, and polished leather shoes.

They had trimmed their hair and beards, which had become unruly during the voyage. Some of them wore wide, flat-brimmed hats sporting a wide black band, and others wore top hats.

The women created a colourful picture on deck, wearing their full-skirted dresses under-layered with petticoats, and their puffed sleeves, collars and cuffs trimmed with lace. They were grateful for their oversized bonnets, intricately tied with pretty ribbon which had been so fashionable in London.

Their attire was fitting for a jaunt through Hyde Park, but not very practical for this leg of their journey. When they saw the casually, comfortably dressed seamen on board the rowboats arriving to escort them off the ship, it was evident that these men were already accustomed to the harsh African climate. They all wore practical, baggy khaki pants and open-collared, loose-fitting white cotton shirts, with rolled-up sleeves and soft leather shoes.

One of the crew assisted Amelia into a small rowing boat. She joined a few other nervous women with small children. Fastening her pretty, wide-brimmed bonnet neatly beneath her chin with a lilac ribbon, her full skirt billowed around her legs as she clung tightly to baby Isabella.

Amelia felt the ocean rise and fall beneath the little boat. The hull of the *Sir George Osborn* towered above them, forbidding and insurmountable. She suddenly felt vulnerable and scared.

Her other daughters, Eliza and Amelia Margarith, along with little Frederick and his cousin Robert, clung to Sampson as they awaited their turn to disembark. Amelia could just make out their little heads peering over the side of the ship. Their eldest daughter, Jane Sophia, chose to stay with her best friend and cousin, Eddie Turvey, and his stepbrother Benjamin Wright. Their mother Julia promised to keep a close watch over the children.

Amelia sat down on the cross plank, cradling the sleeping Isabella firmly with one hand. She gripped the rough seat with her other hand. Closing her eyes tightly, she prayed for safe passage to the beach for her family. The boat rocked them from side to side in the deep waters. There were about ten passengers on board the small vessel. They rowed away from the ship to another larger, flat-bottomed boat.

After a short distance, the passengers had to make the unnerving transfer from the rowing boat into a larger, more stable, transport vessel. For one terrifying moment, Amelia saw nothing but dark water between her and this boat. Trying to support herself and hold onto her baby, she was relieved to feel a firm grip on her upper arm and elbow.

"Don't be afraid, Ma'am, I've got you!" The soldier smiled.

"*Merci beaucoup*," Amelia said, inadvertently speaking French.

The soldier pulled her gently, but firmly, into the boat, leading her to the centre. She made herself comfortable and watched anxiously as the crew lowered her husband and children from the ship. After being transferred from rowboat to the transport boat, Sampson took his place beside her, putting his arm protectively around her shoulders. Feeling suddenly nauseous, she swallowed hard to prevent bile from rising up in her throat.

"I feel sick, *mon cher*. I think I want to throw up," she said placing her hand on her throat.

"Oh God, help us!"

"Not long now, *ma cherie*, and we will all be on land."

He pulled her tightly against him, trying not to let her sense his own feelings of uncertainty. He patted her leg nervously. From his vantage point on the *Sir George Osborn*, he had seen very little sign of civilisation, and this concerned him. The trepidation of the other passengers was palpable.

As the transport vessels carried the settler families to the shore, curious onlookers from the mainland came out to welcome the latest group to Algoa Bay. A small crowd of locals had gathered on the white sandy beach. Beyond them, the newcomers could see a tent town, their temporary abode.

There was not much else.

The British naval officer in charge of the safe delivery of the passengers from ship to shore was patient and reassuring. "Not long now, folks, and we will be on land. Follow the instructions of the soldiers and everything will go smoothly. There have been no mishaps thus far in transporting passengers ashore."

He looked at Amelia and said, "Madam, please be ready to disembark first. We need to get your little one onto dry land, soonest. Once we are past the shore breakers and close enough to the beach, the men are to climb over the side of the boat and wade to shore. I suggest you take off your smart shoes and roll up your trousers."

"But I can't swim, Sir," said a lone voice.

"Don't panic. If there be any amongst you who can't swim, there are slaves who will carry you to land," said the officer.

The sky was powder blue and white clouds rose beyond the distant hills. Storm clouds were building up to the north-east of them. There was a cool south-easterly breeze.

The skilled oarsmen pulled together and the boat surged towards the beach. Amelia noticed the waiting British soldiers, their white skins burnt red, in startling contrast to their black companions who were dressed only in loincloths. A group of honey-coloured men grabbed the front of the boat and pulled it up onto the sand. They steadied it against the waves, which threatened to pull the boat back into the water.

They set about assisting the women and children off the boat, carrying them through the water to the beach. Amelia reluctantly handed over Isabella to a soldier, fearful of losing her baby in the confusion.

A giant Xhosa man, naked to the waist and dressed only in some form of animal skin, reached over the side to assist Sampson with the children. "Papa! Papa! Papa!" Eliza screamed, as the dark stranger reached for her. The man had woolly peppercorn hair and little bits of springy stubble on his dark face. He remained stony-faced at the child's reaction. Sampson was grateful to the man, as he handed over young Frederick, and hoisted Eliza onto his own shoulders.

After months at sea, it took a while for the travellers to find their land legs. Most of them had removed their shoes, and their feet were wet and covered in sand. The bottoms of their trousers and hems of their dresses were soaked. They plonked themselves on the fine sand, before attempting the walk up the beach to the wooden registration hut. They felt giddy with the stimulation of their new surroundings and at being on land again after three months at sea.

The heads of the parties were eager to greet the British officials. Some settlers were nervous to sign allegiance to their new country and its policies. Nearby, there were wagons pulled by spans of big-horned oxen.

Most of the other settlers had arrived months earlier and had already been transported to the allotments in the Albany District, some 130 miles away. In one respect this was a good thing, as there were no large queues of people needing attention. Peter Clark Daniel, as the new leader of the Turvey Party, handled the paperwork on behalf of the Turvey and Daniel families.

With the small contingent of 111passengers on board the *Sir George Osborn*, it meant the disembarkation and registration of passengers went relatively quickly. Both army and navy officials were on hand to assist the newcomers. Resident in the area for the past thirteen years, Captain Francis Evatt, of the 21st Light Dragoons, warmly welcomed them. He explained that Lord Charles Somerset was back in England on two years leave And Sir Rufane Donkin was the Acting Governor of the Cape Colony.

The settlers moved into their tents, erected about a hundred yards from the beach behind the dunes. Dutch transporters would take them to the Albany District in a few days.

"The tents are a bit grubby, *mon cher*," Amelia remarked, placing her large leather carry bag on the sandy floor of the makeshift shelter.

"You must remember scores of other settlers have stayed here over the past few months. These tents have housed many people before us. Let's just get through one day at a time, *ma cherie*," Sampson replied.

Julia Turvey was alone with her children and her elderly father-in-law. Sampson marvelled at her bravery and steadfastness in the absence of that dithering husband of hers.

Ann Mitchley stayed in her own tent with her children.

Benjamin was placed in charge when the children asked permission to go and explore. Being older, he was inquisitive to find out more about his new surroundings. A whole group of energetic youngsters scurried off in search of shells, crabs and other artefacts. They ran with gay abandon on the beach and they scrambled to the top of the dunes. Once at the peak, they slid and rolled down leaving snake-like tracks in the sand. They relished their freedom and wandered off a little too far.

They saw a small group of near-naked small people walking in their direction carrying sticks. The children screamed, and high-tailed it back to the safety of the tents. The Bushmen roared with laughter, calling after the scampering pale-faced children in a language that seemed to be composed almost entirely of clicking sounds.

As the sun set, the group began to settle, gathering around fires. In muted voices, the settlers discussed their new surroundings. "The officials said we will receive our rations and our farming supplies in the morning," Peter Daniel told his party. He caught the eye of Ann Mitchley on the other side of the fire.

"Tomorrow morning," he continued, "family heads can collect ploughs, spades, saws, nails, harrow teeth and whatever else we may need, to get our farmlands going. There is still some seed available. Word has it that some of the settlers are appalled at the conditions they find themselves in at their allotments in the Eastern Cape. We will have to all knuckle down and make the most of the situation. It sounds as though life here will be much harsher than we anticipated."

The women murmured amongst themselves, wondering what they could expect when they left the tent town. A couple of soldiers, including Lieutenant Robert Hart, joined them around the bonfire. The Lieutenant brought out a rough map of the proposed route and explained the journey overland from Algoa Bay to the Albany settlement near Grahamstown.

"Colonel Jacob Cuyler has organised the wagon trains that will take you to Albany. The very first trek he organised consisted of ninety-six wagons with about five hundred immigrants. It was a big group to manage. They have already begun building their dwellings and planting their crops. However, I must warn you, it has not been an easy road for them and, although your group is smaller, it will not be easy for you either. Conditions in the Zuurveld are harsh."

He did not wish to scare the newcomers, but he felt it his duty to let them know they were in for a rough ride and they were not to expect everything to be provided. He made no mention of the hostilities from the locals.

"Depending on your location, and the transport driver of your wagons, your parties might take one of two routes. However, the first night is spent at the Sundays River. The lower route will take you through Jager's Drift and across the Kowie's River near its mouth. The upper route goes through Rautenbach's Drift. At Assagai Bush you will either continue to Grahamstown and beyond to Collingham, and the Coombs, or to the south, to the plots a little further away from the frontier," continued Lieutenant Hart.

"How long will it take us?" asked Sampson.

"With your group of just over one hundred, excluding the *trekboers* and their helpers, I estimate about ten days or so to do the hundred and thirty miles."

There was lively chatter amongst the family members, and their excitement grew with each moment as Lieutenant Hart animatedly explained some of the sights they could expect to see on their journey.

"You have already seen unusual sightings during your voyage – whales, dolphins and the like."

"...and flying fish!" exclaimed an excited Benjamin.

Benjamin had aspirations of becoming a Great Hunter and, before sailing from England, he had asked his mother to find him books on the continent. He had avidly read and re-read the pages of each book she had sourced.

"Benjamin!" said Julia sternly. "Don't interrupt Lieutenant Hart. My apologies, Sir. Please continue."

Hart laughed loudly, amused at Ben's enthusiastic contribution. He could tell the Wright boy would fit in quickly, although he had reservations about some of the other folk.

"You'll be sure to encounter some strange beasts on your wagon journey. Most of them, like the antelope, will scatter as soon as they hear the sound of wagons or see humans. Your transport rider will probably send his scouts ahead to shoot some for the pot, and you may ask to keep the skins. These will prove handy as rugs, bags and belts. The *trekboers* make soft shoes from the skins, which they call *veld-skoene*."

"What?" exclaimed old man Turvey who, at eighty-two, was quite hard of hearing, "are we expected to build our own houses? I thought my son said that we would be provided a house?"

"Yes, indeed, Mr Turvey, Sir," replied Hart, "where you are going, there are no ready-built homes. You will have to employ some of the local tribesmen to help you build walls out of thick branches of trees and daub, or mud, and roofs out of reed grass."

The men were unprepared for this, and the women were shocked. There was consternation and everyone began firing questions at the officer.

"Calm down," said Peter Daniel, "We are all capable people. We have business acumen. We are all hard workers. I am sure the Government will assist us. We will not be abandoned and simply expected to fend for ourselves."

Lieutenant Hart kept quiet. He knew otherwise but decided not to cause undue anxiety. He changed the subject. "One of the more astonishing animals you will see in great numbers as you venture inland will be the African elephant. Many of the males have enormous tusks. Generally, you must be wary of the young adolescents, especially when they are in must."

"What does 'in must' mean?" asked Ben.

"It is when the young males' glands give off a strong-smelling odour as they come into puberty and they can get into an aroused state. They become very aggressive, charging and even challenging older bull elephants. It is a dangerous time to encounter these animals. They can overturn wagons. We know of a soldier who was gored to death by one of these teenaged elephants."

He went on to explain the territorial habits of the enormous animals, marvelling at their strong sense of family. The matriarch was very protective over the herd.

Lieutenant Hart also warned them about bathing in the rivers, to be aware of crocodiles, hippos and snakes. All these creatures could be deadly to man. He asked whether any of the party had guns. When some of them said that they had never fired a gun, he advised them to acquire a weapon and learn how to use it. "In Africa, you should carry a gun with you at all times. You will encounter lions and leopards and other predators, such as hyena."

"What's a hyena?" It was Benjamin. The boy had been listening intently.

"Oh, he is not a creature you want to encounter in a hurry, young Ben," answered the Lieutenant, who was enjoying the young man. "Like the big, ugly vulture birds, they are the scavengers of the wild. They steal prey caught and killed by other animals, and they will fight to the death when ripping a carcass away from another animal."

"What do they look like?"

"They have a face similar to a domestic dog, only more thick set, and appear to have an uncanny, almost playful grin on their immensely strong, thick jaws. Their ears are large and rounded, and they are tawny with spots. You cannot mistake them as they have an unusual way of walking. Their back legs are shorter than their front legs, and they look almost hunchbacked. Hyenas like to prowl at night and make an unmistakably eerie laughing sound. You will be sure to hear them on your travels to the Albany settlement. You will probably smell them before you see them."

The younger children shivered and snuggled closer to their parents as the night air closed in around them. The bonfires dotted around the beach had died down. There were just enough embers glowing in each hole in the sand to carry a dim glow to the faces of the settlers who were about to call it a night.

"Well, that's given us some food for thought," said Sampson, thanking Lieutenant Hart for his hospitality and his tales. The immigrants were all anxious to get started, envisioning life on their one hundred acres of Africa.

As Sampson opened his tent flap, he saw Peter furtively meeting Ann Mitchley behind her tent. Clicking his tongue, he shook his head. Life in Africa would be problematic enough – he wondered why Peter had further complicated matters for himself by taking Ann under his wing. It was his life. His choices.

Amelia settled the children into their makeshift home. All five of them were fast asleep by the time Sampson retired. The exhausted parents, too tired to talk, pushed their camp cots together and held each other. The support poles of the two cots dug uncomfortably into their sides. Determined to lie together on their first night in Africa, Amelia had lined the cots with every soft item she could find, including their big winter coats and extra blankets.

Sampson had found a canvas tarpaulin near their tent. He was grateful that the previous occupant had left this behind, certain it would be useful in the weeks to come.

The unfamiliar sound of the crashing waves kept them awake. Sampson could not see Amelia's beautiful features in the dark, but he could feel her breath against his cheek. Her fingertips tickled his scalp as she ran her fingers gently through his hair. She stroked his eyebrows in a show of affection and comfort, knowing he was concerned about the safety of his family.

He kissed her passionately in return for her affection and thanked her for believing in him and supporting him. He wanted to apologise for bringing her to this harsh land, but decided to keep his anxiety to himself – for the present.

Instead, he asked, "Do you know how much I love you?"

He imagined her smile in the pitch darkness.

"*Oui, mon cher*. Of this one thing, I am certain," she murmured.

At first light, the newcomers rose to the smell of wood fires and the rattle of tin cups. A hot drink would be welcome in the chilly morning air. The soldiers served sweet milky tea with Dutch biscuits called beskuit. After a communal breakfast, Sir Rufane Donkin welcomed the settlers. Lord Somerset was on leave in England.

He explained the allocation of their land, and the approximate distance they would be travelling from the tented camp. The Boer transporter would collect them from the camp. He pointed in the direction of the wooden shed where they could purchase their agricultural implements and seed. Donkin expressed his regret there were no draught animals to pull the ploughs, nor were there horses or wagons available at the land allocated to them. Once at their destinations, settlers could purchase these items.

"How does he expect us to plough the land we are given if we don't have horses or oxen and ploughs? These were supposed to be part of our deposit," asked Sampson.

"You will be required to pay for the hire of the oxen and wagons yourselves and this will be deducted from your deposit – the amount you paid to the Government to get to Africa."

"I don't believe this, Peter!" said Sampson under his breath. "This is not what we were promised when we applied. I am appalled that they are charging us for implements and seed. How on God's earth do they expect us to make our money stretch, when we still do not know what other expenses are ahead of us?"

"Sampson, we are in no position to argue at this point. I suggest we keep our thoughts to ourselves for the time being," Peter tried to calm his brother.

Sampson stormed off. He could not control himself from expressing his disgust at the breach of promises made by the Government even before their departure from the homeland. Peter found Sampson sitting on the beach looking out over the ocean.

"I have invested in this scheme, Peter, and I will not keep quiet forever. The conditions to which we are subjected, are unacceptable. According to Hart, the fact that we will not have adequate, or rather no form of shelter at all when we get to our location is downright despicable! I cannot subject my family to this."

"Let us see the conditions for ourselves before we make a fuss, lad," he said. "You are naturally tired and emotional from the journey and the upheaval. Stay calm. All will be well."

Sampson found it hard to believe, but agreed to keep the peace. He could not promise for how long, though. His family depended on him and his ability to provide for them, in this godforsaken land. He was not impressed with what he had seen so far.

"That wretched Turvey... That no good, conniving son of a ..." he mumbled under his breath.

Sampson again regretted Turvey swaying the family to agree to this ridiculous 'overseas adventure'. He doubted if even Amelia could calm him this time. Waves of nausea overcame him and he retched onto the beach.

CHAPTER 14

TRANSPORT TO THE EASTERN FRONTIER

Wilhelm Meyer was the Dutch transport driver assigned to take them to the Albany district of the eastern Cape. The enormous man took off his hat, his rough, large hands outstretched in greeting. Sampson found his hand clasped in an iron grip by this man who resonated warmth and confidence. Wilhelm had a thick, scruffy red beard that covered his deeply tanned face and laughed heartily as he shook Sampson's hand. "*Liewende God*!" he exclaimed, "*Meinheer*, we had better get you a new boer wardrobe – fast!"

In stark contrast to Wilhelm's comfortable and practical clothing, Sampson wore polished leather shoes, a top hat and a white cravat. Placing a giant arm around Sampson's shoulder, Wilhelm jovially continued, "*Moenie worrie nie,* I'll show you the ropes! *Kom nou*, come, let's go."

Sampson was encouraged by the large man's casual welcome and friendliness. Wilhelm whistled and signalled in the direction of one of his servants, a black man wearing a short skirt of animal skin. He sprang to attention and came running up to the wagon. Sampson recognised him as the man who had assisted his family from the boat. Wilhelm instructed his menservants to assist with the loading of the Daniel family's possessions, including the piano, which they were instructed to handle like a new born baby, or else he would *donder* them.

One of the men lifting trunks and boxes onto the wagon stood next to Sampson. An overpowering sweaty odour wafted from the muscled body.

Beside the ox-drawn wagons, excited dogs, horses, a few sheep and chickens formed part of the procession that rolled out of the tent town, some women and smaller children riding on the wagons while the rest walked. The British men, women and children seemed overdressed in comparison to the burly, casually dressed Dutch transport riders. The Hottentot slaves, slightly built, were scantily dressed while the Xhosa men and the single Khoikoi tracker wore only small coverings of animal skin. As the group moved off, a cacophony of languages could be heard. Various dialects of English were spoken, guttural Dutch, soft clicks of the Khoikoi and the harder ones of isiXhosa. The Hottentots spoke a dialect of their own.

"What's that strange smell?" asked Benjamin Wright, wedged between his Uncle Sampson and Wilhelm Meyer at the front of the wagon. The long yellowwood *disselboom*, the main shaft of the wagon, stretched out in front of them with a span of sixteen oxen yoked to it.

"It's the *khakibos* you're smelling," replied the *boer*. "It's good for putting under your mattress to keep fleas away."

Young Ben asked questions about everything. His favourite words of the moment were, "What?" and "Why?" Luckily Wilhelm was a patient man and tried to answer all of the boy's questions, perhaps realising that Sampson needed to learn as well. Everything in this new country was strange. Sampson realised he needed sound local knowledge if he was to provide for his family. The sights, sounds and smells emerging from the bushveld heightened his senses. He absorbed everything, preparing himself for what lay ahead. He knew that once Wilhelm and his team of helpers left the party at their location, the families were on their own.

After a hard, slow first day on the wagons, the weary travellers reached the banks of the Sundays River where they set up camp. Wilhelm delegated tasks to each party leader, who in turn delegated these to other people. Although a jovial soul, Meyer was a strict disciplinarian in camp. He maintained order that way.

That evening, seated around campfires, the settlers gathered information about those who were already at their locations in the Zuurveld. The news was not always encouraging. The newcomers were disillusioned at their prospects, although, at this late stage, there was little to be done about it.

On the second day, the group stopped in the heat of the day for a much-needed rest. If this was winter, then Sampson wondered what the African summer would be like. He had packed away his thick winter coat and replaced his good shoes with an older pair, which were more comfortable for walking. Comfort and practicality came before impeccable dress. Each day, the slightly built, wiry Bushman tracker, wearing only a leather thong and carrying a pouch of small arrows, ran ahead of the wagons, scouting the road. His sun-wrinkled skin, the colour of honey, looked like it needed ironing. His name was XhipaXe, meaning 'bee-sting eyes'. Meyer explained that the Bushmen were amazingly skilled hunters, patiently following a wounded animal for miles until it succumbed. Their tracking skills were unsurpassed, and finding a loyal scout was like finding a nugget of gold.

XhipaXe came scampering back to Wilhelm like an excited child. He reported a herd of buffalo a little further upwind from where the oxen were tethered. He was pleased with himself, chattering excitedly. His smile showed off a set of fine white teeth, which he cleaned with charcoal from the fire.

Wilhelm grabbed his gun and motioned for a few of his men to accompany him. Benjamin pleaded to join them. "Stay close to me, *seun*" Wilhelm instructed the excited boy, "and make no sudden movements."

The other travellers relaxed in the shade of the trees. Some lay underneath the wagons to escape the sun's rays. The intermittent buzzing of flies mingled with the soft murmuring as people spoke quietly amongst themselves. There was the odd puffing of the horses and the cluck of chickens.

Suddenly, a volley of gunshots shattered the silence. Startled at the sound, some younger children ran for the protection of their mothers and some clambered beneath the wagons.

"Stay calm," said Peter Daniel.

Their *trekboer* leader was nowhere in sight and Julia noticed that Benjamin was missing. She anxiously told Peter. She felt vulnerable and disorientated in the bush. Peter could only assume that ever curious Ben was with Wilhelm. All they could do was wait.

After what seemed like a long time, but may only have been about thirty minutes, the Dutchman came into view through the long grass, his arm draped around Ben's shoulder. Both were grinning from ear to ear. Ben wore Wilhelm's felt hat and had a heavy gun slung over his shoulder. Stripes of blood marked his cheeks, signifying his first kill. "Benjamin, are you hurt?"

"I shot a buffalo!" Ben smiled proudly as the crowd huddled around him.

"*Ja*," said Wilhelm, "he did! This boy is very brave! Come, we must take the wagons and go and collect the meat."

Ben and his newfound hero, *Oom* Wilhelm, sprung onto the front seat of the lead wagon. Adrenalin from the hunt still coursed through their veins. Ben cracked the whip hard, causing the oxen to jolt forward in unison. Wilhelm smiled and nodded. The wagon train was on the move again.

"*Die Rooinek is nou ingebreek*," reported Wilhelm, "the red-neck has been broken in."

Not too far off, the women were astounded to see a huge dead beast. It had a massive set of curved horns. The Hottentot helpers were already skinning the animal. Its tongue hung limply out of the side of its mouth and there were pools of blood where the hunters had sliced open its stomach, allowing the intestines to pour onto the grass. They removed the scrotum and the innards to prevent these from tainting and spoiling the edible meat. It took no time at all for the men to hack the carcass into chunks using large machetes and knives.

"The hide will be used to make a *trektou*," said Wilhelm pointing to a rope on the back of the wagon. The rope would be used to repair broken yokes and for pulling wagons out of muddy rivers and up steep ravines. Due to its elasticity, it was also used for stirrup leathers.

The *boer* promised to show the settlers how to make spiced and salted dried meat. It was the Dutch way of preserving meat. He pulled a piece from his waistcoat pocket and gave it to young Benjamin.

"I always carry a supply with me when I travel, because you are not always lucky enough to shoot an animal along the way."

Wilhelm Meyer left one wagon and a few men behind to cut and load the meat. The rest moved out. The men would make a fire and cook the offal and hooves before catching up with the group. There was always a danger the smell of blood might attract lions and other carnivores to the site of the kill. Wilhelm wanted to get the group far away from the area, quickly.

He was pleased with the kill, though. He would show the new settlers how to prepare an oxtail *potjie* stew, using the tail. Nothing from the animal would be wasted.

That evening, the full moon rose above the horizon and lit up the landscape. Wilhelm sat near the campfire, smoking his pipe and studying the group of pale-skinned English settlers. He realised how much they still had to learn. It was impossible to teach them everything they needed to survive in the days he would spend with them. "Oh, well," he thought, "they will learn the ways of Africa soon enough."

Each day proved interesting and exciting. The rough tracks made by the British soldiers, the Dutch and British settlers who had travelled them before, revealed new sights, smells, foliage and animals.

"How much further?" asked Jane Sophia, who was seven.

"Mr Meyer said between nine to fourteen days, *ma petite*," her mother answered. Those travelling on the front wagons spotted a dead ostrich. It was the biggest bird they had ever seen. The children asked if they could go over to it. Wilhelm stopped the wagon train. Cautiously, they ventured towards the oversized bird, checking the area for predators in the surrounding bush. Seeing no danger, they began pulling ostrich feathers from the tough skin; laughing as they tickled each other with the oversize feathers. They stuffed their hats and clothes with feathers.

The group passed many *kraals*, or homesteads, along the way, groups of huts made from rocks, mud and sticks. Wilhelm explained how the occupants smoothed cow dung over the floors and, over time, the surface became highly polished. This would be one of many useful and practical skills the newcomers would learn for use in their own dwellings.

The Khoikoi women dressed scantily, but this no longer surprised Amelia. "These ridiculous bonnets and heavy petticoat dresses do not encumber the Khoikhoi women," she thought. She began to think of creative ideas for lightweight dress designs and she shared these with Eliza and Julia.

After a few days' travel across rough terrain, they crossed the Kariega River and approached the Theopolis Mission. This hint of civilisation, as they knew it, brought some comfort to those who had lost hope of finding any traces of the English way of life in this strange land. Camping at the mission for two nights meant that supplies could be replenished and wagon wheels repaired. There was fresh water from the river for washing grubby clothes and bathing.

The Reverend John Ulbricht greeted his new acquaintances. He shared some history of his family in Africa, telling the Daniel brothers of the hardships he and his wife had experienced when they first arrived at Theopolis.

On 17 April 1813, the Reverend John Campbell had selected a site on the left bank of the Kasouga River for the Theopolis Mission. It was to serve the *Gonaqua* people and to convert the local heathens. The Reverend taught scriptures, reading and writing to the locals, and schoolchildren had helped to build a dam on the river.

George Barker built his own house at the mission station in 1816. On 13 October of that year, the first European baby was born at the mission to George and Sarah Barker. George caught fish in the Kasouga River, grew wheat and planted peach and fig trees. By 1817, the mission station had a population of three-hundred and seventy-one people and boasted forty-one dwellings. Most residents were Europeans who had abandoned their holdings between the Kasouga and Fish

Rivers due to constant raids by the neighbouring Xhosa.

By December 1818, the Xhosa raids on Dutch settler homesteads in the surrounding areas had become so serious that families left their isolated and exposed farm homes and built dwellings closer together. By February of that year, the population of the mission station had increased to five hundred people.

Reverend Ulbricht went on to tell them how tough it had been for everyone. Some collected seashells which they crushed and burnt, making lime which they could then sell.

"It seems that times are still tough," Sampson remarked.

"About two months ago, a convoy of ninety-six wagons crossed the river at Jager's Drift with a large group of British settlers," the Reverend said, "They passed the mission and outspanned at the Reed River Post. There must have been five hundred settler folk."

The first group to arrive at their destination was led by Lieutenant John Bailey, of the Bailey party, which consisted of two hundred folk from London.

"Young Francis Stanley, a son of one of the members of the Owen's party, drowned while crossing the Kowie River. Be very careful when crossing that river in the next couple of days. Make sure you only cross when it is at its lowest level and the tide has receded, as there is a strong backwash out to sea."

The party arrived at the banks of the Kowie River late the next afternoon. It was too late to cross and the tide was in. They would use the Albany Road to Bathurst the following day, the alternative route some Settler parties had used before them.

"*Mon cher*, look at the beauty of this river mouth. Look there, where it flows into the sea! Such incredibly wide, white beaches," said Amelia. "It's spectacular! Everything is so lush and green." She breathed in deeply, "I can smell the salt air from the ocean. Oh, Sampson, let us stay and build our home here. I love this place."

"*Ma cherie*, we can't just stay anywhere!" Sampson laughed at her naivety, "We must go where the government has allocated us land. Later we can move on, if we want to."

The late afternoon sun shone on the gold dunes on the other side of the river, where dense green and grey foliage spilled over the sand. The children, grumpy from the day's trek, tugged on Sampson's hand and begged to be allowed to walk the short distance along the riverbank to where the river mouth opened out into the sea, vast expanses of unspoilt beaches stretching to either side.

Jane Sophia looked up at him and pleaded with her eyes.

"How can a man resist?" he smiled, placing the palm of his large hand on her bonneted head.

He nodded his approval and looked around for Amelia. It would also give him time to be alone with her, away from the others. Living in close quarters with other families for so long had taken its toll.

Excitedly, Jane Sophia beckoned her siblings, cousins, and new-found friends. "We're going onto the beach. Follow me."

Happy to be free of the jolting and jerking of the ox-wagon, the children raced towards the vast sandy beach. Hand in hand, Sampson and Amelia slowly followed.

"*Maman*!" called Jane Sophia, "look at all the beautiful seashells and the seaweed over there." Slimy green seaweed covered one section of the beach. Jane Sophia squealed with delight and ran over with the cuttlefish, shells and coral she had gathered in her skirts.

Jane Sophia's best mate, Eddie Turvey, came bounding up to her and playfully threw her to the ground. She stood up indignantly and picked up a handful of sand, which she tried to rub into his hair, but he had fast reflexes. He ran off to the foaming white surf, laughing hysterically with his trouser pants rolled up above his knees.

"Oh, *mon cher*, I want to stay here forever," said Amelia tucking her arm through Sampson's and leaning her head against his shoulder. Despite the difficult beginnings and the hardships of the journey from London thus far, she suddenly felt content and secure, knowing they would soon be at their new home. Maybe uprooting the family and sailing to Africa had been the right choice after all. Only time would tell.

Jane Sophia ran alongside Amelia, playfully grabbing her hand.

"*Maman*," she said looking up at her mother, "*Maman*, I want to be called Sophia from now on." This was quite an unusual request and Amelia raised one eyebrow inquisitively. After a bit of thought, "Why not?" It was her French grandmother's name after all.

"You will have to ask your *Papa*," said Amelia, who winked at her husband for his approval.

As the sun began to set, they watched a fine mist roll in from the sea, covering the beach and gently blowing inland up the estuary. The cool night air and the mist reminded Sampson of his days growing up in Ireland. Grey-white smoke billowed into the air above the camp. The smell of a hearty oxtail stew wafted through the cool night air. Wilhelm was cooking his *potjie* over the open fire in a cast-iron pot, along with some other people delegated to kitchen duties that evening. To his pot he added sweet potatoes, carrots and a few beans he had bought at the mission that morning. There was a scrumptious smell of fresh homemade pot bread and the Daniel family was suddenly ravenous.

As they sat around the dying embers of the fire, Wilhelm explained how the Xhosa raids had forced him to move his family away from Albany to Uitenhage in 1817. The warriors had ransacked his house before burning it to the ground. They stole his horses and cattle. He was offered refuge at the Theopolis Mission, but decided to settle at Uitenhage where there was an abundance of water. With only a small population of indigenous people, there was less threat of violence than closer to the Fish River and Grahamstown. Uitenhage was easier to use as a base for trading and transportation in both northerly and southerly directions. Sampson listened intently and made a note of this new information.

"I heard news recently the farmers in this area are expecting a drought. There were not good rains this year," Wilhelm continued, wiping the rich red sauce of the stew from his mouth with the back of his hand. "Not good news for you, Irish." He had given Sampson this nick-name and Sampson took it as a sign of his friendship. "You settlers are supposed to be make it on your own, but it will take at least two years before that will be possible, if ever. The Government will need to look after you and provide plenty of rations through the drought. After all, they brought you here to protect *die ryk mense*, how do you say, rich people, in the Cape. These Xhosa are warrior tribesmen. They are not going to leave you alone. They chased us Dutch farmers away and they will do the same to you." He was silent for a while, then continued, "I don't think the British officials have been honest with you, Irish. Maybe the British Government does not have your interests at heart. You know these government people – I think they have a hidden agenda."

He produced the wrinkled map of the Zuurveld area and pulled the oil lamp closer. It was the map of the allotments allocated for settlers, surveyed by Johan Knobel.

Sampson scrutinised the map. He was concerned that their piece of land was decidedly close to the Great Fish River, which created the natural border between the settlers and the land of the Xhosa tribe.

"Tomorrow or the next day, Colonel Jacob Cuyler will be there to show you your one hundred acres, and to officially welcome you to the Albany settlement," said Wilhelm.

Not in the mood to talk politics after his happy day at the beach with his family, Sampson made light of Wilhelm's earlier comments about the intentions of the British government. Yet, he felt a sense of foreboding. He decided to raise some questions with Wilhelm during the final stage of the journey to Trompetter's Drift in the morning.

That night in the tent, once all the children were asleep, Sampson leaned across and laid his hand on Amelia's chest. Her gentle breathing told him she was in a deep sleep, exhausted from the day's journey.

"Please, God, give me the strength to see this through and the wisdom to make the right decisions. Help me to provide for my family in this hostile land. Keep us safe from harm. Guide my every thought and bring the right type of people across my path to ensure my success in the days ahead. Amen."

Sampson slept lightly. Vaguely aware of the not too distant sound of the waves crashing, he thought of setting foot on his own piece of African soil.

He was undecided whether to be excited at the prospect, or not.

CHAPTER 15

THE TURVEY PARTY ALLOTMENT

1820 – 1823 Despair, Disappointment and Determination

The Daniel family woke to the familiar sounds of cast iron lids clanging on pots of water set to boil on the morning fires. Smoke permeated the canvas tents and the trek oxen bellowed deeply whilst harnessed to the yokes. It was the final leg of the journey.

Dense grey clouds warned of a damp day ahead and the Daniel family wrapped up against the cold with scarves and buttoned-up coats. The uneasiness from the night before still gnawed at Sampson's gut and he was decidedly worried about the fate of his family. He would make sure Wilhelm gave them a seat inside a covered wagon today to make their final journey more comfortable.

There was an unusual birdcall from somewhere in the nearby scrub. Sampson spotted a medium sized grey bird with a triangular-shaped crown on its head jumping from branch to branch. Pointing it out, he asked Wilhelm to name it. His new found friend knew everything, it seemed, about the fauna and flora of the region.

"That, my friend, is known as the Go-Away bird. Listen carefully and you will hear why."

Sampson listened out for the call again, and sure enough, it sounded as if the bird shrilled "go away".

Wilhelm Meyer and his men guided the first three wagons across the Kowie River at the demarcated crossing point. The tide was out, but there was a sense of urgency to get the wagons and people across before the sea rolled back into the estuary, making the river impassable.

Everyone was exhausted, but if they followed instructions, they could reach their location before nightfall. The river was about a mile wide where the oxen entered it, some of the settlers hung onto the sides of the wagons. Small children sat on top, waving excitedly as they passed their parents and friends. The British settlers were more than ready for the final haul.

The Eastern Cape coastline has many rivers running into the sea. Sometimes it was necessary for men and women to strip down to their undergarments so they could swim across. Since the start of their adventure, there had been little room for privacy or alone time. They were a tightly-knit group who depended upon each other. There was no place for modesty amongst the Boers, Xhosa, Hottentot assistants and Khoikhoi trackers.

The wagons followed what was once a steep elephant path lined with trees. Soldiers of the Cape Regiment had cut the branches back to make a passage for the wide wagons. The belt of trees extended for about a mile from the river. The countryside changed dramatically as they veered inland. Tracks became rocky. Broken wagon wheels along the track were silent evidence of the passage of other settlers before them.

Now adept at identifying the countless antelope they encountered, the settlers saw herds of zebra, buffalo, impala and often heard the deep-throated roar of lion at dusk. They were, however, unprepared for the herd of elephant that lumbered in front of them, bringing the wagons to a standstill. There was a collective gasp of awe at the sheer size of the animals. Their mammoth bodies swayed from side to side, as they ambled across the track.

"Look! There's a baby!" shouted an excited child.

"Shh …' Wilhelm hissed.

"Elephant. Be quiet. Let them pass," one traveller whispered to another.

The elephant seemed to take no notice of the watching humans. But for the crunch of dry grass and the snapping of branches, they passed silently. Suddenly, a young bull elephant crashed through the scrub, charging the onlookers. Wilhelm recognised the mock charge as a warning and gave the order to move on before the elephants became aggressive. The wagons lumbered on through the rocky mountain passes. A large male baboon called out a warning from his lofty sentry post. It was a loud frightening call. Ever attentive and alert, Ben spotted the baboon. He pointed it out to young Eddie Turvey as they hung their legs off the back of the wagon. The half-brothers loved the adventure. They had long since removed their jackets and neckties and rolled up their trouser legs to their knees. They wore their shirts un-tucked in with the long sleeves rolled up to their elbows, just like the *trekboers*. Although Wilhelm had made good friends with these *rooineks*, he was eager to complete the journey and return to his Lizelle in Uitenhage. It had been many months since he had been home and he longed for his own bed, his wife and her home cooking.

From his Thorn Ridge vantage point at Bathurst, Colonel Jacob Cuyler spotted the trail of wagons heading in the direction of the Trompetter's Drift post. After the second British occupation of the Cape, he had been commissioned to take over the command of Fort Frederick and the district of Uitenhage from the Batavian officer, Captain Alberti. Soldiers from his regiment had informed him the Turvey party was on their way to their allotments. He would greet and welcome them. They were one of the last parties to arrive. He understood their departure from London had been delayed due to inclement weather and ship damage.

As the magistrate of Uitenhage, he had the task of supervising the dispersal of the settlers to their locations in the Albany settlement. He would show them the surveyor's plan of the properties and issue them with their conditions of settlement. These conditions included their 100 acres of land per family head and the method of drawing rations against their monetary deposits made in England. He would also caution them to become proficient at handling guns.

The Turvey party was allocated land in the Coombs Valley adjacent to the Elliots, Stubbs the farmer, architect, builder and brewer

Mahoney, and trader and fisherman Brown. The area ran roughly from east to west between the Kap River Hills and the Fraser's Camp range, forming the eastern edge of the newly named Albany settlement.

Cuyler knew that living there would prove a great challenge for the newcomers. He pondered the increased tension between settlers and the Xhosa people over the use of the clay pits in the Coombs Valley. The collection and use of the unusual clay deposits was an integral part of Xhosa tradition, as was finding suitable grazing for their cattle. He was concerned about the negative consequences of this on the settlers in the long term, but this was out of his hands.

He resolved to meet with the Turvey group at first light.

The weary travellers were about fifty miles inland from the sea, a few miles from the Great Fish River. The fully laden wagons creaked and rocked as the oxen pulled them along the stony track. They halted in the middle of a dry patch of land covered in scrub-like bushes bearing purple flowers and dotted with red ant heaps.

"*Daar's sy*!" Wilhelm Meyer gave the signal to stop.

"What?" questioned Sampson, "why are we stopping here?"

"This is your new home, Irish. Not far from here is the drift which crosses the Great Fish River into what is known as the Neutral Territory," said Meyer.

Sampson and Amelia stared at each other in disbelief. All they saw was dense scrub, a few trees and patches of bare rocky earth. Pretty Cape *fynbos* was scattered among aloes, cactus-type plants and thorny shrubs as far as the eye could see. The only sign of habitation was the scant remains of a farmhouse and a run-down blockhouse.

Sampson helped to balance Amelia, as she climbed off the wagon. She carried the sleeping Isabella in her arms. This leg of the journey had taken its toll on Amelia and her face was ashen. Isabella had been restless with a bout of colic, crying incessantly.

Sampson immediately sensed Amelia's deep despair even before she expressed it.

"This is hell!" Amelia cried, "There is nothing here, Sampson! Nothing!"

The journey to Africa from England, which began as an exciting adventure for the Daniel clan, more than six months previously, turned to bitter despair for Amelia. The weight of the journey and the burden of the uncertainty which lay ahead finally erupted in an emotional meltdown.

Baby Isabella started to cry and everyone fell silent as Amelia raged. "We gave up our precious home, our comforts, our friends, our church, our life... for what? For this?" Waving an arm over the land.

"Now we are expected to call this God-forsaken place home? *Mon Dieu*! God Help Us!" she wailed.

By their expressions, many of the party members echoed her sentiments, although they did not voice them aloud.

The distraught woman fell to her knees, clutching her infant tightly to her bosom and wept uncontrollably.

Standing helpless before his sobbing wife, Sampson stared blankly ahead. Julia knelt beside her sister-in-law, while the empathetic Ann Mitchley took the crying Isabella from her arms. A cold wind whipped through the wagons. Amelia longed for the lush green meadows of England, for the hustle and bustle of the carriages and clip-clop of horses' hooves along cobbled streets. She wept for the French flower seller at the market, for the family and friends she had left behind in London, and for the stray cats she used to feed at home in Broad Street. She longed for the familiar smell of the theatre and the buzz of backstage during performances. She mourned the deaths at sea of young and old, and that of her dear friend Ellen Burgis, laid to rest at the bottom of the vast ocean.

Julia pulled Amelia's head close to her chest as hot tears streamed down her own cheeks. The two women huddled together for a while without speaking until Amelia's sobs subsided into pitiful sighs.

Around them, Sampson and the others began the tedious task of offloading the wagons. They needed to erect tents before dark, which was sure to bring further challenges.

Several of the men, including Sampson, Peter and John, set off to survey their allotted land. Sampson hung back, already determined to find another place to live, even if this meant breaking his government contract. The children trailed behind him, naively exploring their new environment, oblivious to the adults' concerns.

Sampson caught up with John Burgis, the only experienced farmer in the group. "One hundred acres is only sufficient for a small number of cows and a few sheep. It's never going to be enough for everyone in the party to make a living," Burgis said. Old Mr Turvey nodded in silent agreement.

The men headed back to the wagons to find their belongings unloaded and stacked on the ground. Wilhelm approached Sampson, offering a gnarled hand in farewell, "Irish, it was a great pleasure to have met you. I wish you and your family God speed. May you find your way in this wild Africa. There is a man in these parts called Piet Retief. You will hear of him. He has a great deal of knowledge of this area and when I see him, I will ask him to look out for you."

The Turvey party huddled together surrounded by their few possessions. Sampson placed a protective arm over his wife's shoulder. He could not bear to see her swollen red eyes and blotchy skin. Stunned by their new reality, the group watched Meyer's ox-wagons slowly disappear over the hills. They were on their own in circumstances that none of them had ever imagined.

"What's for dinner?" Ben Wright asked, breaking the deathly silence.

CHAPTER 16

SETTLING DOWN

Amelia woke before sunrise, noticing her own heartbeat and the soft breathing of her sleeping family. She should be strong, she thought, and not break down as she had the day before. The deep-throated bark of a sentry baboon in the nearby hills broke the silence. Startled by this, Amelia woke Sampson. It had rained during the night and the grassy floor of their tent was wet. Others began to stir as Amelia stepped outside. The grass glistened in the early morning sunlight, the dewdrops dancing like diamonds. Shivering in the cold wind, a few of the women made a fire using some of the coals from the night before. They soon had a pot of water on the boil and enjoyed dunking Wilhelm's homemade rusks into their tea for breakfast.

Over the simple meal, the Turvey party members discussed the day ahead. Older children were delegated tasks, while the men decided to pay a visit to Coombs Valley. As they were about to leave, a senior official dressed in full uniform, arrived on horseback.

Colonel Jacob Cuyler and two of his lieutenants came to welcome the party and to issüe them with their conditions of settlement. He was clean-shaven, with a clear, tanned complexion, fair eyebrows and neatly trimmed blond hair. His blue eyes made him appear younger than his forty-five years. Despite the rigidity of his military uniform and his authoritarian appearance, he was a rather likeable man. Sampson instantly warmed to him. He spoke kindly and had a good understanding of challenges facing the newcomers.

"I have opened a store for rations on the north side of Donkin's Terrace. From there you can get your monthly rations of flour, meat, tea, sugar and candles. The military base at Cape Town has shipped three hundred firearms and they will be issued to settlers, along with two rounds of ammunition and one spare round for each firelock, by the provisional magistrate of Bathurst. I urge you to obtain guns as soon as you can. Arm yourselves. There are both human and animal thieves out there," Cuyler said, pointing in the general direction of the river. He continued, "You need to carry a weapon at all times, even whilst tending your crops."

Cuyler unrolled a parchment showing the land surveyor's map of the surrounding area and the demarcation of the 100-acre plots allocated to each party head. He identified where the Turvey party was located, between the Thackwrays and the Elliots and within walking distance of the Irishman, Thomas Mahoney. Thackwray's portion was in the direction of Grahamstown.

"Mr Thackwray and Dr Clarke's wife have fought over the ruins on the property," Cuyler laughed. "Each time Thackwray stores his trunks in the ruin, Mrs Clarke has her men move them out. It has no roof and an old dirt floor, but it's a valuable beginning, especially when there is absolutely nothing else. It seems the previous occupiers were a Dutch family, sadly murdered by the Xhosa."

There was an uncomfortable silence at the Colonel's candour. Sampson preferred not to pursue the matter of the Dutch family for now, as it made him feel ill at ease. Cuyler confirmed the Brown and Stubbs families were to be located about eight miles further down towards the Clay Pits in the Coombs Valley.

The map showed it was about 25 miles to the village of Bathurst. A journey on foot would take about four days and a person would only be able to take home what they were physically able to carry. Cuyler suggested they purchase a cart and horses as soon as possible in order to make life easier for themselves.

"What are the chances of moving to another area?" asked Sampson, rattled by the thought of how exposed his family was to danger.

"You may apply for a pass to leave the area, but you will forfeit your deposit to the British Government in England," was the Colonel's response. "If you have the means, may I suggest you look at relocating your family to Uitenhage? There are plots available for purchase and there is positive development in the town. There are also business prospects there for those so inclined."

Sampson had heard of Uitenhage from his new friend, Wilhelm Meyer, and the thought of moving there had already crossed his mind. Cuyler's mention of the town was perhaps a positive omen. The Colonel took his leave and wished the Turvey party well.

This group of settlers had only been there for a day. Already, the men and older boys had erected the tents neatly and arranged them in a laager-like fashion for protection. There was a central cooking area with crates and boulders circling the fire pit for people to sit on. Their more precious tables and chairs, sideboards and the piano belonging to Amelia Daniel, were sheltered inside one of the tents. There was a stockpile of wood and kindling over to one side of the camp.

"They will be alright," Cuyler thought, as he rode away on his horse. The astuteness of the Daniel brothers had impressed him. Their calm, rational attitude to their situation brought stability to the others in the party. He had heard party leader, Edward Ford Turvey, had not returned to the *Sir George Osborn* at Simons Town before its departure to Algoa Bay. He wondered what kind of leader would delegate the responsibility of his family and his charges to others. He was glad to have met the Daniels. He had his doubts they would be successful farmers, though, especially under these poor farming conditions and considering they were not experienced.

The men of the Turvey party included Sampson, Peter Clarke and John Nevins Daniel, their nephews Benjamin and William Wright, John Burgis, Robert Cartwright, Henry Holland, John Keevey, John Mulligan, John Kemp and Willy Thomas. Together they set off to explore the land and its surroundings, leaving old man Turvey with the womenfolk and the children. Packing some fruit and snacks, including some of Wilhelm's biltong and rusks, and a canvas bag filled with water, they set off on foot in a southerly direction towards the sea, keeping the Great Fish River to their left. They walked along the rough track pointed out by Cuyler, well-used by both mounted soldiers and other settlers. After forty minutes, they saw a group of people moving around on what would be neighbouring land. They crossed a grassy plain towards familiar-looking government-issue tents.

"Goodness! That looks like Tom Mahoney standing next to that wood pile," said Peter, recognising him from the Men's Club in London.

"Yes, Turvey and Mahoney still have a score to settle. I don't think they will ever see eye to eye," agreed Kemp.

Peter Daniel called out to Mahoney, who looked up from his work. He recognised Peter and greeted him and the other men heartily, stretching out his calloused hand.

"It's bloody great to see some familiar faces here. *Caid mille failte,*" he said, welcoming them with the traditional Irish 'one hundred-thousand welcomes!' He was excited to see old acquaintances and glad to know they had come to settle nearby.

"Where's that bloody scoundrel, Turvey?" he asked.

"He was left behind at Simonstown," answered Peter, "and we haven't seen or heard from him since."

"Good bloody t'ing!" laughed the thickset thirty-five-year-old Irishman.

"It serves him bloody right for being such an idiot! Cannot say I would be pleased to be neighbours with him, then. He and I came to blows in the Men's Club. Called me a drunkard he did. I cut him off my party list straight away." Patting Peter on the shoulder, he continued, "But I'm so pleased to see you all made it here in one piece. Come into our beautiful home," he winked, "and have a mug of Mahoney home brew!" He ushered them towards his muddied tent where his wife, Ann, had already put on a pot of water to boil.

"Take that water off the boil, woman! It's homebrewed porter time!" His homemade alcohol was a dark-brown bitter beer brewed from charred malt. He had brought his brewing equipment from England.

Pulling up crates, logs, boulders and makeshift furniture, the dozen or so visitors sat outside the tents. They drank beer as Mahoney regaled them with stories of their sea crossing on the *Northampton* and the challenges they had faced since arriving at the settlement.

"Africa isn't for sissies, that's for sure!" laughed Mahoney. Taking a long sip of his beer, he leaned forward, "The government's put us a stone's throw away from Clay Pits, you know. We went there a few days ago and saw a bunch of Xhosas digging the clay. They use it for face and body paint and for dying fabric and the like." Speaking a little softer, he continued, "I haven't said anything to my wife, as yet, because I don't want her to worry. I was talking to Wilhelm Meyer on the road from Kowie River. He told me about the troubles the previous British and Dutch residents had with the Xhosa people in the area. It seems the government has been trying to push them back across the Great Fish River for years. They keep resisting and then they attack unexpectedly and steal everything they can."

Mahoney then told his visitors a little of the history he had gleaned from the British soldiers stationed in the area. "Before our arrival in 1812, the British formations kept up the struggle to push Chief Ndlambe's Xhosa marauders back across the Fish River, beyond what is known as the Neutral Territory. During the Fourth Frontier War, under the command of Sir John Craddock, the soldiers managed to drive the natives east of the Fish River and to clear the Zuurveld of at least twenty thousand of Ndlambe's followers. On 30 November of that year, the conflict between the British and the Xhosas ended, although the army continued to patrol this area. Since then, the Government has been trying to consolidate it, hence the 1820 Settler Scheme and the real reason why we are here."

The group of newcomers absorbed this disturbing news, while savouring the yeasty flavour and alcohol of the homemade beer.

"The soldiers have been having a hard time here," Mahoney went on, "The local tribesmen are stealing cattle on a regular basis. One young fellow I met when we landed at Algoa Bay told me that just last year there were numerous attacks. Dutch farmers abandoned their homesteads in fear. We've been coerced here by Governor Somerset's bullshit to stop the infiltration of the tribes into this British occupied territory."

The shocking fact that only ten months ago the colony had been at war with the Xhosa stunned the men of the Turvey party.

"Who else has been allocated land in this area?" asked Peter.

"Well, the Elliots and the Thackwrays are next to you. I have it on good knowledge that Knobel did not make proper provision for John Stubbs and John Brown. Word has it they will be located on the far side of my land, northeast of the Kap River and closer to the Great Fish. I'm only thinking that it will spell trouble for them. And ultimately for us neighbours," Mahoney answered. British soldiers, posted at various points along the river, had told Mahoney that the Xhosas cross the river at full moon to collect baskets of the red and yellow ochre clay to be used for rituals. They called the Pits *Embholeni* – the Place of the Red Clay. "John Brown is a trader and a keen fisherman. He is not interested in farming for gain. His partner, Stubbs is a genuine farmer, so I think between them they will work the land and the stock and they hope to trade with the Xhosa people." Mahoney took another big swig of his homebrewed porter.

Sampson spoke up, "Peter and I will be making a trip to Bathurst within the next few days to get firearms. The ones Cuyler told us about."

The three Daniel brothers looked at one another. The mood had turned a little too serious. None of them liked weapons, but it seemed they would have to arm themselves.

"You're here now, so make the most of your African adventure! Cheers!" shouted Mahoney, raising his hand as he bid his visitors' farewell.

Back on their way, the men crossed the undulating, grassy hills, carefully avoiding loose rocks. The terrain was dotted here and there with succulent aloes, whose bright orange flowers glowed against the backdrop of the blue African sky. The men walked in silence, pondering their discussions with Mahoney. Despite the rugged beauty of the countryside, their future in Africa seemed bleak. Sampson felt more despondent than ever. Sampson drew Peter and John out of earshot of the others.

"I don't have a good feeling about being situated so close to the river. We are a sitting target!"

Peter placed a comforting hand on Sampson's shoulder. John Daniel, the youngest and quietest, listened intently as his two older brothers conversed.

"I understand, lad," Peter said, "Nevertheless, remember, the British soldiers have fought the warriors repeatedly. Cuyler told me they have negotiated a peace treaty and an agreement with Chief Gaika. The next time the Xhosa cross the river at full moon to collect clay, there will be a large contingent of soldiers to monitor them to prevent confrontation. The soldiers will ensure they do not take our cattle home with them."

Sampson sighed, "It's not just the threat of attack. It is also our situation. We have no solid dwellings, no schools, no churches and no water for miles. How can we be expected to live in this hostile wilderness?"

Angrily, he pushed Peter away and stalked off, oblivious to the large fish eagle that soared above them.

"Time, give it time, lad," Peter called out. Speaking to John, and trying to lighten the mood, he continued, "I believe a certain Lieutenant Alexander Bisset RN is already well established on his farm called *Croyden.* He has planted two and a half acres of his land to wheat, with one hundred vine stocks plus potatoes, beans, pumpkins, cabbage, onions and other vegetables. We will endeavour to do the same. "Let's be positive. We have no choice. Bisset has been here longer than us and he is still living in a tent."

The brothers caught up with Sampson, and Peter playfully slapped him on the back. "Cheer up old chap! Look on the bright side. You have a wife who adores you and beautiful children who need your strength and encouragement. You have this exquisite countryside around you. There will be numerous challenges, but also many opportunities ahead." Sampson ignored him.

The men picked up their pace. It was getting late. By the time they got back to camp, they decided to pool resources and purchase some form of transport, possibly a horse and a small wagon and oxen, to start with. They would leave Henry Holland and John Kemp to look after the women and children while they made the four-day journey to Bathurst. At the place they began to call Turvey's Post, a happy sight greeted them. The older boys had erected a makeshift lean-to and stacked the firewood beneath it as protection from the rain. There was a makeshift coop to house their chickens, and the ram and two sheep which Wilhelm had left for them were tethered to a thorn tree with buffalo-hide rope. The area around the tents was clean and there was order in the camp. The boys had placed large rocks in a circle and had a huge woodpile ready for the evening fire. A smaller fire was burning to one side and a three-legged cast-iron pot was emitting an aroma of venison, potato and vegetables. Amelia had learnt how to make this on their journey from Algoa Bay. She stood over the pot and smiled at Sampson. He was glad to see her looking a little more at ease.

The younger children sat on a blanket listening to Aunt Julia tell a story, each one wearing a funny-looking, hand-woven reed hat – a craft they had learnt whilst at the Theopolis Mission.

There was an atmosphere of calm and contentment. But Sampson was not convinced.

CHAPTER 17

EXPLORING THE NEIGHBOURHOOD

Trip to Bathurst

A week later, Sampson, Peter, John Nevins, John Burgis and Keevey walked to Bathurst. Their mission: to buy rations, horses and a cart. On foot, the twenty miles to the small village took about eight hours.

When they arrived in Bathurst, they found many other settlers waiting outside the British government issues office. All had similar complaints about the lack of rations, poor soil, scarcity of water and limited resources for building.

As Sampson spoke of his concerns, Captain Trappes, the official on duty, avoided eye contact. He had heard these complaints before and squirmed under the pressure. He was unable to give Sampson an honest answer to his request for a pass to leave the Albany area. Sampson fingered the relocation application letter in his pocket and wondered if he would fare better to hand his request to the more senior official, Cuyler. The seeming lack of genuine support from Trappes was a little unnerving. Disgruntled, Sampson stepped outside the supply office. He saw a boer standing on the opposite side of the rudimentary dirt road, which served as the main street of Bathurst. The man offered two horses with saddles for sale. He wore a wide-brimmed black leather hat and his thick raven beard was neatly trimmed. Crossing the road, Sampson walked over and introduced himself. Shortly afterwards, Peter and the others joined him.

"*Aangename kennis, my naam is* Piet Retief," said the man as he extended his hand in greeting. He studied the well dressed, albeit dusty group of men and realised they must have walked quite a distance.

"We are looking to buy horses and a cart," said Peter, shaking the proffered hand.

"I have just what you need, and more," replied Retief, showing him the *boerperd* mare and a gelding alongside him. "These are good, strong work horses and they have great stamina and endurance. They can easily pull a small buggy, but you will need oxen to pull a wagon. I have these too."

Sampson remembered Retief's name from Wilhelm Meyer, who had spoken highly of him. Retief was well known and a trusted businessman who owned properties and livestock. The men agreed on Retief's asking price and shared the expense of buying the horses. Retief said he had a buggy and a wagon for sale in Grahamstown.

"Is there better quality of land and resources further afield?" Sampson asked Retief.

"Oh, for sure," said Retief, "there is fertile land further northwest of here. There is a place called Uitenhage, which is beautiful and has an abundance of water. I have properties there. It is a safe distance from the Xhosa, too."

"Do you know Wilhelm Meyer from there?" asked Sampson.

Retief answered in the affirmative.

"I am going to send word with you to ask him to find a piece of land there for me. I refuse to stick around here for the Xhosa to slaughter my family, or to die from exposure to the elements. There is no use planting seeds in soil that will not yield good crops. From what Meyer told me, that place is far away from the troubles and there is a small, established community there."

"You are welcome to travel with me to Uitenhage to hunt antelope, Mr Daniel," said Retief, "I go in a month. Then you will be able to see for yourself and make up your mind whether you want to move from the Albany District."

Sampson gratefully accepted Piet Retief's offer of joining the hunting party to Uitenhage.

Piet Retief was the commandant of the Winterberg Ward in the Albany District. He was born in 1770 in the Wagenmaker's Valley to the west of the Cape Colony. He was only a little older than Sampson. He had settled in the frontier in 1814 and acquired his wealth through buying and selling livestock. The Daniel brothers agreed Retief was the right person to speak to on behalf of the frontier farmers. He had experience with the Xhosas and knew the British officers stationed in the area. He was also acquainted with many of the settlers.

Peter Daniel was not keen to head further north. He decided to scout around over the next few months for land of his own, closer to Grahamstown. He liked the lay of the land and saw a future for himself as the business centre grew. He planned to open his own jewellery shop in the town. Sampson had his own choices to make and Peter supported those.

The men accepted an invitation to stay two nights at the home of Piet Retief in Bathurst.

The following morning, Sampson dropped off his letter of application with Colonel Cuyler. In it, he agreed to forfeit his settler deposit in exchange for a free pass out of the Albany District.

After concluding their business affairs, purchasing the horses from Piet Retief, and various supplies, the men headed back to Turvey's Post. Sampson and Peter agreed to meet Retief at a later stage with the prospect of buying his buggy and wagon.

There was great jubilation in the camp when the men returned with the two horses, a dairy cow with calf, two oxen, a bag of crushed maize meal, 200 lbs of flour, sugar and tea and seeds for planting. The government had issued them with two ploughs and some harrows, candle moulds and soap.

Sticks of biltong were a real treat for the children, a gift from Sampson's new Dutch friend along with rusks, made by Retief's wife, for Amelia. Sampson surprised Amelia with an unusual sweet treat. Retief had called them *koeksusters*. They were a syrupy-sweet, sticky dough-like plaited finger dessert. Sampson excitedly told Amelia about Retief, Uitenhage and the hunt. He told her that the application for a pass out of the Albany district was safely in Cuyler's hands. All they needed was patient resilience in the meantime, as weeks rolled into months.

"It's nigh impossible to plough this land by hand," said John Keevey one day, throwing the plough to the side angrily and walking away. The soil was shallow and dry, filled with tubers, roots, rocks and stones. These needed to be cleared before they could make any attempt to plough the land.

Tempers flared and the men had to control themselves to prevent fights breaking out.

"Still no word from Edward?" asked Amelia as she watched the men toil out in the veld.

"Not a word. I am expecting him any day now."

Julia stared into the distance. She shrugged her shoulders in defeat, knowing she was unable to rely on Edward. When Edward failed to return to the ship at Simonstown, she resolved to make the most of a very difficult situation – settling in a new country without her husband and fending for her children. She was deeply grateful for the help she received from her sons and her brothers. They had been pillars of strength for the months of Edward's absence. She received constant support from Rosa, a real gem of a daughter-in-law married to her eldest son William. And of course Amelia Daniel was her steadfast friend.

To occupy the long days whilst the men set about building more permanent wattle and daub dwellings, Amelia choreographed children's performances and gave informal ballet lessons to the girls. She taught the children to sing French songs. Her piano recitals delighted both family and neighbours alike.

Young Eddie Turvey enchanted the audience with his ungainly ballet antics, bringing much laughter to young and old. He was a good-looking boy like his father.

One sunny afternoon, instead of the usual bible lesson reading, Julia and Amelia made the children act it out. They re-enacted the story of Daniel in the lion's den. The eager little actors became vociferous as their teacher, Julia, narrated the events of the story whilst they performed. Amelia had draped them in tablecloths and linen for coats and used hand towels for head scarves.

"But King Darius, I have been nothing but faithful, honest, responsible and trustworthy in your court, yet your officials accuse me of simply praying three times a day to my God, as I always do," pleaded a young Ben playing the role Daniel.

"You are guilty," said King Darius, alias Eddie Turvey, "May your God who you serve faithfully, rescue you." He pointed his finger firmly at the accused man, as he declared Daniel guilty of disobeying the law.

The court officials, played by the smaller children gathered around "Daniel" and gleefully pushed him into an imaginary pit of snarling lions where the narrator said he stayed for 30 days.

"King Darius really loved Daniel, but he was forced to punish Daniel by his deceitful court officials. He had sleepless nights," read Julia, as Eddie paced up and down the makeshift, dusty stage floor.

King Darius marched to the pit of lions, expecting Daniel to be dead. Instead, he heard Daniel call out excitedly, "Long live the King. My God sent the angels to shut the lions' mouths, so they would not hurt me. I have been found innocent in his sight."

"Daniel was saved as he trusted God," read the narrator. The men who had falsely accused Daniel were thrown into the lions' den along with their wives and children.

"*Nec Timeo Nec Sperno* – Neither fear nor Despise!" called out the stage of young actors boldly, as they bowed and declared the Daniel motto.

Julia, Amelia and the other adults watching the open air performance, clapped delightedly.

The sound of horse's hooves on the rocky dirt road caused Julia to look away from her little group of actors. What she saw brought her smartly to her feet.

"Edward?" she exclaimed, not sure whether to be excited, relieved or angry at the sight of him.

There he sat, astride a beautiful dapple grey thoroughbred. He wore a floppy leather hat and a soft leather jacket over his white, open-necked cotton shirt. He sported a long, fair, bushy beard. Julia hardly recognised her husband. His rifle was firmly attached to a sleeping roll behind the saddle. The children gazed curiously at the new visitor.

"Children, the lesson is over," said Julia, dismissing them as she marched over to Edward.

There was an awkward silence as Julia stood with her hands on her hips in front of him, quietly watching him dismount. Silhouetted against the bright winter sun, for a brief moment he appeared as a heavenly apparition. The angelic illusion was soon broken as Edward hooked the reins of his horse over a branch of a nearby acacia tree and removed his hat. He too, felt rather strange seeing his wife after all this time. He tendered no apology, but instead reached into his jacket pocket for a rolled-up canvas. As he unrolled it, Julia saw it was an unfinished sketch of the Theopolis Mission.

"I'd like to return there one day to complete the painting," was all he said.

Julia hardly glanced at the picture. Out of nowhere, she yelled at him. It was an outburst of pent up fury, "You left me alone all these months, Edward! Alone to fend for myself, and our children!"

Her voice rose to a high-pitched crescendo and the others adults ran in her direction to see what the commotion was about. "You did not even bother to send a message! Sampson, Peter and John had to look after us, when they have families and worries of their own."

He sheepishly rolled up his sketch and put it back inside his jacket pocket. He gently touched her face, kissing her tenderly on the forehead.

"I missed the boat in Simonstown," was all he could offer in weak apology.

In some ways, the equilibrium around the Turvey allotment became unsettled and imbalanced for a while. Edward, who had once been the leader of the party on board the *Sir George Osborn* was treated rather like an outsider. So he preferred to keep to himself. He spent much of his time painting. He travelled to Bathurst and Grahamstown, often spending days away from home. Julia always felt cheated when he went away, but she was determined not to let his absence bring her down. She continued with her daily teaching routine. She became used to her husband's long absences and took on the role as the head of her household, even when he was at home. She found it difficult to adjust having him around. He was more of a frustration than a help to the other men.

Edward steered clear of the Mahoney Camp, preferring to keep his distance to avoid conflict with his Irish adversary.

"Mahoney is so self-opinionated," thought Turvey. "If I see him, I will probably take a swipe at him."

Sampson found it hard to understand Turvey's logic and the two men also steered well clear of one another. Turvey appeared to have no plan of action and offered no practical explanations for some of the strange things he had done since re-joining his group.

Sampson observed Turvey from a distance. The jeweller watched the artist dig holes in the ground – rows and rows of them. Turvey then methodically transplanted rows of aloes and then later, rows of trees into the meticulously prepared holes. He took large poles, fashioned from tree trunks and "planted" them in the ground. When asked by the other men what these poles were for, he told them to "mind your own business." Eventually, the other members at Turvey's Post all but ignored him and left him to his own devices.

He certainly was an unusual character and lived in his own quirky world.

One morning, two strangers arrived at the Turvey's Post. They introduced themselves as the surgeon, Alexander Cowie, and his associate, Benjamin Green, explorers of the African continent. Edward welcomed them and Julia offered them tea along with fresh bread baked in the makeshift oven, fashioned from a clay antheap. They perused Edward's collections of paintings, including the unfinished one of Theopolis, and another he had done of Fort Wiltshire.

They had heard of Turvey's artistic abilities. As such, the men invited him to join them on an exploratory expedition into the interior to document fauna and flora, agreeing to pay him well for his drawings and sketches. It was an opportunity the eccentric Turvey simply could not resist. Without much thought, he jumped at it, showing little consideration for Julia's needs. He persuaded her this would be the right thing for him to do, and it would bring in much-needed funds for the family.

Julia knew Edward was not happy at Turvey's Post. Everyone else had realised early on he had no interest in farming or tilling the soil, let alone taking on the responsibility of earning for his family. They hardly gave him the time of day anymore. It was not in his make-up to build buildings or to cut wood or to plant crops. He considered himself an artist. He would rather take a twig or a log and carve an image from it before chopping it up for firewood. Whilst the other men in the camp busied themselves with completing their dwellings out of mud and wattle wood to provide shelter for their families, Edward Turvey daydreamed, painted and played.

Julia had no option but to agree to support her husband's new venture. The men said that they would only be away for about six months. They promised that when they returned Turvey would have enough money to make his family comfortable.

The following morning, Julia and her children watched as Edward rode away on horseback with his two new partners. Benjamin hugged his mother and she rested her head wearily on his tall shoulder.

"Everything will be alright, Mother. William, Rosa and I will help you with the children. You'll see."

Alone that night, Julia thought of her brothers and how different they were, yet such close friends. She feared they, like Daniel in the bible story, had been lured into the lion's den of Africa. She worried if any of them would survive this new life in Africa.

Peter and Sampson shared the costs of hiring Khaya, who had arrived unexpectedly at Turvey's Post with his wife and two children. Khaya had presented a note from Wilhelm Meyer.

"I have sent Khaya to help you with building. His wife can help Amelia with chores. Feed him and shelter his family. Bring him back to me when you come to Uitenhage. Stay strong, Irish." The note came with a sack of biltong and some homemade rusks.

Piet Retief had obviously conveyed Sampson's message to Wilhelm. The Irishman smiled to himself. He was glad to have formed a good rapport with the Dutch people.

Khaya the Xhosa was a quiet, hardworking man with the strength of an ox. It was difficult to tell his age, but he seemed to be around thirty-five years old. His wife, Thembisile, helped Amelia and her sister-in-law Julia with domestic duties, and showed them where to find wood and how to store and protect it from the damp weather. Together, they harvested edible berries, roots and bulbs from the bush and Thembisile showed the ignorant *umlungus* the poisonous plants. She was bemused at how little they knew about the bush, which was second nature to the woman who had been born on the other side of the nearby Fish River. She was adept at making a fire and had no qualms about wringing a chicken's neck before plucking it. Thembisile soon became invaluable to Amelia and the other women.

With the help of the Xhosa couple, Sampson and Amelia finished building their first home. It was a wattle and daub house with a reed thatched roof. They planned to replace the reeds with corrugated iron once supplies arrived from England to Grahamstown – if they stayed that long. Sampson was still waiting patiently for his pass from the government.

For now, they made their living area as comfortable as possible. There was always a hand-embroidered linen cloth on the tea tray, brought from England and a bowl of freshly picked wildflowers on the rosewood leaf table Sampson had carefully reassembled.

"Surely Edward thinks of the children?" Amelia asked her sister-in-law Julia, one morning while they were collecting gooseberries. "He should have sent you some money from the sale of his sketches by now."

"No, not a word," replied Julia, shrugging dismissively. She had known she could not rely on Edward. This time, she was not sure that she would even see him again.

Months after Edward's departure, a wooden trunk of books arrived at Turvey's Post. It was addressed to Julia from her eldest son John Wright, in Ireland. She took the welcome collection of books out one at a time to read. She wanted to savour them, reading each one slowly and lovingly. Early one morning, a few days later, an excited Eliza woke her mother. "Mother, I had a vivid dream last night. I dreamt that there was some money between the pages of one of the books that John sent us."

Julia looked quizzically at Eliza and then thought about the feasibility of that. When the trunk of books had arrived, they had unpacked them to check that there was no damp or damage and then carefully repacked them never thinking for a minute to check between the pages of each one. Mother and daughter raced each other to the trunk and hurriedly unpacked the books again. They methodically flicked through each one. Between the pages of *Harry and Lucy* they found a large wad of pound notes and a letter from John, stating that the money was income from her estate in Ireland.

Julia screamed with joy and bear-hugged Eliza tightly. The two danced around with sheer delight.

"Thank you, John, thank you, thank you!" she yelled as tears streamed down her face.

CHAPTER 18

THE CLAY PITS IN THE VALLEY OF THE COOMBS

Xhosa – "i-Qumrha" – the Place of Many Olives

Old Year's Night – 31, December 1821

On the eve of 1822, the Daniel camp was deathly silent. Grey clouds hung low in the night sky hiding the moonlight. With a blanket wrapped around his shoulders and tucked up over his ears, Sampson stared into the dying embers of the cooking fire. The family had long since gone to bed and the sounds of insects were his only company.

Sampson Daniel was unable to sleep. His head was spinning in turmoil. Amongst other things, he was plagued with thoughts of the recent tragic murder of Benjamin Anderson, a local youngster who was murdered by a lone Xhosa tribesman whilst on his way to visit John Stubbs at the Clay Pits. A huge detachment of mounted Cape Regiment, 150 infantry and twenty mounted burghers, including Piet Retief alerted to the news of the missing man, found the body of Benjamin in a secluded area of dense bush in close proximity to the Stubbs plot. He had been stripped naked and repeatedly stabbed, then buried in a shallow grave in the bush.

As he sat alone under the night sky, Sampson took a drag on one of Peter's cigars. He seldom smoked, but tonight he felt a false sense of comfort as he drew the rich tobacco smoke into his mouth. Slowly, he puffed out white mini clouds and reflected back on the significant events of the past year, 1821.

Sampson's mind drifted back to February and the early parts of 1821. He remembered walking with Amelia. The parched dirt road between the Turvey location and the Clay Pits was dry, like cracked lips waiting for moisture. There had been no rain for months and the crops planted by the settlers on their arrival had failed. Sampson and Amelia walked side by side in silence. The hardships of the past eight months since their arrival in this foreign land had taken their toll on them all. Although they had managed to build a three-roomed settler cottage out of wattle and mud, it was far from what they had imagined they would live in, when they had first heard of the settler scheme back in Edinburgh. Under the circumstances, Amelia made their home as comfortable as possible. Sampson was set in his resolve not to spend all the money they had brought with them from England on this location. He had seen other settler families falling on hard times through lack of resources. He was biding his time, waiting for his pass to Uitenhage.

The irritating buzz of flies around his head added to his frustration and he gave up swatting at them. The heat of the midmorning sun during their walk did nothing to ease his bad mood.

"We should have left earlier," mumbled Sampson.

Aware he was grumpy Amelia had suggested they walked to the Clay Pits to visit the Brown family, and to witness the Xhosa clay-collecting ceremony. According to John Brown's wife Ann, it was quite a colourful sight. She had admitted to being quite unnerved the first time a large group of Xhosas from across the river arrived, unannounced, to collect clay, but afterwards she said she had rather enjoyed the gaiety of the gathering. John Brown had taken full advantage of these visits to trade beads, buttons and brass-wire for ox-hides, horns and elephant tusks.

Sampson reluctantly agreed to accompany Amelia. As they crossed the open veld, they noticed a herd of zebra grazing silently in the shade of a thorny tree. The couple was so close they could hear the thick tails of the striped, horse-like animals swishing away the flies. As soon as the herd sensed the presence of the humans, they spun around in unison and ran off in the opposite direction.

On route to the Clay Pits, the husband and wife passed close to the Elliots' property, which bordered on the farm of Thomas Stubbs. The Mahoney homestead was to their right. They waved and called out a greeting to Mrs Mahoney who was outside in her yard. Sampson smiled as he thought about Mahoney's entrepreneurial spirit. The man tendered for every Government building project and had a successful home brewery on the go. He traded whatever he could, whenever he could, always quick to turn a buck. Although complete opposite in character to himself, Sampson enjoyed visiting this loud, rough Irishman. He was good for a hearty laugh from time to time.

"Mr Brown is a bit like my brother, Peter," said Sampson as they approached the clearing leading to the Brown house. Amelia turned, looking at him inquiringly.

"He likes women… very much," Sampson continued, bluntly, "his mistress, Charlotte Whitfield, lives with him and his wife. In fact, she has a number of children from Mr Brown already."

Amelia clicked her tongue and rolled her eyes as she walked on. "I know. I heard," she snapped back. "I would never allow another woman into my kitchen, let alone allow her to share my husband's bed." Indignant at the immorality, she held an imaginary cattle whip in her hand and gestured wildly. "I would beat her black and blue until she begged for mercy!"

Sampson laughed out loud. His mood lifted immediately at his wife's animated actions. They walked down the well-trodden path to John Brown's humble homestead.

Mr Brown had planted a hedge of Kei Apples around the neat stone building and his wife had created a pretty garden, despite the harsh drought. Sturdy walls were fashioned from the local stone and the roof was made of reed. Considering the hardships, many settlers managed to make their dwellings homely, with a distinct taste of Ye Olde England.

Mrs Brown warmly welcomed them into the tastefully furnished home. She introduced them to Charlotte, who was young enough to be her daughter. The two women appeared quite accepting of one another. Only Sampson noticed the slight flair of Amelia's nostrils as she shook Charlotte's hand, and he smiled at his wife's prudish morality.

They ate lunch at the polished mahogany table set with white linen, fine china, silver and iron spoons. Mrs Brown proudly served the homemade soup, mashed sweet potatoes and pumpkin, produced from her own garden. She treated her guests to a side of venison and roasted wild pig, shot a few days before. Dessert was a scrumptious apple pie. Mrs Brown's kitchen had all kinds of modern equipment which they had shipped with them from England and her husband had a toolbox filled with specialised tools. Noticing a shelf filled with books, Amelia commented on them.

"My sister-in-law has taken on the role of governess in our area. I don't know what we would have done to educate our children without her. Julia Turvey encourages all the neighbourhood children to read."

Charlotte showed Amelia a trunk filled with books and kindly invited her to borrow some for Julia. Being an educated woman herself, Charlotte said she was the governess in the Brown household. She taught both the Browns' and the neighbouring Stubbs' children to read and write. The school established in Grahamstown was too far away and hence impossible for the children to attend daily.

"I am sure you teach Mr Brown a few things, too," thought Amelia, her one raised eyebrow hinting at her thoughts.

"I am greatly encouraged by what you have achieved since you have been here, John," said Sampson as the group left the farmhouse after lunch and followed the pathway that led to the Clay Pits. The land was dry and the grass stood tall in some places, but the path was well worn. Sampson could see the neighbours visited one another regularly. Brown and Stubbs had formed a partnership when they left England and were the best of friends.

"As you are well aware, there have been hardships, Mr Daniel," said Brown. "Drought, the rust on the crops and the locusts have all but ruined me. It has been nigh impossible to turn this virgin bush into farmlands. Once we get to the Clay Pits, you will see that Stubbs and I have taken to trading with the Xhosas in order to make a living, although this is frowned upon by the authorities."

They approached a small herd of cattle and Sampson enquired about the animals.

"I keep persevering with my cattle, but this Kap River bush is alive with Xhosa," he said matter-of-factly. "We are constantly on the alert to fight them off and to take measures to protect our stock. We have tried to keep them out and reason with them, but they continue to break the conditions of any peace treaty and cross the neutral zone to collect their traditional clay from the Clay Pits. I do not have a problem with them coming to collect clay. However, I do have a problem when they take some of our cattle back across the river. We used to keep out of their way, but now we have to do something about it. It is occurring too often."

The men walked in silence for a short time.

"The Xhosas have obtained permission from Colonel Wiltshire to collect clay here today. You will see for yourself what happens." Brown shook his head and as he continued, "Solving the problem is easy. These people want our cattle, our iron, our alcohol spirits, our buttons and beads. Above all, they want open access to collect the red clay from the Clay Pits. They have been free to do so for years before the white man came. Both Stubbs and I have agreed to give them what they want … at a price. The government officials forbid direct trade between settlers and the tribesmen. However, there is so much corruption. The officials ensure our hands are tied with their bureaucracy. In this way, it is them who can turn an underhanded profit, not us. This is unfair practice and creates much contention. Times are tough for the settlers, Mr Daniel, but we go on. There is nothing else to do but make the best of the situation we find ourselves in. We will trade with our black neighbours, but I fear this will come at a high cost."

Sampson kept quiet. His philosophy was rather different. Instead of succumbing to the temptation of dealing illegally behind the authority's back to make a living, he admitted to Brown that he had applied to the government for a pass to leave Lower Albany to seek greener pastures.

"I am a businessman, Mr Brown, not a farmer. I will not subject my family to the constant threat of Xhosa attacks, or theft of my livestock. The fact is, many families live very close to the tribal lands and are vulnerable. The Xhosa do not think the same way as we do. We are from different worlds with different cultures. We have intruded upon their land and yet, we expect them to understand and conform to our ways."

He paused for a moment before speaking his truth.

"I have decided, in the best interests of my financial wellbeing, and for the safety of my family, to move further north. I have found land at Uitenhage."

Mr Brown stopped dead in his tracks and looked his counterpart in the eye.

"Times are hard, Mr Brown, but I intend to make them easier for myself and my family." Sampson sensed Brown's open warmth dissipate.

The two men continued walking in silence. Brown eventually spoke out.

"Mr Daniel, John Stubbs and I will NEVER give in to these Xhosa. I will stand my ground. This is my land and I will make it work for me and my family," he said emphatically.

Each to its own, thought Sampson, but it may just cost you your life. Aloud, he said, "All I am saying is my life and the safety of my family comes first."

Sampson felt no guilt at the decision he had made. This place truly was the forlorn hope described by most of the settlers. He had no desire to hang around longer than necessary to find out if it was true. From Brown's homestead, steep rocks flanked the path which descended through dense thicket, finally opening up to reveal a beautiful valley. It was a land of sharp contrasts.

The womenfolk caught up with the men as they approached the Clay Pits. They heard a multitude of voices and were astounded at the sight that greeted them as they parted the long grass. There was a throng of dark bodies, mostly women, digging vibrant red ochre from the abundant clay deposits. The Xhosa woman sang melodiously while they worked, watched over by some uniformed soldiers of the Cape Regiment.

The women laid clay crush into large piles, as the Xhosa men sat on their haunches, keeping vigilant watch, knobkerries in hand. These men were not doing any of the hard, physical work. Some bartered skins and ivory for beads and buttons from a few of the settlers, including John Stubbs who was at the forefront of the negotiations.

Major Pigot, who lived a few miles away, frequently complained about the risks involved in allowing so many Xhosa into the Kap River bush area at one time. Hence, the soldiers built a fort there, and the area was frequently patrolled. This only stirred up conflict and animosity between the residents and their Xhosa neighbours. Even after the army patrols ceased, the animosity continued unabated.

John Brown and his neighbour Stubbs, however, had different views. They believed they had developed a good understanding with their tribal neighbours and their leaders. They felt assured of their safety. Sampson was not as certain. He felt trading with the unpredictable Xhosa was a dangerous gamble and he told Brown this.

Brown brushed aside Sampson's pessimism and bent down to pick up a few pieces of the dry clay, which he handed to Sampson. The surface of the clay felt surprisingly smooth and silky between his fingers. A fine red powder rubbed off onto his hands. Sampson was dumbfounded that lives had been lost because of fights over the abundant clay deposits in this small area.

"Is this what the conflict is all about?" he asked Brown.

"Oh, aye!" responded Brown, "this is not just any kind of stone, Mr Daniel."

He spat on a piece of clay and rubbed it on Sampson's hand, leaving a rich red ochre mark on the skin. "This clay is used for body adornment and for protection from the sun by the women. Water is added and it is rolled into small, pea-like balls, which they use in their hair as beauty accessories, much like your fancy hat pins!" Brown laughed. "They also decorate their houses with the clay. There is a mustard-yellow stone and a brown one. So you see, Mr Daniel, this is a precious commodity and we must take advantage of this. I do not have a problem with them collecting the clay. I just wish they would leave my cattle alone!"

Sampson was impressed. He was a businessman, but he was not a great risk taker like Brown and Stubbs. Therefore, when Brown invited him to invest money in trade with the Xhosas and other tribes, Sampson cautiously declined. The concept of producing paint from the clay fascinated Sampson. He mulled over the idea of how, in future, one could turn the clay into a profitable paint business. He put some pieces of clay into his coat pockets for the children to use as colouring sticks before the walk home with Amelia, back to Turvey's Post.

As the early morning rays of sun peaked over the horizon in the east, marking the beginning of the new year, Sampson continued his reflection of events during 1821.The terrible drought firmly set in early in the year. Plants and crops died as the days were stiflingly hot. There was little respite from the harsh rays of the sun. Some poor settlers were destitute, but the British Government provided little or no help. Fellow settlers helped where they could, but they too, were lucky if they managed to eke out a living for themselves.

George Bonsall, a member of George Smith's party became incurably ill. His wife Sarah begged the authorities to send the family back to England, as they were entirely without subsistence and there was no other family to help her.

The three first months of 1821 passed as things became progressively worse for many settlers without additional means brought from England to sustain them. What crops they had planted, failed. They had little and sometimes even nothing to eat. Their clothes were threadbare. Things were dire and many people died.

The neighbouring Xhosa tribe also suffered the negative effects of the drought which created additional burdens on the settlers. On 31 March 1821, when Thomas Mahoney rose at dawn to check on his herd of cattle, he discovered that fourteen head had been stolen by a group of Xhosa. The tribesmen had crossed the river under the guise of collecting clay. At the discovery of this loss Mahoney looked up at the heavens, clutched fistfuls of his thick hair and bellowed with rage. Red-faced and angry, he cursed at God, as if needing someone to blame. His immediate instinct was to collect his gun and pursue the culprits, but he knew it would prove fruitless and dangerous to attempt this on his own. Things were tough enough for the settlers. And now this. As with others in the vicinity, he was at his wits end with the thieving marauders. There was little hope of ever recovering his cattle.

A few days later, on Friday 6 April, the late afternoon sky grew dark with clouds closing in on the months of oppressive heat. The families at Turvey's Post took shelter inside their dwellings, amidst screams from frightened children as lightening forked down to the earth in a violent flashing rage of its own. It seemed as if the earth around them shook with the great rumblings of thunder and the heavens opened. After months of drought, the rain poured in torrents. The settlers could only stay sheltered indoors and wait it out.

After relentless days of torrential rainfall, there was a welcome calm after the storm. The earth was muddy, soft and saturated. The fresh crisp air had an unusual earthy fragrance all of its own. The canvas of blue sky was cloudless in the warm sunshine. Sampson walked outside to the covered wood pile to replenish logs for the fire. As he lifted the canvas cover, he heard the hiss before he saw its source. Less than a few feet away, he had almost stepped on a grey-and-yellow patterned snake. Camouflaged with red mud, the thick, sluggish puff-adder with its large, triangular-shaped flat head, the size of a saucer, lay dangerously close.

Startled by the presence of the reptile, Sampson stumbled backwards over the chopping log, falling onto his elbows. He quickly scrambled back onto his feet, with adrenalin coursing through his veins. Keeping his eye on the deadly snake, he put a safe distance between it and himself. He knew that one venomous strike from the reptile could cause a painful death. He picked up a large rock and moved slowly towards it, careful to stay out of striking range. He threw the rock at the snake's head, crushing its bulbous skull. The stocky, fat body twisted and writhed as its head was trapped beneath the weight of the rock. One blow from Sampson's axe severed the body from the head, and the snake ceased moving. He picked up the remains of the snake with his shovel and threw it into the bushveld, grateful for his lucky escape.

On 16 June that same year, a violent hurricane hit the area. Extensive flooding destroyed houses and some of the settlers sunk even further into despair. Despite the incidents of cattle theft from his property, the Daniel's neighbour, Thomas Mahoney seemed to fare pretty well. Looking for opportunity amidst the chaos of stock loss and inclement weather, he tendered for government building projects. Mahoney's wealth grew considerably. He bought Lot number 5 in York Street, Bathurst and in October of 1821, he built a cottage on that property, which was situated much further away from the more frequent attacks by the neighbouring Xhosa community.

In November of 1821, a heavily pregnant Amelia gave birth to baby daughter Luisa, the couple's fifth child. Whilst Julia Turvey was tending to her sister-in-law and the new family's new addition, they heard raised voices and a commotion outside the house.

Julia looked out, she saw two Xhosa men scrambling out of the chicken coop, and another one snatching clothes off the piece of buffalo hide rope tethered between two trees. Her son Ben, who had seen the thieves, grabbed a gun, ran outside and fired a shot at them as they ran away in the direction of the river. The culprits fled holding a squawking chicken by its feet in each hand. Ben watched them scamper surefooted over the plain in the direction of the Fish River. He re-loaded the weapon, and fired another shot, as the third thief raced barefoot over the stony bushveld carrying items of clothing.

This incident strengthened Sampson's resolve to move away from the Zuurveld. That day he advised his sister Julia to relocate to Grahamstown. Their brother Peter had already identified another property at Grobbelaars Kloof, and he was preparing to move there with his wife Eliza, his mistress Ann Mitchley and all of their children.

The situation was desperate. The Daniel family heard of many accounts of similar incidents. Cattle theft was a regular occurrence.

Stubbs and Brown continued to trade illegally with the Xhosa neighbours.

Throughout the year, Government officials waited for the promised shipments of flour and other essential foodstuffs, but nothing arrived. For months there was a shortage of seed for planting and rations. Some settlers died of malnutrition.

The Turvey party was frugal with their supplies, living off pumpkins, potatoes, onions. Ben shot guinea fowl and antelope for the pot. He was an excellent horseback rider and an accurate shot like his stepfather, Edward Turvey. The family learnt to master the art of food preservation, such as drying venison and pickling vegetables, for the lean times when they could not obtain fresh food. There was strict household rationing.

On 11 December, word reached the Daniel clan that forty-four cattle were stolen during a raid on Thomas Timms' farm near Clumber. The theft of livestock and attacks on homesteads by the Xhosa was spiralling out of control. The attacks were becoming more brazen and frequent as the people across the river became more desperate for supplies and food themselves.

It was a bleak Christmas for everyone in the Coombs Valley. Settler morale was at its lowest ebb.

Turvey, their one-time leader, had absconded. Nobody had heard from him in months. Not that it seemed to matter much. The men looked up to Peter Daniel as their leader. He was more organised than Edward Turvey, whose contribution to the success of the party since leaving London had been negligible. Sampson noted early on that Turvey had his own agenda. Although he was concerned about his sister living without the support of her husband, Sampson had not been sorry to see Turvey ride off into the distance with the botanists. He wished them all luck.

Sampson hoped the government's permission and his official pass to leave the area was granted soon. He saw no future for himself and his family in the Zuurveld. His Dutch friend Wilhelm was right.

"The meaning of the name Zuurveld is Sour Field...." Wilhelm Meyer had told his Irish friend when he had dropped the Daniel family off on the plot of land called Turvey's Post. Sampson was beginning to believe he was right. Sour indeed.

As the sun rays lit the land around him in a golden glow, he puffed on the cigar again, blowing out a large puffy cloud of white smoke. Holding the fat cigar between his thumb and index finger, he stared at the red glow at the end of the cigar.

"Come on Daniel. Focus!" he chided himself, "Opportunities for you here are few and far between. You are here under duress. You fear for the future of your children, and the safety of your wife. You feel a responsibility towards Julia and her children. You feel loyalty to your brothers..." He knew there had to be better opportunities out there.

"There has to be more," he said, shaking his head when he realised he was talking aloud to himself.

His heart was set on moving to Uitenhage. There was plenty of water, flourishing fruit trees and abundant crops. There were brick houses. There was structure and order in the village. Piet Retief had told him there were plots for sale and Sampson had the resources to purchase his own piece of land. It was time to cut his losses and let go of his investment in this barren wasteland.

After their father died in Ireland, Peter, being the oldest son, received a substantial annual income of £2000 from John Daniel's estate. Sampson knew Peter would prosper, as he planned to establish a jewellery business in Grahamstown with his inheritance and work the farm at Grobbelaarsdal with Ann Mitchley. He was uncertain about his half-brother, John Nevins' future plans, yet.

As the last embers of the fire burned out, Sampson stubbed out the cigar in the dirt beneath his feet. On reflection, 1821 had been a horrible year. In the new year he would press for his permit to leave the Zuurveld. It would be painful breaking away from his close-knit family and friends. They had endured much together over the past two years, but he could see no other way out.

He looked at his pocket watch. It was just past five in the morning. The distinctive churring whistle of the nocturnal Nightjar bird had ended as abruptly as the darkness. Sampson stepped into his humble mud dwelling to light the fire to boil water for the family's morning tea.

CHAPTER 19

COOMBS VALLEY UNDER ATTACK

1822

While Sampson Daniel pondered his future into the wee hours of morning, Thomas Mahoney crouched in the dense bush nearby, fearing for his life. Sampson was about to snuff out the flame of his candle when a loud, frantic knocking at the front door roused the entire household. A dishevelled Mahoney almost fell inside when Sampson opened the door.

Mahoney's clothes were mud stained and his jacket was torn. Blades of grass and blackjack weeds stuck to his trousers and he was missing a shoe. Amelia, keeping close to Sampson, took one look at the distraught man and hurried off to make the tea. With a cup of hot tea in his trembling hands, Mahoney recovered enough to explain what had happened.

"A couple of bastards accosted me during the early hours of this morning. I was on my way back from a dinner at the Stubbs' house. They jumped out of the bushes next to the road."

Over the years Mahoney's temper had landed him in many a brawl, and his previous experiences had served him well. He managed to beat off his attackers, before running for his life in the direction of the Kap River, losing a shoe in his haste. He heard his aggressors searching for him in the dense thicket, but they could not find Mahoney who hid in the bush next to the river.

"I believe Gaika sent the men. I was too scared to go home, so I headed straight for Grahamstown for help. I saw candlelight as I passed your place. I decided to seek refuge here."

Mahoney wanted to warn John Brown about returning too late in the afternoon on his own. It was no longer safe to travel alone on the Coombs Valley road. "Just before Christmas day, one of Stubbs' assistants, Edward Driver, was abducted by some of Gaika's warriors on the other side of the Great Fish River. They took him to the chief's kraal. The chief confiscated the trade goods on the wagon and sent Driver packing, with a threatening message to Stubbs. Gaika told him to get me to supply some brew and brandy on the next delivery, otherwise he would report us to the authorities for illegal trade," Mahoney explained.

Brown, Mahoney and Stubbs traded with the tribesmen despite the heavy penalties they could incur for the illicit trade. Sampson was glad he had refused to join them. He was concerned about their continued business dealings with the Xhosa throughout the past year, despite warnings from the authorities. The ever hot-tempered and truculent Mahoney had begun to trade his homebrew and imported brandy with the Xhosas for cattle, skins and ivory. Chief Gaika was greedy and wanted more.

In the meantime, John Brown, sensing trouble, stayed over at a friend's house in Grahamstown. He, too, feared reprisal from the Xhosas. The tribesmen were becoming hostile towards them. The trade deal with Gaika had soured and the chief made it known that he would retaliate.

A month or so after this incident John Stubbs went to the Drostdy in Uitenhage to explain his dealings with the Xhosas. He left his wife at home with their eldest son John, who was fourteen, and their younger sons Thomas, William and their other siblings. Their twenty-two-year-old cousin was also at home. The family was still living in tents. John Stubbs had been too busy farming cattle and trading with the Xhosas to set up any solid dwellings.

It was around mid-morning, when Ann Stubbs heard low voices and saw a group of about twelve Xhosa men, armed with what appeared to be *knobkerries*, approaching one of the tents.

"Thomas!" she yelled, "Call your brother, John, quickly! Then run to the Browns' house for help."

The youngsters were working in the garden about five hundred yards from the tent. When John and his cousin reached his mother's side, the group of men had advanced and was much closer to them. Ann instructed their cousin, who was the eldest, to approach the men and see if they were friend or foe. As she spoke, she loaded a gun and waited. The older cousin hesitated.

"If you don't go, I will go myself!" said Ann Stubbs, looking him squarely in the eyes.

Perhaps abashed at his cowardice, the young man approached the group who, it turned out, were all women, carrying sticks. They greeted him in bastardised Dutch, "Morrow, Morrow!"

He returned the greeting then walked with them back to where Ann Stubbs waited.

When she saw they were women, she hid her gun and stepped forward to greet them. Motioning for them to sit, she gave them water and bread. Since she could not understand them, she was not able to find out the reason for their visit. A while later, a number of men from the neighbouring properties arrived, including Mr Brown, Thomas Mahoney and some mounted soldiers from the fort.

Without formality, the soldiers rounded up the women, finding more of them at the Clay Pits. All of the women were escorted back to Grahamstown where some farmers hired them as labourers. One woman escaped across the river, back to the neutral territory and her tribe, reporting the incident to the chief's induna. The incident did not augur well for future peaceful relations between the Xhosa and the settlers.

On 22 February 1822, British troops withdrew from the Clay Pits. In the meantime, Mahoney worked hard at fortifying his property against future Xhosa attacks. At a roof-wetting ceremony, he named the new structure Mahoney's Castle.

The British Government formed a settlers' committee in Cape

Town to address the plight of distressed settlers. Letters poured into the committee and sent to the British government office Cape Town, telling of hardships and the poor conditions of the Lower Albany district.

One sunny midday, a handsome young man, sitting upright in his crisp soldier's uniform, rode onto the Turvey property. He had soft, smiling eyes and he sat comfortably in the saddle astride a magnificent black thoroughbred.

"Good afternoon, Madam," he greeted Amelia, swinging his leather-booted foot over the horse's rump to dismount. "I am Lieutenant Robert Hart of the Cape Regiment at your service." He extended a gloved hand in greeting. Amelia curtseyed respectfully.

"Good afternoon, Lieutenant. My husband will be on his way back from our neighbours, the Mahoneys, shortly. They had trouble with the marauders yesterday."

"So sorry to hear of your troubles, Mrs Daniel," he said, taking in her classic features as he tethered his stallion to a nearby tree. "I believe the Xhosa in this valley have been quite restless and troublesome lately. However, I come bearing some good news. The Government has approved a pass for your family to leave the settler programme, at your leisure. It is signed by the Colonial Secretary for the Cape Colony, Colonel C.C. Bird."

He held out the official pass document to Amelia. Amelia who could barely contain her excitement. She supressed the urge to hug and kiss the handsome Lieutenant.

"*Mon Dieu. Merci, merci*!" she cried. "We have been praying for this day. Thank you for the good news, Sir!" She knew Sampson would be ecstatic.

"May I offer you a cup of tea while we wait for my husband?"

Knowing it was unbecoming for a woman to be alone with a strange man, Amelia excused herself for a moment to call Julia, who was outside collecting chicken eggs.

"Join us for tea, Julia. We have something to celebrate."

While Amelia was gone, the young lieutenant looked around the simple dwelling. The mud-and-stone structure was basic. There were two doors leading off to what he expected were bedrooms. He wondered how many children the Daniels had. He could not help but notice Amelia's strong French accent and the sweet aroma of lavender in the home, which Amelia grew from seed brought from England. He saw the bowl of wildflowers on the drop-leaf table next to the tea tray, with its white embroidered linen tray cloth. There were delicate porcelain cups, saucers, and polished silver spoons. He could only imagine what this family must have left behind in England.

Hart was secretly glad that they had been strong enough to stand up to Lord Somerset. Now the family were free to leave this God-forsaken Zuurveld and the volatile Lower Albany. He wished only the best for this lovely young woman and her family.

Amelia could not wait for Sampson to return. She broke the seal on the official envelope. The pass document was dated 8 January 1822. It confirmed that they could move around southern Africa freely, "By Command of His Excellency".

On 30 June 1822, the Government established a fund to address the desperate plight of the British settlers. Letters addressing the indescribable poverty, lack of rations and resources, continued to pour in to the Impoverished Settler Committee.

Relations between Chief Gaika and the Cape Corp remained unfavourable. The military prohibited Chief Gaika from grazing his cattle between the Fish and the Keiskamma Rivers. Nevertheless, two of his sons, Maqomo and Tyali, defied the regulations. Colonel Scott ordered Major Fraser and a troop of the Cape Corps to advance and drive off the Xhosa who grazed their cattle in the area. Maqomo refused to move and a skirmish ensued during which twelve Xhosa were killed and their cattle impounded by the British soldiers.

Later, in a gesture to appease the Xhosa and rekindle better relations, the officials organised a trade fair at the Clay Pits on 31 July, although relations between the British and the Xhosas remained strained.

After months of living in tents, the Stubbs family started work on their house. Whilst the Stubbs boys were mixing the mud for the walls, a Hottentot interpreter appeared with an official document from an officer at Fort Wiltshire. The document gave permission for 500 people to collect deposits from the Clay Pits, close to their proposed homestead. John Stubbs was not impressed. However, he would use the opportunity to barter with the natives.

The following day, a contingent of Xhosa men under Chief Ngqeno crossed the Coombs River about three miles away. The men rode oxen and the women were on foot. The military refused to give the settlers protection and, that day, old man Stubbs forbade his sons from sending their cattle to graze.

Stubbs traded forty skins, two buffalo horns and two tusks of ivory for permission to take three wagonloads of dry clay. Later that afternoon, Stubbs and his sons Thomas and William met at the chief's kraal and traded a further eighty bell buttons for a large elephant tusk and seventy-five buttons for a large red ox. It was a successful trading day for both parties. Everything went off smoothly, although the chief was not present.

A week later, a company of soldiers of the 6th Regiment, under Captain Duke, pitched camp near the Stubbs property. While building a fort close to the Clay Pits, a soldier fired shots at the Xhosa collecting clay. Unharmed, the men scurried off back to their temporary camp across the river.

On 23 August 1822, forty-five-year old Richard Freemantle, an employee of Thomas Mahoney, took a wagon close to the river to collect wood. Richard, his two sons, John and Samuel, and Dick Wilton, stopped beneath a large clump of trees just beyond John Stubbs's place, between the Clay Pits and the Coombs River, close to the military post where the 6th Regiment was stationed. No sooner had they tethered the oxen to one of the trees when a dozen Xhosa rushed out from the thickets. One man lashed out at Richard Freemantle, repeatedly puncturing his body with a short stabbing spear. Another tackled his son, John, who was leading the oxen. The aggressor stabbed John five times in his chest, before he had a chance to retaliate. Dick

Wilton jumped off the wagon, wrestling one of the other attackers to the ground in a fight for his life.

Freemantle's assailant made off into the bush for safety. As Samuel reached over to grab the musket on the wagon, another man stabbed him in the leg. He wildly fired a shot into the air and the attackers fled through the dense thicket, making off with the cattle they had cut loose. On hearing the shot and the men's shouts, Thomas Mahoney ran towards the commotion. From his homestead, his daughter Eliza also heard the shot and, fearing for her father's safety, grabbed a weapon and ran towards the trees.

Although severely wounded, Samuel gathered his brother's limp body in his arms. He carried him for about a half a mile towards the fort, but was forced to stop and rest at frequent intervals. With no option, he left his bleeding brother on the ground, not far from the site of the attack. Samuel stumbled on towards the Clay Pits Post to summon help from the soldiers. Richard Freemantle was dead by the time Eliza arrived at the scene. His torn body was slumped lifelessly against the wagon wheel and there was blood everywhere. Hearing her father's familiar voice, she frantically walked in the direction of the Post and saw John lying in the long grass. He was barely breathing, bubbles of blood and spit oozed from his mouth. She gently lifted his head and rested it in her lap as she witnessed his life drain away.

By the time Mahoney arrived at the Clay Pits, the soldiers had already loaded Samuel onto the wagon. They took him to Kaffir Drift Post, where the surgeon attended to his wounds. Mahoney wondered if the attackers had mistakenly attacked Freemantle instead of him. The delicate understanding between the settlers and the Xhosa was no more. This violent act of savagery forced out all thoughts of accommodation. No longer would the Xhosa be allowed to collect the clay they so desired.

Young Samuel was able to identify one of the attackers as being among those who had accompanied Chief Ngqeno to the last fair. Uneasiness settled in the Coombs Valley. Working two day shifts at a time, groups of settlers patrolled between the Kap and Coombs rivers, searching for stolen cattle and raiders.

Eliza Mahoney felt unsafe after this incident. She and a few friends went to Bathurst to prepare her father's new cottage as a safe house. It was her refuge, should things become worse.

A little too late for Richard Freemantle and his son. The Clay Pits Post was once again heavily garrisoned.

CHAPTER 20

"IT'S THROUGH ADVERSITY WE GROW"

1823

The government seemed nonplussed by the multiple deaths occurring in the district. Johnson was butchered to death whilst tending to John Stubbs's cattle near the Kap River. No sooner did the settlers bring cattle back from the monthly markets in Grahamstown, than the local Xhosa stole them. The situation was out of control. Stubbs had run out of funds and he was becoming desperate.

Early one morning, on his way to trade with the Xhosa, he saw Sampson coming from Mahoney's homestead. Sampson greeted Stubbs, but he could tell the man was in a hurry to get somewhere.

"Where are you off to then, John?"

"I am off to trade with the chief," he replied, "men and even innocent boys are getting murdered in this area and the government does nothing about it. I am at the end of my tether, Daniel. I have tried reasoning with the officers to let us do an honest trade, but they refuse. They allow the soldiers to antagonise and intimidate the Xhosa without just cause, especially at the Clay Pits close to where I live. When this happens, the Xhosa retaliate. Who suffers? It is us, while they sit in the safety of their fancy houses in the Cape. Quite frankly, I've had my fill of the authorities."

"Don't do it, Stubbs," pleaded Sampson, "you put your life at risk every time you cross the Fish River and venture past the neutral territory. There must be an alternative solution. I do not accept it either. It is only a matter of time before I pack up my family and relocate to Uitenhage. I have negotiated to buy a piece of land next to Retief and, although it is nowhere near 100 acres, it will be in a safe environment where I can set up a general dealer and a jewellery store. Think of your wife and children, man. Do what is best for them."

"I am thinking of my family, Daniel. I don't care what the authorities do if they find me trading with these damned heathens – a man must do what's necessary to keep his family alive and make an honest living!" With that he leaned over the horse's wither, looked Sampson in the eye and gave him a firm handshake. Sampson grabbed the horse's bridle in a bid to prevent Stubbs from riding away.

"Goodbye, Daniel. Wish me luck."

He kicked the horse hard in the ribs and the animal bolted, forcing Sampson to release his grip on the leather cheek strap. He watched as Stubbs and three other men rode away on horseback in the direction of Trompetter's Drift. Stubbs, his son John, Edward Driver and Tom Hood each carried bags of buttons and beads to trade for cattle and ivory with the Chief. Sampson felt uneasy feeling as he walked the few miles home.

The following day, he received the shocking news. John Stubbs had been found dead not far from the Clay Pits with an assegai through his neck. Authorities had arrested John Stubbs junior and Thomas Hood for illicit trading. Devastated by the tragic news, the settler community in the Coombs Valley spoke at length of the incident.

Evidently, as the story unfolded afterwards, on the return trading trip, John Stubbs was riding at the back of the herd. He had bartered eighty head of cattle from Chief Gaika in exchange for his buttons and beads. His men tied ivory tusks to the backs of some of the cattle. Stubbs sat back triumphantly in his leather saddle, feeling very satisfied with his business transaction. The group of men were just about at Fraser's Camp on top of Trompetter's Hill, when John junior saw a fire burning ahead of them alongside the road.

"We'd better alert Father and Driver," said young John, and he galloped to the back of the herd with Thomas Hood.

"Hottentots!" they shouted, pointing back in the direction from where they had come.

The older Stubbs told the young men to hang back until he returned, then he rode up ahead to the waiting group. Members of the Cape Corps immediately surrounded him.

"Stubbs! We are here to place you under arrest for illegal trade in cattle and ivory."

Fury filled Stubbs' being confronted and accused of illicit trade. He retaliated and began to argue back.

"How dare you! It is my God-given right to trade and make an honest living in any way I can. How else can I feed my family in this miserable, God-forsaken place! Be damned! All of you! Just try and stop me!" He picked up his weapon and pointed it at the group. "I will shoot the first person to lay a finger on me!"

His face turned scarlet. He was as furious as a raging bull.

The men backed off and began rounding up his cattle. He rode away to look for the others, but only found Edward Driver.

"Where's Tom and John?" he shouted. "These bastards want to arrest us and confiscate our cattle!"

Driver shrugged. They both assumed the youngsters had gone home. The two men hurriedly rode off through the bushveld in the direction of the Clay Pits. When they reached the edge of a steep gorge, they saw another herd of cattle. John Stubbs rode on to investigate and soon realised that they were his stock. Driver, feeling rather unnerved after the day's activities said he would meet Stubbs back at his house and he rode off, leaving Stubbs alone.

Stubbs rode towards his cattle, sensing something horribly wrong. The cattle were restless and moving in different directions. He grabbed his weapon and laid it across his lap. The next moment, a Xhosa broke through the thicket and mercilessly stabbed Stubbs in the groin. Shocked by the suddenness of the attack, the wounded man felt something like a hot iron plunge into his back. An assailant behind him pierced him between the shoulder blades with an assegai. He saw another dark silhouette approach from the front and he lifted his rifle, but it misfired.

Wracked with pain, he clenched his knees together and clung to the horse. In sheer desperation he lifted the gun by the barrel and wildly swung the wooden butt end. He fought as a man possessed, but was outnumbered.

The first assailant delivered the deathblow. He stabbed John Stubbs again, piercing his jugular vein with the razor-sharp weapon. Stubbs collapsed, his limp body swung down over the left side of his horse, his feet caught in the stirrups as the blood drained from his already lifeless body.

The Xhosa cut the stirrup straps and John Stubbs fell to the floor like a sack of flour, the short stabbing assegai still embedded in his throat. The thieves tethered his horse to the tree and made off with the cattle.

At about eleven o'clock that evening, a frantic knocking at the door alerted young Thomas Stubbs. He ran his skinny fingers through his dark wavy hair and wiped the sleep from his eyes. He wondered who could be knocking at this time of night. He was barely fourteen but had a maturity beyond his years. He grabbed a large kitchen knife off the table and called out.

"It's me, Driver," he heard the unexpected visitor whisper hoarsely.

On opening the door, Thomas ushered in a weary and pale Edward Driver. He collapsed into a chair, requesting water. The distraught man put his head in his hands. Thomas could barely make out what he was saying.

"... cattle have been confiscated by the Hottentots. I left your father, John, and Tom Hood behind. I hope they will be here soon."

The late visitor woke Mrs Stubbs, sleeping in the next room. Dressed in her nightgown, she came into the living room and stood next to her son, her hands folded across her ample bosom. She had warned her husband not to go out trading that morning. When would the man learn any sense?

Somewhat recovered, Driver spoke earnestly to young Thomas, "Take this letter to the Hobsons for me. It is urgent. Go at once. If you meet anyone along the road, rather destroy the letter than give it up. Remember, it's important."

Thomas Stubbs saddled his horse and galloped through the darkness. It was eight miles to the Hobson's place, where he delivered Driver's letter, much to the surprise of a bleary-eyed Mr Hobson. Thomas was confused but surmised the letter must have something to do with the transactions with the Xhosa. It probably contained confidential information best kept from the authorities.

Thomas, meanwhile, turned on his heel and started to make his way home. As he descended the steep hill just opposite the Dredge's house at Driver's Bush, he saw a number of unusual silhouettes in front of him. He called out nervously, unsure if the shapes were animals or human.

"Who goes there?"

There was no reply from the darkness. However, by the light of the moon, the shapes seemed to be making their way towards him.

"Who goes there?" he called, louder this time.

He felt his heart beating hard in his chest. He tried to turn his horse to ride back up the hill, but it refused to budge. In desperation, Thomas dismounted and picked up some stones as, in his haste to leave home, he had forgotten his rifle. Just then, a voice called out.

"Friend!"

He lowered his hand and waited for the men to approach. He was astonished to see the group of mounted Hottentots. Hood and his brother, John, walked in their midst, their hands shackled.

"Where's Father?" asked Thomas in a low tone.

"There was trouble earlier. I have no idea where Father is," replied his brother.

There was no time to elaborate, as the commander of the party gave the order to march on towards Grahamstown. Thomas headed home with a heavy heart. When he arrived there, his mother was still up, but his father was not yet home. He gave Edward Driver the letter of response from Mr Hobson. Without sharing the contents of the letter, a distraught Driver left the Stubbs' residence, and headed home to the Nottingham Party, not far from Bathurst.

After a couple of hours of restless sleep, Thomas and William milked two of the cows. They were very worried, as their father still had not returned home. As the youngsters herded their few remaining cattle into the veld, they saw soldiers from the 6th Regiment heading in their direction. They bore a stretcher with the body of their father, John Stubbs.

His wife, Ann, was inconsolable. The distraught woman wailed loudly and pummelled the chest of the soldier who brought the tragic news. Her eldest son and her nephew were in prison in Grahamstown and her husband lay dead before her. Her little daughter, Mary Ann, was barely two years old. This would never have happened if he had heeded her warnings. The poor woman wept as the men stood around helplessly. Her sons Thomas and William were shocked. They did what they could to console her.

Reverend William Geary buried Thomas Stubbs in Grahamstown on 25 June 1823. Sampson and Amelia Daniel attended the funeral with more than a little sadness. Some of the townsfolk stayed away, fearing association with the man who had dared to challenge the laws of the government. Others paid their respects, admiring the man's tenacity at trying to make a living.

He had fought hard – and lost.

The Landrost allowed John Stubbs junior and his cousin, Tom Hood, to attend the funeral. The local magistrate found the young men guilty and sentenced them to six months' imprisonment. All the cattle, horses, ivory and guns were confiscated.

In an unusual turn of events, Hood later turned state witness and the two men were freed. Hood exposed Boesak, the Captain of the Hottentots, for his own participation in illegal trade on that fateful day. He stated that when the Cape Corps apprehended the men in the Stubbs' trading party, the Hottentots were also in possession of a wagonload of ivory, which they themselves had recently purchased from the chief.

After a mock trial, it was proven that Boesak and his men were gainfully employed by Harry Rivers, the local magistrate. He had permission to trade with the chief, under the pretence of going into the neutral territory to shoot elephants. The authorities confiscated their load of ivory and the affair ended. Boesak continued in his office as the Captain of the Hottentots.

The government did nothing to apprehend the cattle thieves or to bring Stubbs' murderers to book. Instead, they sent Field Cornet Currie to the Stubbs' house to take an inventory of his possessions with the intention of removing them. Ann Stubbs protested vehemently and the authorities allowed her to keep everything until she died. Thereafter, the officials would deliver them to the Orphan Chamber in Cape Town.

The savagery in the area raged on unabated.

On 19 August 1823, two young boys, Mark Sloman and Thomas Donovan, were murdered while herding cattle. A few days later, a search party discovered their decomposing bodies in thick bush, a short distance from their home, after their parents raised the alarm. Buttons had been removed from their shirts and their knives were missing. Their family was devastated. At their funerals, mourners noted that they had been settler children who had arrived on the ship *Belle Alliance* as part of Thomas Wilson's party.

Torrential rain drenched the colony during the first week of October. An incredibly strong wall of water surged down the Kap River wiping out everything in its path. Several houses in Grahamstown were flooded and some destroyed. Mr Cadle, a local townsman, drowned in the floodwaters.

With the devastation in the wake of the floods and continued attacks by the Xhosa, many farmers moved to the towns of Bathurst, Grahamstown and Uitenhage.

In December, the troops of the 6th Regiment abandoned the fort near the Clay Pits. The vulnerable, fatherless Stubbs' family were open to attack from the enraged Xhosa. The family decided to move into the completed section of the fort for safety.

There was no respite. Marauders attacked again, stealing the

Stubbs' remaining cattle. John and Thomas bravely chased after them. While they were tracking the thieves, they heard William desperately calling them back.

"Come quickly! Mother has died!"

The months of hardship and trauma had claimed another victim. Ann Stubbs suffered heart failure.

The lives of the three boys and their eight-year-old sister Eleanor, six-year-old Richard, two-year-old Mary Ann and baby George, were shattered. The youngsters lived from one nightmare to another. Neighbours in the area rallied to support them.

Amelia Daniel, Julia Turvey and Thackwray's daughter were among those who assisted the orphans. In time, the British Orphan Chamber arrived to take over the Stubbs' possessions. After their mother's death, as decreed by the British authorities, Stubbs' personal belongings from England were sold to the highest bidders at an auction in Grahamstown. The items included top-quality bed linen, a beautiful mahogany table, silver spoons and an ample supply of kitchen equipment. There was also a collection of tools and farm implements and two violins.

Julia Turvey bid on and secured a box of books, which she returned to the Stubbs children. She was angered that they received none of their parents' belongings from the state. The Stubbs orphans had lost everything.

Thomas and John relocated to stay with John Brown for a while. The Daniel family took in young William. Ben Wright, now twenty-one, had opened his own saddle business in Grahamstown with his father's inheritance. He offered to arrange an apprenticeship for the boy, but first Julia Turvey insisted on teaching William to read and write.

One evening, at about eight o'clock, while the other Stubbs children were staying with Mrs Brown, ten Xhosa armed with assegais surrounded the house.

"Long John. Long John," they shouted out the name they had given John Brown.

Nervously, his wife explained that her husband had gone to Grahamstown to plead for the release of Chief Kassa. He was one of Ngqeno's tribe, arrested the previous evening when a Hottentot patrol had apprehended them near the gorge at the Clay Pits. Brown went to beg the authorities for the release of Kassa, or his family would be at grave risk.

The enraged men forced their way into the Brown's homestead, unwilling to listen to reason. They violently stabbed assegais into the mattresses, ransacked the house and demanded food. They cleared out the food store and ate like ravenous dogs. Taking up sentry points around the house, they waited for Mr Brown to return. Unharmed but intimidated, the Stubbs boys made a plan to move closer to Grahamstown.

In Grahamstown, Thomas Stubbs received a note from his good friend Rafferty, who was camped near the Fish River. A Hottentot *voorloper* delivered a note saying his friend was completely out of supplies. Rafferty listed the food and other equipment required. He pleaded with Thomas to send the goods to him at Bothas Drift as a matter of urgency.

Thomas rode into town on his favourite animal, Skewbald, his late father's pack ox. Collecting a horse from Ben Wright he managed to get a few apples, mielie meal, rusks, biltong, a tin of tea, sugar and a live chicken before heading off in the direction of Bothas Drift. He was in high spirits as he sat astride his new horse, pulling chunks off a loaf of bread, freshly baked by Julia Turvey. The *voorloper* walked ahead with Skewbald in tow.

At Bothas Drift, Edward Ford Turvey rested on the banks of the river. He had finally returned from an excursion to Natal, two years after his departure from the Turvey location. He was in the company of William Thackwray, whom he had met up country, hunting elephant and lion.

The party of hunters were outspanned at Botha's Drift alongside the Fish River, resting their animals for a few days before the final haul to Grahamstown.

A gaunt, suntanned and travel weary Turvey was shocked at the sight of his old acquaintance, Rafferty, also camped at the river. The man had run out of food and supplies. His clothes were in tatters, his body skeletal and his gaunt cheekbones accentuated his face. Rafferty told Turvey stories of how desperate the situation was for some settlers. They were starving to death. He shared tales of attacks and settler murders by the Xhosa raiders. Edward Turvey was astounded at the news. Hearing of Rafferty's terrible plight, he invited him to join the hunting party for a meal that evening. He regaled Rafferty with tales of his adventurous exploration along the coastline over the past two years.

The following day, as Thomas approached the river, he saw a great number of people and wagons on either side of it. These included soldiers, civilians and womenfolk. The Hottentot *voorloper* pointed out Rafferty's wagon on the opposite bank. Thomas' friend spotted him across the river and excitedly ran to the water's edge, waving both his hands in the air. He motioned Thomas to come across the river to the other side. Stubbs firmly fastened the grocery-filled leather bag to Skewbald's head. The *voorloper* held tightly onto the ox's tail as he swam behind it to the other side of the swollen river. Thomas swam across alongside his horse.

Dripping wet, he had hardly stepped out of the water, and was shaking Rafferty's hand in greeting, when he was surprised to see old man Turvey striding purposefully in his direction. Turvey reached Rafferty's camp as Thomas was wringing his shirt dry. Thomas hardly recognised his long-lost neighbour. The older man's sun-streaked hair was long and stringy, and his deeply tanned skin was more wrinkled than he remembered. His wispy beard was wild and unruly.

Edward Turvey remembered Thomas as one of John Stubbs' boys from the valley. Even before enquiring about the boy's wellbeing, he felt no qualms at asking Thomas for the use of his horse to cross the river. When Thomas first looked down at Turvey's stretched-out hand, he smiled. He thought the man was carrying a small pistol. Then, he remembered how Turvey shook hands – with his pinkie and ring fingers turned into his palm and the other two and his thumb sticking up in the shape of a small firearm. He took Turvey's hand and squeezed it firmly. Turvey winced at the young man's strength, as his bent fingers pushed back painfully into the palm of his hand.

"Lend me your horse, boy," he demanded, abruptly, "I'm in a great hurry to get to Grahamstown, to see my wife and children."

Thomas wondered what Turvey's hurry was. He had heard the Daniel family talking about how the head of their party had taken off with some botanists a couple of years before, and not been heard of since. As far as he knew, Mrs Turvey was coping quite well without him – as she had given him homemade bread that day. His younger brother William was working for Turvey's stepson, Benjamin Wright, who was the saddler in town.

Thomas reluctantly lent him the horse he had just received as a gift from Ben. He instructed Turvey to leave the steed with his stepson at the saddle shop. He would ride back to town with his friend Rafferty in a few days and collect it. Without so much as a thank you, Turvey prepared to leave by stripping naked. He kept his worn leather hat on, tightening the strings securely beneath his chin. He then rolled up his bundle and clothes into the saddlebag, and tied it to the saddle. He led the horse into the swollen river and slowly disappeared below the muddy water, much to the amusement of the people near him. The horse followed suit. With flared nostrils, it began treading water, as soon as it could not feel the riverbed with its hooves.

Halfway across, the horse threw its head back and the rein slipped from Turvey's hand. The man had no option but to keep swimming across to the opposite bank. He believed the horse was following right behind him. The horse, however, headed downriver with the current and returned to the riverbank where Thomas stood watching. Turvey did not notice and carried on swimming. A large crowd gathered on both sides of the river to watch his antics.

Exhausted from his strenuous swim, Edward Turvey crawled out of the river onto the opposite muddy bank, on his hands and knees. Digging his elbows into the ground, he rested his head on his hands exposing his naked butt to the sky. The gathered watchers erupted into raucous laughter. There stood Edward Turvey in all his glory, muddy, naked and dripping wet. He lifted the soggy brim of his hat, squeezed the water from his beard and looked around for Stubbs' horse. He spotted it happily grazing on the opposite bank. The saddlebag containing his clothes had come adrift and washed downstream.

Nonplussed, Turvey looked around at the amused faces and smiled. He spotted Mrs Sergeant Major Brown sitting on the *disselboom* of one of the wagons, gaily watching his shenanigans. Not at all shy, she cocked her head to one side and eyed Turvey with a wry smile. Placing a hand over his crown jewels in a token attempt at modesty, he walked boldly up to her, pointing his other pistol-fingered hand in her direction.

"Good day, Ma'am," he said, a smile with his near-perfect row of white teeth lighting up his weathered, but still handsome face, "May I borrow some clothes?"

Highly amused, she handed him one of her shirts and instructed some of the soldiers to donate their clothes. They collected a jacket and a pair of trousers for the seemingly unperturbed Mr Turvey. He painted a rather odd-looking picture in his borrowed clothes as he eventually set off for town.

After his return, Julia and Edward Turvey bought a house in Grahamstown, although Edward was seldom home. When he was, he spent most of his time pottering around in his garden, or painting. He sold some of his sketches to the surgeon Andrew Steedman for use in his book, *Wanderings of South Africa.*

Peter Daniel bought a house in Grahamstown and moved there with Eliza. He established a jewellery business and purchased a farm at Groblaars Kloof, which he called Beggars Bush, after their family home near Dublin. Peter visited Ann Mitchley on weekends, on the farm where she lived with her children.

The Daniel clan and the Turvey's, along with some of their close settler friends and neighbours, gathered at Peter Daniel's farm for an emotional farewell to Sampson and Amelia.

CHAPTER 21

UITENHAGE OR BUST

1822 – 1833

Finally, there was reason to celebrate. With the pass from the Colonial Secretary's office, Sampson was ready and free to move around the Colony without fear of arrest.

The first thing he did was arrange an overland excursion to Uitenhage with his Dutch friend, Piet Retief. The Uitenhage District was beautiful, lush and green with an abundance of water. The village was well established and well run. He bought one *morgen* of land in the centre of the picturesque town.

In 1802 the Cape Colony had been declared by France and England as being under the rule of the Batavian Republic of Amsterdam and The Hague in the Netherlands. Councillor Jacob Abraham Uitenhage de Mist, the Commissary General of the Batavian Republic established two new districts; one of them being Uitenhage. The government of the day purchased 3000 morgen of land for four hundred pounds from Mrs Betje Scheepers. She was the widow of the Dutch farmer, Gerrit Scheepers, who was murdered by Xhosa raiders in 1799. The marauders had burnt down Dutch settler homesteads and laid some four hundred and seventy farms to waste.

The Scheepers farm and its surrounding land was the perfect site for a new village, as it had abundant water, fertile soils and suitable pasturelands alongside the Zwartkops River. Mrs Scheepers negotiated to live rent-free in her cottage on the land for as long as she lived. De

Mist permitted her to graze her cattle on the commonage. She grew grapes, figs, peaches, melons and other fruit and farmed oxen and sheep.

The town itself was formally established in 1802. Uitenhage lay some one hundred and sixty miles southwest of Grahamstown, far enough away from the Zuurveld with its constant threats of Xhosa invasion. The town planner drew a military-camp style plan of the town showing equal one morgen plots lining the new streets: Caledon, Cuyler, St John and Baird streets. There was an area for the market square allocated in the centre of the town.

The Batavian government gave these plots to Dutch burghers on the proviso the owner built a house on it within six months. Otherwise, the land would be re-allocated to another person by the government. Being free of political and cultural violence, Uitenhage had developed into a thriving, prosperous town by the time the British took control of the Cape again in 1806.

As the family's wagon approached the town, Amelia felt at peace, convinced that their decision to move to Uitenhage was the right one. They went straight to the official Drostdy – the office of the local Cape Colony government district in Uitenhage. The beautiful whitewashed building was situated in a lush expanse of manicured gardens with an abundance of fruit trees and sprawling farmland before it. Amelia was fascinated by the gracious Cape Dutch gable and the flanking stairs leading to the stately solid mahogany door with its highly polished brass handles. It looked very grand indeed, especially when compared to the humble abode that was their homestead. The elegant building and tasteful furniture reminded her of London.

Neatly dressed, the Daniels waited for Colonel Cuyler in the large entrance hall. Recognising Sampson, the Colonel extended a hand in friendly greeting.

"Mr and Mrs Daniel! How wonderful to see you again. You have come to collect the documents for your new property, I am told? I am pleased you have chosen to make Uitenhage your home."

He ushered them into his office, directing the children to play in the garden where they could pick and eat some fruit. Amelia watched through the office window as Sophia took charge of her siblings and made sure Frederick did not spill peach juice on his shirt.

"I trust you will find our garden town a haven of peace and tranquillity compared to the stress of living in the dreaded Zuurveld," said Cuyler. He was only too aware of the many difficulties and tragedies the settlers had faced. He admired the fortitude of these decent people and understood Daniel's desire to establish his family in a more secure environment. When the Colonel asked about his plans, Sampson responded, "Well, I'm a jeweller by trade, qualified as both a silversmith and goldsmith. I do watch and clock repairs and I have been managing financially by trading and selling fresh produce, chickens and livestock to others. My wife bakes bread, rusks and biscuits, and she also sells eggs."

Sampson pointed to the ornately carved yellowwood grandfather clock behind the Colonel. "I see it's not working," he said, smiling, "I can easily repair that for you. I'll take a look when we're done, if you like."

"I would appreciate that, Mr Daniel. Yes, there are many opportunities for trade in Uitenhage. I see possibilities for a jeweller as well as a general trade store." Cuyler sorted the documents in front of him, continuing, "Most of the town's inhabitants are Dutch burghers and you will do well to learn the language."

Before the couple left, Cuyler gave them a hand-drawn map of the town and pointed them in the direction of their newly acquired plot at 32 Baird Street.

"Congratulations, Mr Daniel. You are now the proud owner of a property in Uitenhage. Welcome!"

Amelia could hardly contain her excitement. She lifted her skirt above her ankles and ran over to where the children were playing. She hugged them each in turn and then stretched her arms wide, spinning in circles on the lawns beneath the oak trees – her beaming face looking up towards the sun. She felt like an eagle, soaring high above the earth on the thermals. A huge weight lifted off her shoulders. She felt free.

Piet Retief was given two erven in Uitenhage in 1814, long before the arrival of the British Settlers. He owned numbers 5 and 15 Baird Street. He was the government contractor at that time. Retief had built many of the houses the Daniel family saw as they walked along the wide streets. One year later, he had sold both his properties for a profit and had bought three additional erven in Caledon Street at a public auction.

Sampson Daniel walked with his head held high, street map firmly in one hand and baby Luisa on his shoulders, holding tightly onto his thick, silver hair. His wife walked behind like a mother goose with her five goslings trailing noisily. Sampson had not seen Amelia and the children this relaxed in a long time. The excited family passed the large sandy square where the markets were held. Sampson looked forward to the Saturday market days with its congregation of wagon traders, townsfolk and farmers. He could almost hear the noise of the oxen, sheep, chickens and people, all gathered in one place and the thought took him back to memories of the Cows Gate market in Edinburgh.

They walked on past Market Street and then turned left into Baird Street. Sophia ran ahead, reading out the numbers painted on stones in front of each plot.

"Here's Oosthuysen," she said, battling to read the Dutch surname on the wooden board at the entrance to number 11. A little further on she called out number 15, Retief's property. Uitenhage was a flourishing town. If residents were buying and selling land for a profit, there had to be a future for development and growth.

Sampson looked beyond Sophia, Eliza and Amelia dashing from one side of the street to the other, working out that number 32 was at least ten more plots along on the left-hand side. They had one more street to cross. According to the map, the newly registered Daniel plot was located on the corner of the next street. The Meyer family lived directly across the street while the Moors owned the house diagonally opposite.

The girls squealed in delight when they found the stone with the number 32 on it. Sampson paced out the one-morgen plot, which was 150 feet wide. It had a small, rickety wooden structure on it, which would serve as a shelter to sleep in for the meantime and a store for his tools, while he built their house. There was a wetland on the other side of the road at the back of the property. This meant the land would not be developed. They could enjoy the natural open veld, something they had become accustomed to in the Zuurveld.

The family held hands in the middle of their plot of land while Sampson prayed. It was a prayer of thanksgiving for the promise of their deliverance from the strife-torn Coombs valley. It was for blessings and prosperity in their soon-to-be-built new home. It was a prayer for peace, guidance and wisdom for the future. Amelia's unborn child moved within her.

They chorused 'Amen' in unison, except for four-year-old Frederick, who had lost concentration and was fidgeting and pulling at the bows on Isabella's dress. Sampson wiped a tear from his eye and Amelia squeezed his hand reassuringly. She sensed her husband finally felt in control of his own destiny.

They heard the clip-clop of horses' hooves on the dirt road and saw a burgher pulling up at the house opposite.

"Irish!"

Sampson heard the familiar booming voice of Wilhelm Meyer, the Dutchman who had transported them from Algoa Bay to Albany. He beamed as his friend dismounted and lumbered towards him, hefty arms outstretched for a bear hug. He lifted each child into the air, in turn, and gently shook hands with Amelia.

"Dankie Vader! Ek kan dit nie glo nie, julle is uiteindelik hier!"

It was an emotional reunion. Any doubt Sampson may have harboured about the move to Uitenhage dissipated. Wilhelm Meyer was confirmation he was in the right place.

Over several months, Sampson completed his house with the help of other members of their party. John Kemp the sawyer, Robert Cartwright the carpenter and his good friend from London, Henry Holland, the gem cutter, offered their assistance. It was after the latter the Daniel's second son was named. Henry Holland Daniel was born in 1824.

Sampson opened his jewellery business, importing exquisite pieces from England, collecting shipments from time to time at the port of

Algoa Bay, some twenty miles away. With Amelia's help, he became a successful farmer, and the couple sold fruit, vegetables, live and dressed chickens, and eggs. Amelia made her popular lavender shortbread and French bread, which she sold at the market.

Altogether, there were thirteen pianofortes and one organ in Uitenhage, so it was easy for Amelia to join forces with other women who enjoyed music. Occasionally, one could hear sacred pieces by Handel and other composers drifting through the streets. To supplement their income, Amelia was happy giving piano and ballet lessons to local children.

She bought lace-making spindles and extra cotton. Her handiwork was much sought after by the women of the town. She invited her new friends to visit, serving lavender shortbread and local rooibos tea in her exquisite silver tea set. She used the silver teaspoons Sampson created for her in his shop.

The young Frederick assisted his mother when she delivered fresh vegetables and eggs to the market. As he grew older, he showed the makings of a fine entrepreneur, delivering the goods alone and keeping meticulous records of his transactions.

On Sundays, the family attended the Methodist Church with about forty other parishioners. The Daniel family lived in Uitenhage for over ten years, sometimes visiting Grahamstown to see family and for business. As the years went by, these visits became less frequent, but they still worried about family in the strife-torn Albany District.

Julia Turvey
Grahamstown

Sampson Daniel Esq.
32 Baird Street, Uitenhage
1834

Dear Sampson and Amelia

It is with great sadness that I write to tell you of the death of my Ben at 48 years. He was my life. He will be buried tomorrow.

His wife, Ellen (Eleanor Ann Adkins Bradfield) is grief stricken. She has six little ones to fend for. I will, of course help her where I can, but I am not as young and energetic as I used to be. I miss you both terribly.

My son William and John Bradfield are the Executors of the Estate and Ben's 2000-acre allotment in New Gloucester. It is being offered for sale.

My Edward remains the same. He spends his time pottering around in the garden and chatters to the passers-by. He continues to dabble in art, and lives a quiet, almost reclusive, life.

Write soon. Send us news of your life in Uitenhage. Your loving sister

Julia

On a Friday evening, 1st December 1837, Julia Turvey died in Grahamstown. Sampson received a copy of her obituary published in the Grahamstown Journal, which read:

Departed this life, on Friday evening, 1st December, MRS JULIA TURVEY aged 60 years, deeply regretted by her numerous off-spring. She was a tender mother, a faithful wife and a sincere friend. Her early prospects ill fitted her to combat with an adverse world but it brought her nearer to her God, and enabled her to triumph over Death and the Grave, imparting a happy consolation to her bereaved partner, to whom a union of 32 years only served to increase her affection – and who leaves this testimony of her worth.

Edward Ford Turvey, continued to charm the ladies who passed by his humble abode in Grahamstown. Alone, he continued to live in what people called his ramshackle mud hovel and to tend his manicured garden. Cowper Rose described him as an old artist who "hawks about his drawings in vain", and "whose pencil fails to keep him in Cape brandy."

Empathising with the old man who seemed so lost without his wife, pedestrians would stop to admire his well-kept garden with its many exotic and indigenous plants. When they did, he was sure to tip his hat and ask them to wait a moment while he selected a rose or a flower for the lady. Despite his idiosyncrasies, Turvey was a polite man.

In the early evenings, he would take his dog, Bonzo, for a walk and then retire to the porch to enjoy a snifter of fine brandy. He carved a rather lonely figure since Julia's death He sometimes regretted he had not paid her more attention during their time together. She had been such a gentle soul. So loved by the community. She was a good mother. He wondered how differently their lives might have turned out had the deal with Akin and Mcgrath not gone sour all those years ago.

CHAPTER 22

JOY TURNS TO SORROW

John Montgomery was born in Dublin in 1803. He was a thickset man with a large round face and thin lips. With bushy, dark eyebrows and wild raven hair that framed his sun-weathered face, he looked fiercer than he was. He had a handshake like a bear and the strength of an ox. He stood out in any crowd. He was unruly, by his own account. Montgomery was known as a tinker, a trader, a farmer, a hunter and an explorer. He had tried his hand as a jeweller, a shoemaker and a blacksmith. He was a veritable jack-of-all-trades.

Montgomery arrived on the ship, *Fanny*, in May 1820. He married Susanne van Zyl when he was only nineteen years old. He was a *smous*, a travelling trader, and he travelled north and across the Orange River with the Dutch traders.

Sampson Daniel, dressed in his finest suit, saw Robert Daniel's future father-in-law talking to Thomas Webster near the entrance of the Colesberg Church, on a sunny day in February 1838. Sampson was acquainted with Montgomery. He liked his mischievous streak and infectious belly laugh. Sampson walked over to Robert and placed his hand firmly on his nephew's shoulder, "I'm proud of you, boy. Your father is sorry he missed this fine occasion. He sent you this."

Sampson handed Robert an envelope from Peter Daniel, which contained a letter and some money to help the newlyweds set up their home. "I am sure that your mother Eliza is also smiling down on you from the heavens and your Aunty Julia, God rest her soul, would have been very proud of you today."

At 25, Robert Daniel was no longer a boy. Handsome, tall and well-built, he could ride as well and as hard as any burgher and was a skilled shottist. Robert had learned many of his bushveld skills from John Montgomery, who was known amongst the settlers as a fearless man.

"Mr Montgomery is a fine man, Uncle Sampson," said Robert, "since August last year I have been assisting him as a *smous*. He has taught me so much about trading and business. He has shown me how to fight. I have a lot of respect for him."

Sampson admired his nephew's confidence. He had always been a fearless lad with strong opinions. He just hoped that he would be cautious in future adventures with his father-in-law.

Sampson had a calming presence whilst the groom waited for Sara. She was the eldest of Montgomery's children. Like her father, she was a capable person. As a child, she had travelled by wagon with her parents as far as the Orange River to the north. Her father traded clothing, coffee, sugar and matches in return for livestock. Montgomery sold biltong, bags of fat, sheepskins and ostrich feathers in Port Elizabeth and the interior, including the regions around the Vaal and Hartz Rivers.

Robert told his uncle how he met Sara. "I rode one of the trading wagons for Montgomery. Mr Le Mare, a German botanist and doctor who had his own wagons, accompanied us. We were later joined by a man called Mr Von Abo, a land surveyor from Graaff-Reinet."

In August 1837, Montgomery had invited young Robert Daniel to accompany him on a trading trip into the interior. A few days before their scheduled departure, Robert reported for duty at Montgomery's farm, Doorn Hoek, situated in the picturesque Bamboesberg Mountains near Stormberg. The older man had acquired this farm and the adjoining farm, Spree Kloof, when his father-in-law, Jan Benjamin Van Zyl, had died.

"Get that wagon loaded, lad. We will be leaving at sunrise tomorrow so that we have a chance to catch up with those crazy Dutchmen heading for greener pastures! They'll soon be needing some of what I'm selling," Montgomery had ordered. Robert had tipped his leather hat respectfully, and continued to load supplies of matches, coffee, sugar, blankets and clothing. He bent down to check that the coupling on the wagon was properly fastened.

"Besides, some of them owe me money and I aim to get it back," added Montgomery.

As Montgomery left to collect some twine from the shed, his fifteen-year-old daughter, Sara, walked over from the house to the wagon, carrying a tray of fresh, sweetened lemon juice and some homemade bread smothered with *konfyt.* She longed to join the party as she had done on many previous *smous* expeditions, but this time her father had insisted she stay behind, as it would be dangerous travelling into the interior. They would be crossing the great Orange and Caledon Rivers. There was the threat of attack by wild animals or tribesmen hungry for food, weapons and cattle.

Sara balanced the tray on a nearby rock and invited Robert to join her. "My father's a hard man and demands a lot when he's out trading. But he's a fair man, and if you treat him with respect, he will look after you in return."

Robert felt the blood flow into his cheeks and shyly thanked Sara. He had grown up with girls, his own sisters and Uncle Sampson's girls, Sophia, Amelia, Eliza and Isabella. He felt at ease with them, but felt awkward, yet excited, whenever Sara came near him. He was looking forward to his time with Mr Montgomery. Uncle Sampson had told him to be teachable and to learn as much as he possibly could about the *smous* business. He was eager to be in charge of his own wagon and oxen, and to learn to hunt and fight off attackers if necessary, as well as how to make money from trading.

Montgomery returned with leather ropes and Sara helped Robert and her father tie down the canvas tarpaulin covering the numerous crates and wooden boxes. By late afternoon, Robert's wagon was ready for the early morning trek. All that remained was for the Hottentot helper, Aaron, to span the sixteen oxen. Then, with a crack of his whip, they would be off at Mr Montgomery's command.

After a hearty dinner of roasted beef, sweet potatoes and sweet, yellow butternut, Robert bade the family and his other travelling companions a good night. He lay on the rudimentary bed of hay in the shed outside the house, his mind racing with excitement at the prospect of catching up with the burghers who were trekking north.

His thought of Sara, her quick wit, strength and bold character. She could ride a horse with ease and was not afraid to roll up her sleeves and help around the farm when necessary. He liked her… a lot, and wished she were joining them on the trip.

Montgomery's wagon train *outspanned* at a mission station called Beersheba, after crossing the Orange and Caledon Rivers. Then, after reaching the Platberg, he instructed Robert to go on to the Chief of the Basotho, Moshoeshoe. Robert later joined Montgomery at Zuikerboschrand.

The excited groom continued to regale his uncle with his bush travel stories, to keep his wedding nerves at bay. "One night near Jammerberg, Mr Montgomery spied a few Bushmen making off with a couple of spans of their oxen. Mr Montgomery told me to accompany him up the mountain, telling me that we would let the Bushmen kill one of the oxen for food, then retrieve the rest of the livestock and leave the cattle thieves in peace.

"Over the mountain, the two men saw the Bushmen kraal. They watched the triumphant thieves dancing and celebrating their ill-gotten gains. Montgomery and I bided our time and waited until most of the fires went out.

"Mr Montgomery sent me right into the Bushmen kraal. I removed the bushes placed around the cattle and cautiously guided them in the direction of our wagon. I wasn't worried about them hearing the cattle moving, I was more worried that the Bushman could hear my heart thumping in my chest!" he laughed heartily.

"We managed to retrieve all the oxen without being detected and without bloodshed. It was Christmas time after all, and the Bushmen still had plenty of meat left over. We and the team of helpers, arrived back at *Doorn Hoek* just before midnight on 31 December, driving 650 head of cattle. The Montgomery family and guests were celebrating the New Year. Sara was there, helping her mother in the kitchen, and she offered me a meal of beef and sweet potatoes and those tasty Dutch green beans ..." he looked at his uncle and smiled knowingly.

"Sara and I sat outside listening to the sounds of the pianoforte and the fiddle, and the gaiety of the New Year's celebrations inside the farmhouse. We talked into the early hours and watched the sun come up. The two of us drank a toast and welcomed the dawning of the New Year with steaming mugs of hot coffee."

Whilst the two men inspected the cattle later that day, Robert could hardly contain himself and asked Montgomery for his daughter's hand in marriage. Montgomery had witnessed the maturity, loyalty and respect of the young man over the past months and he gave his consent and blessings.

Sampson had no doubt that Robert would make a fine son-in-law for John Montgomery and his wife, Susanna. Living in Uitenhage, it had been easy for Sampson and Amelia to attend their nephew's wedding in Colesberg and Sampson was glad to see the young groom's pride and joy. "Love your wife, Robert. Cherish her and always make sure that her needs are met before your own, and then she will make you a happy man!"

The Colesberg church bells chimed loudly, the cue for the two men to await Robert's beautiful bride.

Over the years, Peter Clarke Daniel's jewellery business grew steadily. He spent more and more time at his house in Grahamstown, although he also kept a keen eye on the farm, Beggars Bush. It was his mistress, Ann Mitchley, who had become the avid farmer. She produced good crops of wheat in 1834 and supervised the completion of the homestead. She raised her own ten children by Peter as well as those from his wife, Eliza.

By mid-1838, life in the agricultural areas around Grahamstown had become untenable. The Xhosa attacks continued unabated and the farmers were under constant threat. Life had become exceedingly difficult for Ann Mitchley and she penned a letter to the Government dated 21 July 1838. Her plea was urgent and heartfelt:

> *I have been plundered of cattle, horses, goats, Indian corn, pumpkins and much more, to a large amount, since War by the Xhosa*

and have been reduced from relative opulence to penury, having a farm (and a family) with 10 children. I am suffering under a dangerous, long and expensive illness. I am asking to be paid back for two horses loaned to the Government during the Frontier War, one of which has never been returned.

Over the years, this strong, capable woman had put her heart and soul into making Beggars Bush a viable working farm. She had been with Peter for almost twenty years, raising his wife Eliza's children as her own, as well as caring for her own children from Peter. Because of Eliza's ailing mental health, Ann Mitchley also had nursed her. At forty-nine years of age, her once fresh and vivacious face was haggard and drawn. It was dotted with sunspots and etched with deep wrinkles from the harsh climate and from spending hours outside in the sun, tending the land. The years of hardship had taken its toll on the beautiful English rose.

Even after Eliza's death in 1833, Peter did not marry Ann Mitchley. She was a brave woman, but after years of extreme hardship and hard work, the fight had left her. Her brave and dogged fight for survival eventually led to incurable sickness. Ann Mitchley died on 26 September 1838.

In her will she stated,

I bequeath all my possessions to my dear friend, Peter Clarke Daniel, with whom I have for many years resided.

The will listed her children fathered by Peter Clarke Daniel as: Thomas b.1811; Sampson b.1813; Eliza b.1816; Ann b.1818; David b.1821; Frederick b.1824; Jane b. 1826; John b.1828; Peter b.1830 and Sara b. 1832. Her will made special reference to Peter's son Robert, born of Eliza, pointing out that "although Robert Daniel is not of my body, I loved him as if he were my own son."

Robert Daniel was the blue eyed boy and remembered by all with fondness.

CHAPTER 23

TURVEY'S POST – 1840

"Run, Sophia! Run!"

Sophia, hanging up the washing on the line in the yard outside the house, whipped around at the sound of her sister's warning screams. She saw a man running past the shed, carrying a squawking chicken under his arm. Shocked, she dropped Edward's wet white cotton shirt onto the sand.

Sophia saw her sister's petrified face before Isabella ran for cover through the doorway of the cowshed. Spinning around to see what frightened Isabella so, she felt an excruciating pain as something smashed into her face. The last thing she remembered was the contorted, angry face of the man who hit her. She recognised him as he had been to the house the previous day, begging for food. She had given him some water to drink.

Sophia blacked out, falling face down onto the freshly swept ground beneath the wash line, blood pouring from the gash in her face. Isabella watched from the small, low window of the cowshed, cowering in relative safety from the thieves. The intruder, a well-built man of about twenty-five, stomped a number of times on the small of Sophia's back with the cracked heel of his bare foot. Then, he ran off through the veld, followed by four or five others, all wielding short stabbing spears. Their near soot-black bodies were clothed only in buckskin loincloths. Their skin shone with sweat and their eyes were wild with vindictive intention.

Once the intruders were out of sight, Isabella cautiously crept from the cover of the cowshed. She first hid behind the milking cow tethered to the thorn tree in front of the shed, then sprinted over to where Sophia lay in a crumpled, lifeless heap in the dirt. Her sister's face was caked in fresh blood and sand, the thick red liquid forming a cake-like crust on her face.

"Sophia! Sophia!" she cried out, stroking the hair back from her sister's face and gasping at the gaping wound. Taking a deep breath to calm herself, she took stock of the situation. Eddie was at the Thackwray's delivering eggs, so she had to take charge of the situation. She filled a metal bucket with clean water and with a hand towel she gently wiped the blood from Sophia's face and eyes.

Her older sister was mercifully unconscious and the tender skin around her eyes was starting to swell. Isabella grabbed a dry white linen sheet and tore off a piece of the fabric with her teeth to make a bandage. Folding the towel, she placed it over the wound to stop the blood flow. Working as gently as she could, she wrapped the makeshift bandage around Sophia's head, wad of towel and all. Her disorientated sister stirred.

"Sophia," said Isabella in a low voice, "you've been attacked. They hit you over the head, but everything's going to be alright."

"I can't open my eyes. I can't see you, Sis. Why can't I see you?" Isabella heard the panic rising in her sister's voice.

Sophia pushed herself up, first onto her elbows and then into a sitting position, her long skirt bunched around her ankles. The small of her back was burning with pain.

"You have a bloody gash across your face and I've wrapped your head with a bandage."

Sophia staggered blindly, then steadying herself on one hand, she lifted her other hand and put her palm over her face, feeling the bandage. "My baby!" she cried out.

"He's still in the house. They came for the cattle." At least the attackers had not gone inside where the new-born Edward Henry lay sleeping. Isabella took Sophia's hand, "Let me guide you back to the house."

Slowly she led her badly injured sister to the house and sat her down in a chair in the living room. She poured her a glass of water from the pitcher and stirred in a teaspoon of sugar to help with the shock. She had seen their mother Amelia mixing this concoction before when one of the children had fallen out of a tree and broken an arm.

Sophia began to panic, her world was in darkness and her eyes painfully swollen shut. She sensed something was horribly wrong and knew she urgently needed the doctor.

"Everything will be fine, Sophia," said Isabella, placing a hand on her sister's knee.

"Go! Go to the neighbours and call Edward, quickly," Sophia said, "he must send for surgeon Campbell."

Isabella guided Sophia to the bedroom and helped her to lie on the bed. The baby, just a few months old, still slept soundly in the crib at the foot of the bed, oblivious to the trauma unfolding around him.

Isabella saddled the chestnut horse and raced off in the direction of the neighbour. The horse's hooves pounded the loose sandy soil and grassy knolls. She did not feel the usual excitement of seeing Mrs Thackwray and sampling her homemade scones. Instead, she rode with a heavy heart.

Since the brutal farm attacks during the Sixth Frontier War of 1834 to 1835, along with Mr Mahoney's vicious murder and the burning of his house in 1834, Isabella had felt insecure about the future. She was terrified at being out on the road alone. For all she knew, the Xhosa attackers could be lurking in the scrub, waiting to ambush her and take the horse.

Relieved, she saw Sophia's husband Edward Mortimer Turvey approaching Turvey's Post from the opposite direction. His friend Thomas Webster was riding with him.

"Something's wrong!" Edward shouted to Thomas, urging his horse into a gallop.

"Eddie! It's Sophia. She's badly hurt!"

Edward sent Thomas to fetch the surgeon from Grahamstown. His horse lunged forward in the direction of home, with Isabella riding close behind.

As they dismounted in front of the house, Isabella briefed him about what had happened. He ran into the house, finding Sophia in front of the porcelain basin, carefully removing the blood-soaked bandage. Cupping both hands together, she began washing the caked blood and sand from her wounded face.

"Sophia?"

Edward was shocked at the sight of her swollen and discoloured face. With tears in his eyes, he gently wrapped her in his arms. "Sophia, my darling. I am so sorry! Doc Campbell will be here as quickly as he can, I am sure."

Sure enough, a short while later they heard the sound of horses' hooves and the rumbling of buggy wheels on the hard earth outside. The muffled sound of voices grew louder as the doctor and Thomas Webster entered the house. Neighbours also gathered outside the house, the men carrying loaded weapons, talking excitedly about the attack on Turvey's Post.

The kindly surgeon tended to Sophia's wound, stitching up the gash using stitches as small as he could manage to minimise the scarring. The womenfolk prepared tea and soup for the traumatised Turvey family.

The men, mostly newlyweds and young fathers, discussed the immediate dangers, which had become part of their life.

"If our parents had known that the Xhosa had chased the Dutch Settlers off the Zuurveld in 1819, just one year before we arrived on these shores, I'm damn sure they would never have agreed to leave the comfort of England."

"Agreed!"

"It was Somerset who deceived our parents. He lied to them about Africa being the land of milk and honey. They used our families as a human shield between the Xhosa on the other side of the Great Fish River, and their lofty towers in Cape Town."

"It's despicable!"

The unprovoked attack on Sophia angered the community and

stirred up anger. She was a gentle, kind young woman, who gladly helped others, no matter their race or creed. She didn't deserve this.

Tucked up in bed later that evening, long after the last of the concerned neighbours and family members had left, Sophia listened to Edward's restless breathing beside her. The bandages soaked up her tears as she cried.

Edward turned restlessly onto his side and put his warm arm over her stomach. Her baby was sleeping in the next room with Isabella who had offered to stay over and help with the infant.

"Tomorrow," she reasoned with herself, "I will get up and do my chores. I refuse to be downtrodden by these people. Forgive them, Lord, for they know not what they do."

She prayed silently. "Thy will be done, oh God. May I continue to bring you glory all the days of my life, no matter what happens. I am grateful that, even though I may lose my sight, my life is spared. Strengthen me in the dark days that lie ahead and help Eddie to accept."

Sophia slept fitfully. Her body ached.

Sampson and Amelia received a letter from their daughter, Isabella, a few weeks later.

Sampson read and re-read the letter, trying to make sense of the news.

... the Doctor removed the bandages today. I thought I would only write and tell you of the incident, once we knew the extent of Sophia's injuries. Thankfully, the swelling has gone down and the gash across the top of her nose where the Doctor stitched her face has healed well. I am sure there will be very little scarring.

As for her sight – it appears that she has lost eighty percent of her vision. At this stage, she is only able to see shapes and shadows. She cannot distinguish colours or features.

But, be assured, she is in high spirits and has determined not to let this disability detract from her usual, bubbly self. You, yourselves know our Sophia – she has always been a positive, caring person and I am sure this will enhance her beautiful personality even more. She has said that she will just have to take extra special care to fine-tune her other four senses!

When she is feeling stronger, we will plan a trip to visit you and the family in Uitenhage and introduce you to your new grandson. Chubby little Edward Henry is simply adorable.

Ever your loving daughter,
Isabella.

Sampson breathed in deeply. He slowly slid his round reading glasses off his nose as he handed the letter to Amelia. When he and Amelia had moved to Uitenhage in 1823, his only regret had been that his daughters had moved back to Grahamstown in search of love. Only their son, Frederick had stayed with them.

Even as children, Sophia and Edward Ford Turvey had been inseparable. He was saddened when they had opted to stay at Turvey's Post after their marriage on August 1, 1837. He had written many a letter, urging them to move to safer pastures. The Albany frontier was still volatile.

Worrying about the safety of his family weighed heavily on his shoulders.

CHAPTER 24

FOR EVERY DEATH, THERE IS A BIRTH

Amelia dropped the enamel pot she was washing and it fell clattering to the floor. She had never heard Sampson cry out like that and rushed to the living room, still carrying an embroidered dishtowel. Sampson stood in the middle of the room, face ashen and clutching his head with both hands.

He wailed, "No! No! Oh my God! Why?"

"What is it?" she grabbed his shoulders, "What?"

Sampson was too distraught to respond, his face contorted in grief. As Amelia guided him to an armchair, she scanned the room for the source of this unprecedented outburst. There it was! She picked up the newspaper that lay on the floor. It was the *Grahamstown Journal* dated 27 February 1840. Scanning the pages, she read the headline, "COLESBERG – Awful and Fatal Occurrence."

As she continued reading, her blood turned cold. Their favourite nephew, Robert Daniel, was dead.

2 February 1840 – Spree Kloof (near Molteno)

As the first rays of sun peeked through their bedroom window, twenty-five-year-old Robert Daniel woke his wife Sara with a hot cup of freshly brewed coffee. He gently pulled back the sheet from her exquisite, naked body, and kissed her stomach playfully. She groaned softly, smiling sweetly as she opened her eyes. She looked down to see Robert grinning, a wisp of blond over one eye, and his cheek resting on her abdomen.

"I'm just kissing my baby good morning," he teased.

Sara had told him the previous night that she thought she was pregnant and that her mother had confirmed she was expecting. "If it's a boy we will call him Robert, if it's a girl, we will call her Robertina!" her husband had joked as he spun her around in circles until they fell dizzily onto the bed.

The couple lived on the farm Spreeu Kloof, adjacent to John Montomery's farm, Doorn Hoek. Not only was their home a generous gift, John had also made sure they had several pieces of good wooden furniture and a large feather bed. Close to the Bamboesberg, Robert ran a large head of cattle, whilst Sara bred chickens and sold farm eggs and produce. They made a formidable team. They were a happy and energetic couple, always laughing and bantering with one another.

That morning, February 2 1840, Robert and his brother-in-law, Adriaan van Zyl, had planned to take a large sack of wheat to be milled at a neighbouring farm. Robert had primed the young Aaron, to have the horses saddled early in the morning. Sara packed a small leather satchel with a light lunch for the riders. The young men tethered the two packhorses together, and the very large sack of wheat was placed half on the back of one horse, and half on the back of the other. Fourteen-year-old Aaron rode behind Robert, with Adriaan taking up the rear.

They had barely left the homestead when the temperature suddenly dropped and dark clouds rolled swiftly towards them. "Back to the farm!" Robert yelled, not wanting to get the sacks of wheat wet. They wheeled the horses around and made tracks back to the house. In no time at all, a huge storm broke with large hailstones hurtling down, crashing into men and beast, bruising their lightly clothed bodies.

"Ouch, ouch, *eina*!" the men yelled as they raced home. Safely in the shed, Robert and Adrian dismounted and ran across the yard to the house, nursing red welts on their arms and legs. Despite being stung by the hailstones, the two of them doubled over with laughter at the expression on Aaron's face as he rode in. The whites of his eyes were as big as saucers in his brown face. With the loaded pack horses, he taken longer to get back, screwing up his face as the hail beat down on his exposed limbs.

Sara, caught up in the frivolity of the moment, brought out an old frock of hers for Aaron to replace his saturated long pants and cotton shirt once he finally made it inside. His disgust at the comical outfit, way too large for him, only made his companions laugh even harder.

Sara insisted that they enjoyed breakfast while they waited for the storm to pass. They sipped hot coffee and ate scrambled eggs with freshly baked bread and homemade wild gooseberry jam. Robert told stories about his travels into the interior with his father-in-law. He never tired of telling the stories of his adventures and planned to take Sara and her brother up north one day. Eagerly, he regaled them with stories of wild animals, like the leopard which had attacked their packhorses. He described the special wild dog trap that Montgomery had devised to catch the prowling animals. To do this, he would secure a leg of mutton on top of a cage with a rope attached to a door, kept open with a stick. The door would slam shut, trapping the wild dog as it knocked over the stick in an attempt to grab the meat.

Around midday, the sky cleared and the threat of rain seemed to have passed. There was still time to reach the neighbour's farm and, as the horses were already saddled, the three intrepid riders set off once again. Robert blew his wife a kiss.

"Look after my baby!" he shouted playfully.

The three rode happily away, chatting and gesticulating animatedly. Sara watched as they disappeared behind the rise beyond the house. She was startled by a sudden flash of lightning. The deafening crack of thunder seemed to come from the rise itself. Sara felt a strange foreboding. An eerie silence filled the air. Attempting to shrug the feeling off, she was about to turn for the house when she saw something moving in the distance.

Unsure of the movement she had seen, she sent her maidservant to investigate as she busied herself with her chores. It wasn't long and she heard the woman screaming frantically.

"It's Aaron! *Daar's iets fout*! *Die Baas en baas Adriaan*, they all fall down! Lightning!" Arms flailing and crying hysterically, the poor woman was barely coherent. Falling to her knees before Sara, she wailed, "The god in the sky, she angry! The horses too, they lie down... *Haauw, miesie, haaauw, miesie*!"

Sara raced inside to grab a clean cloth and a bottle of vinegar, thinking that one of the men must have been injured. As she headed towards the rise, she encountered a disorientated Aaron. His normally dark complexion had turned ashen grey. Dazed and shocked, he stumbled and mumbled incoherently.

"The *baas* .... hy is *dood* ... he's dead," he screamed.

"Oh, no! No, no ..." Sara ran over the rise and was greeted by a scene of mayhem.

Robert and her brother lay near each other on the earth, both flat on their backs with legs and arms splayed out. Four of their horses lay next to them, stone dead. Robert's horse, Champion, had a scorched chest and the leather saddle was perforated as if it has been shot through with bullets. Adriaan's shoes had been blown off his feet by the impact of the lightning strike. He was still fully clothed except for the smouldering fabric on his chest, where his upper abdomen was still burning.

With a pounding heart and gasping for breath, she ran over to where Robert lay, calling his name to try to stir him from his unconsciousness. She fell to her knees and leant over her husband's lifeless body. Sara placed her hand over one of his, which lay palm down across his heart. She felt no movement. His other hand still held onto the reins of the dead horse beside him. The face she adored was perforated with small, black holes as if he had been pelted by birdshot, the blood crimson as it trickled from each tiny hole. His clothes were in tatters, shredded bits of smoking rags hanging from his body. His feet were bare and Sara noticed his shoes some distance away. The force of the lightning strike had blown them off his feet too.

Sara carefully poured vinegar onto her cloth and lovingly wiped

Robert's face. The vacant blue eyes that had attracted her to him were wide open, staring vacantly into the vast African sky. Beads of tears had squeezed from his tear ducts and settled on his cheeks. Small glimmering pools of apology for leaving her so soon.

Sara wiped away the tears and the trickling blood. As she moved down towards his chin, the shattered bones in his lower jaw crumbled under her fingers. Sitting back, suddenly aware of the futility of her actions, Sara allowed the thought that Robert was dead.

Thunder rolled ominously in the distance and the midday air was still. It seemed as if the whole world had stopped breathing in the aftermath of the storm. The maidservant was still wailing uncontrollably and Aaron crouched under a tree, staring helplessly at her.

Sara took in a deep breath and screamed, *"Aaron! Aaron! Skrik wakker! Ry! Vinnig! Nou!"*

She checked that Aaron was registering what she shouted, "*Vat jou perd en ry, vinnig, na Baas John toe.* Ride to *oom* John. Tell uncle John to come, quickly!"

Her father would know what to do.

The hooves of Aaron's horse kicked up clods of dirt as he galloped away and Sara stretched herself unashamedly across Robert's lifeless body, crying out in agony. Only this morning they had wondered whether their unborn child would be a girl or a boy, and what they would name it. Then she had laughed with him and her brother and young Aaron when they were caught in the hailstorm. Now her Robert was gone. For good. Her senses were numb in disbelief.

The maidservant, respecting her mistress' grief, sat beneath an acacia tree, her body shuddering in silent sobs. There was no concept of time for Sara as she grieved. A while later, the urgent cracking of a whip broke the deathly silence as Sara lay still, asleep with her head on Robert's chest. She barely saw her father's horrified face through her swollen eyes as she heard his comforting voice. Murmuring softly, John Montgomery and his men loaded the wagon with the dead. Sara took Robert's hunting knife from his saddlebag and cut a ringlet from his shoulder-length blond hair from behind his ear. Later, she asked her father to make a small hole through the top of a brass bullet cartridge. She placed the locket of hair inside the empty casing and sealed it with a piece of cork. She wore the bullet, strung on a shoelace from his boot, as a pendant around her neck.

The Grahamstown Journal gave a full report of the tragic incident. The newspaper also reported that Robert Daniel, a son of P. C. Daniel of Grobler's Kloof in Albany, and Adriaan van Zyl, were buried on the 4th February, and followed to the grave by a number of inhabitants of the Field-Cornetcy of Groote River.

A few days after Robert's death, Sara commissioned a transport rider to deliver her letter to Sampson and Amelia Daniel, along with a copy of the *Grahamstown Journal.*

"He was like my own son, Amelia…" Sampson, sobbed uncontrollably.

"Oh, Sampson!" she whispered, throwing her arms around him. They both cried and held each other tightly for a long time.

Amelia went through to the kitchen to make a pot of tea, but when she returned with the tray, Sampson was gone.

Every fibre in Sampson's being was numb. He walked out of the door of the homestead and into the neighbouring fields. His footsteps were like lead. The ache he felt in his heart for his nephew would never go away. He looked up to the heavens, threw his hands angrily into the air and cried out, "Why, God? Why Robert?"

Wild Africa had robbed him yet again, he thought, as he sank to his knees.

CHAPTER 25

"FIGHTING TOM" WEBSTER

The War of the Axe – Albany District 1846

The Xhosa forces outnumbered the colonialists by ten to one.

After a fragile period of peace between the neighbours, war broke out in March 1846.

Eddie Turvey's close friend, twenty-one-year-old Thomas Webster was given the leadership of a burgher commando, which was mobilized to prevent further the continued Xhosa onslaught. He and his friend, Jan Greyling set out on a horseback to track the spoor of a group of Xhosa responsible for a spate of local farm attacks in the Albany District. Tom rode his palomino horse. The young man was hailed as a strong and wise fighter. He was feared by the Xhosa tribesmen who called him the "white man who rides the yellow horse."

As the two scanned the surrounding bush, Jan caught an unusual movement from the corner of his eye and alerted Tom. At that moment, a gunshot rang out and a bullet whizzed over their heads.

"Take cover," shouted Tom as he saw a group of warriors armed with traditional weapons charge out of the scrub. One of them held a gun. The two burghers dismounted and sought protection in the dense bush around them.

"There's one to your left," whispered Tom, his body charged with adrenalin. He fired over the top of his horse, killing one of the attackers. The air was electric as the boys reloaded and fired again. Bullets flew around them in all directions.

"Thank God the one with the gun can't shoot straight," grimaced Thomas.

The words were hardly out of his mouth, when he heard Jan call out. He turned to see his friend crumple in pain, dropping to the ground. A bullet had ripped through the flesh on his hip and blood oozed between his fingers as he clutched at the wound.

"*Blixem*!" he screamed, "*Donder, man*."

Webster grabbed his friend by the shirt collar and the leather belt on the back of his pants, dragging him to the safety of a rocky outcrop. For now, they were safely surrounded by dense thicket and boulders. He barely had time to gauge their risk when he saw two of their attackers closing in on them. He fired two shots, killing one and seriously wounding the other.

"*Ga hulp halen. Verlaat my, Tom*," said Jan in Dutch. "Go and get help. Leave me here and save yourself."

"Not a chance," replied Tom peering out between the rocks, "we are a team. The rest of the commando is not far behind. They will have already heard the shooting." Tom held his rifle in his right hand, pressing a crumpled neck scarf against the wound in his friend's thigh with the other. "Here, press hard," he said. Raising the rifle, he took aim, shooting and killing another Xhosa man.

There was a deathly silence. Nothing moved. Thomas slowly scanned the bush around him. He identified the position of an enemy crouching behind some thickets. He reloaded his weapon, waited for the right opportunity and fired. He had to make every bullet count. Jan was not able to back him up. A relieved Tom heard a loud whistle and shouting heralding the arrival of the back-up commando. At the risk of revealing his position, he called out, but the remaining attackers melted like shadows into the undergrowth.

Jan's sigh was audible. Tom turned to his friend whose eyes were screwed up in pain. "*Dankie boetie*," Jan said' "you saved my life."

"You would have done the same for me," said Tom, mopping the blood from his comrade's wound.

Uitenhage District 1846

It was Thursday, 13 August 1846. Twenty eight year old Frederick Daniel cradled his newborn son, while his wife, Lydia rested. The couple had married in Uitenhage on 7 July 1845. His wife was the daughter of James and Mary Urry.

"We named him after you, Papa," said Frederick to his father, Sampson Daniel. "His name is Sampson James."

Frederick handed the tightly wrapped bundle to his father, who beamed with delight. He hoped this little boy would help to fill the void left by the untimely death of his nephew, Robert, almost six years before.

Uitenhage had been home to Frederick for almost twenty years. Having grown up in a predominantly Dutch community, he spoke the dialect fluently. He had become a successful trader and assisted his father in their General Dealer store. Quietly spoken, with dark features like his French mother, Frederick was a sensible, stable man. He had a mop of thick jet black hair and a big beard. He was hardworking and eager to please. He and his Lydia spent many an hour in the comfort of his parents' home, enjoying his mother's cooking. As he grew up, little Sam as he was called, became the apple of his namesake's eye, spending hours in his grandfather's company.

Shortly after little Sam's birth, Sampson Daniel received word of the renewed unrest in Albany from his youngest daughter, Eleanor, who lived at Fort Armstrong. She was engaged to "Fighting Tom Webster", as he became known after he had courageously held off the Xhosa attackers and saved his friend's life. The bad news of the renewed unrest, and the fact that the British government were planning to prevent the Boer Commandos from retaliating against future Xhosa attacks, cemented his decision to move even further north to the greener, safer pastures of a place he had heard about, called Bloemfontein. A number of the trekboers had relocated there prior to mid1830 and the Voortrekkers migrated north beyond the Orange River in a systematic colonization between 1835 and 1846. Sampson had heard positive feedback of successful settlements, lucrative farm lands and general trade opportunities.

Amelia argued with her husband about another big move when he suggested it. She was settled and happy in Uitenhage. She used her children to try to entice him to stay, but her argument was weak.

"Amelia, our children are all grown up with lives of their own. Sophia and Edward Turvey are making ends meet at Turvey's Post for now, and Isabella is living with them. She will soon marry Edmund Bradfield. Eliza is married to John Crook and Amelia is married to Henry Morrell. Luisa and George Whitfield Thom are settled. Albertine is with John Biggs in Fort Beaufort and our Eleanor is engaged to Thomas Webster and living in Fort Armstrong," he said.

"Frederick and his wife, Lydia and our grandson little Sam will come with us."

Sampson and Amelia's youngest child, Charles Augustus, who was born in Uitenhage, was their only dependent child at 12 years old. Amelia gave up trying to argue with her husband. His mind was made up.

On 7 November 1845, Sampson Daniel placed an advert in the Eastern Province Herald.

> *Being about to leave this place (Uitenhage) Daniel Esq. has instructed HH Rens to sell by Public Auction on Wednesday 25 November at his residence; dwelling house, situated in Baird Street. Large garden. Also, 2 plots of ground in John Street. Also assortment of furniture."*

His decision was final. This Daniel family was going to follow the voortrekkers across the Orange River.

The Eighth Frontier War – Albany District 1850

The Xhosa were on the warpath once again. They bitterly resented Sir Harry Smith's recent annexation of their lands and had been secretly preparing to renew their struggle for freedom. After the current Chief Mgolombane Sandile of the Ngqika (Gaika) tribe refused to attend a meeting called by Sir Harry Smith, the British governor deposed him and declared him a fugitive, replacing him with a local magistrate named Mr Brownlee. In December 1850, a large number of gun-bearing Xhosas attacked British troops sent to arrest Sandile. The soldiers were driven back by the warriors. However, this led to the outbreak of the Eighth Frontier War, started with a brazen Xhosa attack on settlers in the border area on Christmas day.

Thomas Webster had set up a small business in Fort Armstrong. The responsibility of his wife, Eleanor, whom he had married on 31 May 1849 at the Mankazana farm, and the threat of Xhosa invasion weighed heavily on him. He was aware how vulnerable the small community was. The couple, along with thirty people, were given permission to move. Tom and Eleanor moved to Whittlesea, where his parents, Thomas and Mary Webster, lived with his ten brothers and his sister, Mary. They were far from safe. Soon after their arrival the village was surrounded by a horde of Xhosa.

The attacks on the settlers were brutal. The besieged village was cut off from outside assistance. As ammunition and food supplies dwindled, the desperate men resorted to melting the family silver to make bullets.

"I know all the back roads in this area," Tom Webster volunteered, "I'll try break through and get help."

The elders of the town agreed. Under cover of darkness, Thomas Webster quietly stole away from Whittlesea. Out of earshot of the enemy, he mounted his palomino and galloped towards Cradock, some 90 miles away. Sweat soaked and exhausted, he reached Cradock in record time.

The burghers and British forces gathered to ride to the aid of the besieged community at Whittlesea. Tom was able to eat a hearty meal, bathe and rest while the troops assembled. One of the Boer women gave him a fresh shirt and placed a food parcel in his saddle bag. The salted ribs, rusks and dried fruit were welcome on the return journey.

Fighting Tom rode with the troops as they sped towards the town of Whittlesea. Drawing near the town, a group of angry Xhosa warriors attacked them. The troops took cover and fired back at their assailants.

Tom fought like a man possessed with thoughts of his wife and family trapped and endangered in Whittlesea. Before long, the fallen bodies of their enemies lay scattered on the ground.

From behind the cover of a large rock, Tom saw a British officer, Lieutenant Robert Jefferson, whom he had befriended on the ride, tumble to the ground when his horse was wounded by stray bullets. Jefferson hit his head on a rock and lay bleeding on the ground. Tom rode over to the injured man, sliding his left boot from the stirrup and shouting, "Grab my stirrup!" Jefferson grabbed hold of the metal with both hands and Tom dragged him to shelter behind the large rock.

The fighting lasted a few hours before the enemy conceded defeat.

The British soldiers and burgher commando relieved the town of Whittlesea. Hearty cheers erupted from the townsfolk as the troops entered the town. Lieutenant Jefferson, supported by his new friend Thomas Webster, the wounded man shouted, "Three cheers for Fighting Tom!"

The crowd rallied around Tom, cheering wildly and the men lifted him onto their shoulders. Shy Eleanor hung back, but glowed with pride and relief. Tom caught her eye over the heads of the crowd and winked reassuringly.

CHAPTER 26

BLOEMFONTEIN

Cautioned by the news that his old Dutch friend, Piet Retief, had been brutally murdered by Zulu King Dingane in 1838, Sampson Daniel did not take the move north across the Orange River to Bloemfontein lightly. Bloemfontein was officially founded in 1846 as a fort by the British army Major Henry Douglas Warden. It was a central place from where he could administer the area, situated across the Orange River. It was a vast open veld, densely populated with wild animals. It was occupied by trekboers, Griqua and Basotho tribes' people.

Many of the Dutch Voortrekkers had pushed on and travelled further north-east, into the land to be known as Natal. Some of the main expeditions carried on even farther north. Many survived, but large numbers didn't. Despite these hazards, Sampson Daniel cut ties with the Eastern Cape and followed in the footsteps of his Dutch counterparts, in search of better future prospects and safety for his family. Daniel and his sons Frederick and Charles Augustus, joined the English-speaking pioneers of the newly established Bloemfontein community.

The migrant groups set up camp on the fertile land above the junction of the Caledon and Orange Rivers. As more and more farmers moved into the area, they tried to colonise the land between the two rivers, even north of the Caledon, claiming that the area was uninhabit-ed. Chief Lepoqo Moshoeshoe, paramount Chief of the Basotho, got wind of the Voortrekker settlement above the junction of the two rivers and said, "... the ground on which these migrants are settling belongs to me. I have no objections to their flocks grazing there, but only until such time as they are able to proceed further. On condition that they remain in peace with my people and recognised my authority."

Instead of building huts made of reeds, which were temporary structures, the Dutch migrants began building solid structures out of clay. They planted their own food crops in the fertile soils and traded less with the Basotho, showing their intention to settle permanently in the region.

In 1848, Sir Harry Smith proclaimed Bloemfontein the seat of the Orange River Sovereignty.

Andrew Hudson Bain was tasked to draw up a plan of the proposed town. The earliest parts of the village occupied the so-called water erven – the plots lying on the south side of the Bloem Spruit. The southern boundary was St. George's Street with the Presidency grounds to the west and Fraser Street to the east. When it was first established, wild animals roamed the streets and huge herds of antelope covered the vast open plains and surrounding hills. Hunting was a part of daily life in Bloemfontein, with lion hunting the most popular. From a dusty and isolated settlement, Bloemfontein grew, over time, from a village to a thriving town.

Warden erected the first *raadsaal* or council chamber in 1849, a thatched, whitewashed hall where the community could gather. Warden was an amicable person with the difficult task of trying to please independent and truculent trekkers and loyal colonials. There were numerous quarrels between the groups. The Orange River Sovereignty prevailed for a period of about six years.

Young Sam told his grandfather what he and his friends had been up to. Sipping rooibos tea and nibbling on Amelia's home-baked shortbread biscuits, Sampson heard how his grandson and his friend, Jacob Stoltz, went to play in the Bloemfontein market square. They met with Sophie Leviseur, who joined the small group. Sam brought the clay wagon and span of oxen which he had made with the help of one of the herd boys on the land where they lived. Together they had modelled a team of toy oxen made from *dolosse*, the knuckle bones of dead cattle, and tied these together with leather twine and small twigs. The oxen were attached to the jawbone of a zebra by a long leather *riempie*, or thong. Carpal bones were used to represent the wagon driver, brakeman and the leader of the span.

The Market Square was a large open space surrounded by several houses. A small market house doubled as an office. Children spent hours playing on the sandy square in the village, pretending to be ivory traders and travellers. That afternoon, Sam had brought along a bucket of spare bones, and the children used them as soldiers pretending to fight off Basotho warriors.

Jacob soon became bored with the game. He took some carpal bones and slipped them into the pocket of his breeches, moving away from his friends. He set up a tin can and began shooting at it with his catapult. Holding tightly to the thick, y-shaped stick, he aimed higher and higher, to see how far he could shoot the bones. He became so engrossed in his play that he inadvertently shot a bone through the window of the Market Square office.

The irate Market Master stormed out of the office, flailing his arms and shouting obscenities at the group of children.

"Watch out!'" shouted mischievous Sam, "here's Mr Cameron! Run for it!"

The children scattered as Mr Cameron stormed across the yard. He caught one of the fleeing youngsters and held him by the scruff of the neck. On hearing the terrified screams of their playmate, the other children stopped dead in their tracks. They turned to see Mr Cameron throw Jacob over his shoulder.

"He's a pig and I'll sell him at the market tomorrow!" yelled the Market Master, as he walked away with the young boy hanging upside down over his left shoulder.

The terrified children scattered in different directions, to report the awful fate of their friend to their parents.

Sampson Daniel threw his head back and laughed loudly, "I'm glad it isn't you, Sam, who will be sold as a pig at the market tomorrow!"

Sampson heard the sounds of the thriving market as it came alive. The market square would soon be a bustle of wagons, oxen, carts and people buying and selling wares. New stocks arrived periodically from Grahamstown, Uitenhage and Port Elizabeth on the East coast. Laden with goods, large wooden wagons noisily rumbled into town in clouds of dust. With cracking whips and the loud bellows of oxen, the traders lined up along the wide dirt streets for each market day.

From the comfort of the living room in the first house he bought in Bloemfontein, Sampson could hear the lively commotion a few streets away, while he read *The Friend*, the local newspaper.

Mr A. H. Bain, the Town Planner who Sampson knew, owned many properties in the district and wished to sell some of them. His advert in newspaper read:

> Important Notice to Land Purchasers
>
> Mr AH Bain, being about concentrating his affairs, offers his most valuable property in the Sovreignty for sale. Mr Bain, from his long residence here has been enabled to become the fortunate proprietor of the most valuable farms in this district, which he now offers to those Stockbreeders who may wish to make this most desirable part of the country their future home.

The properties advertised included Tempe, Bain's Vlei – an easy hour's ride by horse from *Bloemfontein, Quagga Fontein (Zebra Fountain), Leeuw Fontein (Lion Fountain), Wolf House* on the *Modder River* and the *Hartebees Hoek* farm.

Sampson read the article aloud whilst his seventeen-year-old son, Charles Augustus, sat opposite his father, listening carefully.

> HARTEBEES HOEK – this is an extensive piece of land adjoining the farms Bains Vley and Quagga Fontein and from the abundance of wood, a rapid fortune might be made supplying the Bloemfontein market.

> The farm Leeuw Fontein adjoining the above, its capabilities for stock of all descriptions are excellent and makes a valuable addition to the farm called Hartebees Hoek.
>
> Sale, by order of the court, in front of the Civil Commissioner's office, on Wednesday 31 October 1850 at 11 o'clock, will be sold at WINBURG to the highest bidder at a credit of 6, 12 and 18 months before a special...

Before he had finished reading the notice, Charles pleaded with his father to attend the sale. Sampson was pleased with Charles enthusiasm. Charles had always shown an affinity for farming, particularly sheep and cattle. A jovial young man with fine facial features, young Charles was much more suited to the outdoors than his older brother, Frederick. The two were so different, yet both were good, honest, hardworking people. He was confident that Charles would make a good farmer and saw the potential for grazing stock on the Haartebees Hoek farm, as well as offering wood for sale. He knew the farm had an abundance of water.

"I will make an appointment with Mr Bain later this morning. We will ride with him to view the land and make him an offer, Charles," said Sampson. Besides, Sampson thought, he could buy Charles a few head of sheep and cattle to get him started with the farming venture.

Another article in the newspaper confirmed Sampson's ideas.

> The whole of the Orange Sovereignty is perfectly quiet and no further disturbances have been heard on the Modder.

The news that there was no political or tribal unrest in the area, augured well for a bright future and good farming prospects for Charles. Sampson felt confident the timing was right to purchase the land. Further reports confirmed the region of the Orange River Sovereignty was perfectly suited to the rearing of the finest sheep. Should he acquire the farm, Sampson could get hold of John Montgomery for advice on farming Merino sheep.

Sampson was still concerned about those of his family living on the

Eastern Frontier. He worried even more when he came across another news snippet on the same page as the Auction Notice.

"Listen to this, *ma cherie*," he said to Amelia, who was sat quietly with her embroidery, "The Xhosa tribesmen on the eastern Frontier of the Colony appear to be in a very unsettled state."

"We can only pray for them, Sampson," replied Amelia, "it is such a long trip to get there by wagon. They had the opportunity to follow us here where it is so much safer"

Amelia promised to write to each of her children urging them to join them in Bloemfontein should things became too difficult, or too dangerous. She would reassure them that their father would assist them if they ever felt the need to relocate.

Previously, Eleanor had written that Thomas Webster killed more than forty Xhosa marauders during recent skirmishes. At the end of the 8th War, the British Government rewarded him for his valour. He was given first choice of a farm on the Eastern Frontier for his unflinching bravery in the face of danger. In addition to his ferocity in battle, he courageously went to the rescue of the wounded. Despite this recognition, war is never fair neither necessarily right. There are no winners in war.

Charles disliked aggression of any kind, and the talk of war made him feel uncomfortable. He excused himself and joined his friends at the market, where he found them talking of a lion hunt. Evidently, a rogue lion was terrorizing the local kraals near Bains Vlei on the outskirts of Bloemfontein. Residents had heard the deep throaty call of the ferocious male lion at dusk the previous night.

"Charlie, we are hunting lion tomorrow morning," said Lukas Dreyer, a longstanding friend of Charles Daniel. He was a transport rider and hunter who traded in skins and ivory. "Are you coming as well?" he asked.

Lukas told how one of the drivers who worked for him, a Basotho named Ditsheho, meaning 'laughter', was resting at his kraal. Ditsheho and his brother lingered at the open fire once their family had gone off to bed. The two men watched the flames shooting sparks of fire into the night air, sharing stories over a clay pot of home-brewed beer. Near midnight, the embers of the fire died down. The men were about to turn in for the night. Suddenly, a massive lion lunged out of nowhere, from the darkness and locked his powerful jaws around Ditsheho's neck, dragging him backwards through the grass.

Ditsheho died instantly when the powerful predator pierced his jugular with its razor-sharp incisor. Ditsheho's brother screamed for help and the other men of the kraal ran out to help. They grabbed still burning logs from the fire and hurled them in the direction of the beast. The lion lay protectively over its prey, its giant paws pinning the lifeless body to the earth. It fiercely held its ground, snarling at its assailants. By the light of the moon the helpless men could make out Ditsheho's body, a tangled heap of blood and intestines which spilled from his gaping abdomen. The lion fed, unperturbed by the fruitless efforts and shouts of the men who beat their sticks in vain attempts to chase it away.

At first light, the men retrieved what remained of Ditsheho's body for burial.

The group of men listening to Lukas were shocked, shaking their heads at this unprecedented attack on a human. Fearing further attacks by the rogue lion, a group of local residents agreed to join the farmers in the hunt for the beast.

Monday dawned, the air crisp and fresh as the sun peeked over the distant hills beyond Bloemfontein. Fine puffs of mist hung in the cold morning air in front of Frederick Daniel's General Dealer Store. A small group of family and friends of the slain Ditsheho also gathered in front of the building. As Charles Daniel and his father, Sampson, rode along St Georges Street, they passed the cottage of Major Blenkinsopp of the 45th Regiment and that of Captain Bates, and passed the barracks with its solid red brick shed that was used to stable the grey horses trained to pull the big guns. Veering westwards, the two men passed the butcher's shop, the jailer's neat cottage and the jailhouse. This building was in a poor state with the plaster falling off and bird droppings covering the walls. The thatched cottage just before the

Daniel's General Dealer store was run down and needed to be demolished. Frederick stood on the verandah of his store and he greeted them as they stopped to collect freshly baked bread from Frederick for their trip to Bains Vlei to view the Hartebees Hoek farm with its current owner, Andrew Bain. Mr Schindehutte had opened a boarding house nearby, and Mr Colley's canteen sold food and drink. On the west corner of the street, Charles noticed the handwritten sign bearing the name of the local doctor, Dr Fraser.

Mr Bains joined them not long afterwards and the three men road passed the cottages of Lieutenant Dawson and Mr Colley, their yards boasting abundant vegetable gardens and many fruit trees. They caught up with Lukas Dreyer and his hunting party, en route and determined to avenge the death of the loyal Ditsheho. The dead man's brother rode up front with Dreyer, his rifle strapped across his back. The group of horsemen left the village behind them and rode for about 15 miles through vast open plains with small rocky hills and clusters of trees.

After a long while, with the sun high up in the sky overhead, Charles grinned and pointed out across a large tract of land, his blue eyes shining like diamonds in the bright sunlight. "Look out there, Papa. I will own that farm, Hartebees Hoek, one day."

Thomas Bains smiled and Sampson chuckled, letting young Charles dream on about the herds of livestock he would own and whether he would grow wheat or maize in the rich, red soil. The three men broke away from the hunting party, veering left along a rough track. Lukas Dreyer and his posse pressed on in the direction of Kimberley, where the rogue lion had last been sighted.

It had rained heavily the night before and the ground was saturated, turning the rough red soil of the dirt track to slippery mud in places. It took the remainder of the day for Sampson, his son and the owner of the land to cover the vast tract of over nine thousand morgen of the Haartebees Hoek farm. It was early evening by the time the men returned to Bloemfontein. With a weary but firm handshake, Sampson Daniel agreed to the purchase of the Hartebees Hoek farm from Thomas Bain.

CHAPTER 27

FORMATION OF THE ORANGE FREE STATE

Sampson read the copy of the *Grahamstown Journal*, dated 22 May 1852. It accompanied a letter from his daughter Sophia, informing him of his brother, Peter's death. A snippet of the article read:

"The present season has proved a very unhappy one along this frontier. The measles have been very prevalent, scarcely a family in Grahamstown has escaped its attack and in many cases they have terminated fatally. In our obituaries today we have to record the names of two of our oldest inhabitants...one being Mr P. C. Daniel (Jeweller) being one of the British emigrants of 1820. The measles leaves in many cases a species of low typhus fever which cannot be too carefully guarded against. Sudden atmospheric changes are a powerful and predisposing cause of this and should be countered by non-exposure as far as practicable. Measles often leaves encephalitis....."

It appeared Peter had died from a heart attack in the fields at *Glenwyn* farm, as a result of contracting measles. Sampson was deeply saddened as he read the news.

Sampson wondered yet again why his brother had not married Ann Mitchley after Eliza's death. Peter continued to have affairs with various women over the years, one of them being Ann Pote with whom he had a daughter named Charlotte, on March 28 1840. Peter did not marry Ann Pote either. He chose, instead, to marry another woman, Ann Smith when she fell pregnant with his youngest child. In a letter to her parents, Sophia related that Ann Smith had divorced Peter when he had an affair with yet another lady. It was all too much for Sampson who had never understood Peter's carrying on with so many different women. He wasn't sure how his brother had kept it up all these years. By the time he died, Peter Daniel must have sired some twenty children in his lifetime.

"Dear old Peter, he never did change his ways!" Sampson sighed under his breath as he put down the newspaper.

Thaba Bosigo – the Mountain at Night

In 1824, the leader of the Basotho tribe, Chief Lepoqo Moshoeshoe led his people up the steep, rocky mountain pass, onto the flat-topped mountain of Thaba Bosigo, about ninety three miles away from Bloemfontein. There, he established his almost impenetrable mountain kingdom fortress. The sandstone plateau covered an area of almost one-and a-half square miles, and was large enough for the leader of the tribe to build a village for his people and keep cattle. The lofty mountain fortress was accessible by a number of passes, but the Chief blocked them with large rocks, leaving only one route to the top. The rocky cliff face and steep terrain made it difficult to attack the kraal at the top, and made it easy to defend. From the top of the mountain the defenders had views of the plains and slopes below, in all directions.

Born in 1786 in a place called Menkhoaneng the young Lepoqo Moshoeshoe rose in the ranks of the Mokoteli branch of the Koena, or crocodile clan. His mentor was a philosopher named Chief Mohlomi, who encouraged the young man to follow a path of peace during his lifetime.

In 1820, the Korana, a group of Khoikhoi settlers, attacked the Basotho and Moshoeshoe retreated from his father's house to a place called Butha-Buthe. Here, through his centralised authority, he became the Father and ruler of the Basotho, before moving his followers, on foot from Butha-Buthe, for nine days to the mountain called Thaba Bosigo.

In 1833, Chief Moshoeshoe welcomed a group of French Evangelical Missionaries to his area. He allowed them to build a mission station at the base of the mountain. While documenting the Sotho language, they introduced him to Christianity and the cultivation of grains and vegetables.

In 1845, the Basotho Chief signed a treaty with the Dutch settlers, giving recognition to the white settlers to his area. No specific boundaries were drawn between them and his kingdom. Moshoeshoe believed that the predominantly Dutch Voortrekkers were just passing through on their way to the greener pastures of Natal.

The British proclaimed the area between the Orange and the Vaal Rivers, calling it the Orange River Sovereignty, in 1848. Land and border disputes broke out between the tribes and the British. According to British rules, a discernible boundary between the two nations became a necessity to prevent conflict. The Warden Line, as it was known, stretched from the Cornet Spruit and the Orange River, through Vechtkop, Jammersberg Drift and on to the Caledon River. The British troops claimed sole rights to this fertile Caledon River valley, which had once served as a rich agricultural area to both the European immigrants and the Basotho.

Both sides found this borderline unacceptable, and conflict broke out between the Chief's warriors and the British troops. In 1851, the British officers underestimated Moshoeshoe's significant stronghold at Thaba Bosigo. He and his warriors defeated Warden's army at the battle of Tihela.

After a second battle at the Berea Plateau, where the British suffered severe losses at the hands of their Basotho rivals, the cost of maintaining the territory became too great for the British Government. Later that same year, Moshoeshoe formed an alliance with the Voortrekker leader, Andries Pretorius.

This battle, together with Moshoeshoe's alliance with the Dutch Boers who called themselves Afrikaaners, sealed the fate of the Orange River Sovereignty. In 1854, after negotiations with the Voortrekker leaders, the Sand River Convention was agreed upon, and the British territory was signed over to the Afrikaans Boers. The land beyond the

Caledon River became known as the Orange Free State.

The pioneers and early Voortrekkers who had settled in the Bloemfontein area between 1836 and 1846, finally received their freedom from British rule, their intention since leaving the Cape Frontier. This, however, caused further conflict over the undefined land boundaries with the Basotho, who regarded themselves as the rightful owners and continued to use the land for grazing as they had always done, before the arrival of settlers. Moshoeshoe maintained his stronghold on the natural mountain fortress, Thaba Bosigo, the mountain at night, which remained unconquered by British, Afrikaans Boer and other opposing tribes.

Josias Phillipus Hoffman was appointed as the first President of the new Orange Free State in 1854. Being early pioneers and founders of Bloemfontein, along with other Boer leaders, Sampson Daniel and his eldest son, Frederick, were present at the thatched raadsal in St George's Street, to witness the swearing in ceremony of the Orange Free State's newly elected President. During his inaugural speech, Josias Hoffman announced the signing of the Bloemfontein Convention.

The first steps had been taken by the Voortrekkers to establish an independent republic. A huge community festival was held in the Market Square to celebrate this auspicious event.

The Friend reported:

> This day, 23 February 1854 was an uncommon, if not unique one, in the history of the world, and to us, it is the birthday of our Independence.

Although he desired to retain his sovereignty over his people, Chief Moshoeshoe set about arranging a meeting with the new President of Bloemfontein.

The Basotho Chief was known as The Jackal, and for good reason. He would vigorously defend his territory at all costs, although he was not a great risk-taker.

He constantly re-evaluated situations and made plans to secure his long-term security. He was notoriously hard to read, as the new

European settlers would find out. President Hoffman received an invitation to visit the mountain kingdom of Thaba Bosigo. Moshoeshoe intention for the meeting was to broker a deal to secure guns.

After a short term of only nine months in office, Hoffman was replaced by the second President, Jacobus Nicolaas Boshoff. Hoffman was thought to be on the side of Moshoeshoe when he visited the chief bearing gifts of guns and gunpowder. As a builder, Hoffman had also assisted with building the chief's house and the Bloemfontein town council found his exchange with the chief unacceptable.

19 August 1857

Despite the political bantering between boers and Basothos, Sampson Daniel was generally satisfied with his family's move to Bloemfontein. It was 19 August 1857. Sampson and his family sat at the head of a long oak dining table, reminiscing with his guest and old trading friend John Montgomery on the verandah of his redbrick farmhouse on the Haartebees Hoek. He beamed with pride as his family and friends gathered to celebrate the marriage of his youngest son, Charles, to Margaret Holmes, the daughter of his 1820 Settler friend, Thomas Holmes.

The Holmes family had sailed from England on board the Aurora from Gravesend, London, on February 15 1820, with the Sephton Party. They had moved away from the Cape Frontier and were settled at Kaffir Rivier. Holmes' wife, Frances Maria Feagan, had travelled to the farm to join in the festivities. Frederick's wife, Lydia, was deep in conversation with Amelia and their grandson Sam kept making a turn past his grandfather's chair, to find out whether his grandfather needed anything, which lifted Sampson's spirits. He admired his favourite grandson's good manners and thoughtfulness.

Sampson's son-in-law, Fighting Tom Webster, sat to the left of him and he was pleased that his daughter Eleanor had made it to her brother's wedding.

"How's that new farm of yours, Tom?" asked Sampson, "Is it out near Kimberley?"

"It is surprisingly arable and we're doing well there. I didn't want or expect any rewards, you know, for doing my duty, but I was not about to turn down such a promising piece of land," he laughed.

"Have to say, it's great to have my own farm all paid up with no debt."

Wine and homebrewed beer flowed freely. The smell of roasted meats and vegetables cooking in three-legged black pots over the open fires added to the festive atmosphere. Amelia had baked a selection of cakes, including *melktert*, *koeksisters* and her favourite rusks. There was fresh fruit salad and thick farm cream.

After lunch and a cup of strong coffee, Charles took his older brother, Frederick for a walk to show him the new cattle-dipping tank that he had built out of sandstone rocks. He pointed out the proposed site for the new borehole. As they walked away from the farmhouse, they could hear the sound of the piano, their mother playing as the guests sang along. There was ample woodland at Haartebees Hoek and the vast expanse of farmland was proving ideal for farming Merino sheep and cattle. The size of Charles' herds had grown steadily and the farm was self-sufficient. The rich red soils on the flat, open plains were ideal for maize and Charles had plans to plough and plant a crop soon.

As they walked and talked about Charles's plans for the farm and his marriage to Margaret Louisa Holmes, the mood became serious and Frederick grew quiet.

"Is something wrong?" Charles asked. There was a pause before Frederick replied, "The other day, when President Boshoff resigned, there was much merriment in town and I even donated two buckets of wine to the celebrations. Hyman, myself and a Hollander whom you do not know, were asked to draw up a new Constitution for the Orange Free State Republic. I was also approached by the local Volksraad about a week ago to ask whether I would stand as president."

"I know," replied Charles, "I saw the article in the newspaper. There was some indignation over the fact that the only citizens capable of drawing up the new Constitution were an Irishman, a German Jew and a Hollander. It is strange that a boer was not chosen."

Charles encouraged his brother to accept the Presidency. Frederick was well liked in the community and he was an astute businessman, blending in well with both the British and Afrikaans settlers. He was also involved with the development and promotion of the new school and assisted in setting up local churches. He was a regular attendee at raadsaal council meetings, often liaised between the British and the Boers and spoke both languages fluently.

"You know, Charles, I don't really enjoy being in the public eye. I much prefer the affairs of business to politics. I have my reasons, but must decline."

Charles laughed, remarking that he was virtually the president anyway.

"I don't enjoy politics, but sometimes you have to laugh at people's reactions," Frederick said, "during a meeting over the Constitution, one of the burghers of the community shouted, 'I don't want any God-damned Constitution. The Ten Commandments is good enough for me.'"

Margaret Daniel bore Charles two sons, Thomas Edward and Charles Sampson. After less than five years of marriage, Charles was devastated by the death of his wife on 20 July 1862, at only twenty-two years of age. She had been visiting her parent's home at Vaal Bank on the Kaffir River with their two boys. Her sister, Sarah Holmes, who nursed her during her short illness, later told Charles that Margaret had been in excruciating pain for about eight days prior to her death. The doctor had been unable to find the cause of her illness. Sarah volunteered to help Charles to raise the two boys at Hartebees Hoek. Charles consented on condition that they got married, which they did later that same year, and Sarah moved to the farm to take the place of her sister.

CHAPTER 28

THE BATTLE OF THABO BASIGO

Frederick Daniel's good friend, Johannes Henricus Brand, took office as the fourth president of the Orange Free State on February 2 1864.

During his inaugural speech as President, Brand said, "*Alles zal recht komen als elkeen zijn plicht doet*" (All will be well, if everyone does his duty).

President Brand's appointment was celebrated by the entire community. The whole town turned out in the market square and Sampson and Amelia were there to join in the festivities with their family. Charles and Sarah were also present with their sons Thomas Edward, Charles Sampson and Percy Walter, who was a mere two months old. Tom and Eleanor Webster travelled from Boshof and Frederick and his wife attended with their son, Sam, who was no longer a teenager, and their daughter Lydia.

Frederick stayed involved in politics and supported Jan in the Bloemfontein Town Council, but his focus was on his own businesses. He acquired several farms in the surrounding area, including Floradale and Glen Lyons. He established a wheat mill, a sawmill, a lathe and a wool dealership.

Sampson Daniel watched with pride as the young ones laughed and played with friends under the African sun. A square had been set up with food, drinks and fun sporting events. Young Sam first took part in the shooting competition – which he won – before entering the horse race.

"Go Sam! Remember my promise!" his grandfather yelled in his still strong Irish lilt, as the boy urged his horse around the tracks on the outskirts of the Market Square.

The old man held onto his rabbit-fur hat. His heart thumped in his chest as Sam rounded the last corner of the track in a cloud of dust. His voice hoarse, Sampson yelled, "Go, boy!" He hugged Amelia tightly as Sam belted across the finish line only inches in the lead. As promised, Sampson bought the gelding Sam had picked out at a recent livestock auction, his prize for winning the race.

Thanking his grandfather, young Sam said, "Papa, can you ask Pa if I can join the Harvey Rangers? I want to ride and shoot with the burghers."

"I will ask your Pa to talk to Uncle Jan for you," said Sampson, knowing that Frederick was a close friend of the President. He would pull strings for the boy, although he was not sure that it was a good idea. There had been a lot of unrest with Moshoeshoe's people in recent years.

Jan Brand agreed to Frederick's request and, in turn, asked the Commandant of the Rangers, Louw Wepener, to ensure the boy's safety. "Make sure that you take the *Engelse boytjie* under your wing. Treat Frederick's son, like your own," instructed Brand.

When he took over the Presidency of the Republic, Jan Brand endeavoured to keep the peace with his neighbours. He realized that British arrogance in the Albany District had greatly contributed to the difficulties with the native community and had not helped relations. However, in January of 1865, Leawana, Moshoeshoe's nephew, raided boer farms in the Bethlehem area. President Brand demanded seventy two cattle as compensation. Then Poshuli and Moorosi began raiding farms near the Wittenberg range of mountains. Before long, plundering broke out in all parts of the Republic. Most of it was driven by the shortages of food the Basotho were experiencing. Later, Mopeli captured three farmers north of the Caledon River. After having them tortured and thrashed, he released them with a warning that if they came near Lesotho again the Basotho would kill them.

President Brand wrote to Chief Moshoeshoe to keep his Basotho people within the designated land boundaries, and demanded that the perpetrators of these acts of hostility be delivered to Bloemfontein, together with a fine of fifty cattle. When Moshoeshoe refused to comply, Brand felt compelled to take up arms against him and declared war at the beginning of June 1865.

Commandant Louwrens Wepener called his Harvey Rangers to arms as the burghers prepared to attack the mountain fortress of the Basotho.

The day before Sampson Daniel's eighteenth birthday, August 12, he woke in high spirits. He had heard that burghers had been mobilised to fight against the Basotho people based on top of the Chief's mountain kingdom at Thaba Basigo. From Seringboom to Winburg, Louw Wepener rallied burghers to join him. Some volunteers were already camped at the base of Thaba Bosigo. The Boer commander needed all the help he could get to defeat Moshoeshoe and the young Sampson Daniel was more than ready to join the fight.

"There is no way you are joining Wepener, Sampson!" his mother yelled when she learned of his plan to join the burgher forces the next day, his birthday. "You are not yet eighteen," she continued, "Go to your bedroom. Stay there until I say you can come out!"

The concerned mother locked Sampson into his bedroom. Lydia naively thought that this punishment would prevent her son from joining the commanders on their ride to war with the Basotho in the morning.

Sam waited until the household was asleep, escaping through his bedroom window in the early hours of morning. Quietly, he saddled his new horse, Champion II, taking his father's gun and a belt full of homemade ammunition. He joined the other young Rangers, called *Die Spreeus*, or The Starlings, in front of the raadsaal.

"Rangers!" commanded their leader, "Follow me! We ride to the Night Mountain."

"*Waar daar gevaar is, sal ek nie se 'gaan' nie, maar 'kom'*," said the Boer leader, telling his men he would lead them in the face of danger and not expect them to go ahead of him.

The men had all heard about the cunning and skilful Moshoeshoe, who was yet to be defeated in any battle. There was an unsuccessful assault on the mountain refuge by burghers on 8 September 1865.

"The top of the mountain is a grassy plateau. It is a stronghold for Moshoeshoe and not an easy place to gain access to. He is a cunning leader of his people. We will camp overnight and attack at first light," the Boer Commander said. The men were aware that the mountain passes were inaccessible and that the top of the mountain was a fortress against attack. They had confidence in their leader.

He looked around the group of hardened burghers. His gaze fell on young Sam Daniel and their eyes locked briefly. If Commandant Wepener had concerns about taking the younger men into battle, he hid them as he swiftly wheeled his horse about. Sam's uncle, Fighting Tom Webster, was at his side, and Tom's presence made him feel invincible. Sam rode close to Louw Wepener, alongside Jacob Stoltz, the coloured *agterryer*. Sampson was one of the youngest burghers there and his friendship with Jacob went back to childhood.

"The Commandant is determined to flush out Moshoeshoe this time." Jacob said.

The wide, golden grassy plains of the Orange Free State, dotted with rocky outcrops and framed by the snow-capped Maluti Mountains, stretched out beneath a vast cool blue sky. The men gathered in a rough formation, their horses fresh and frisky in the cool morning air. As they approached it, the mountain loomed sharper and became more defined. They could see the tented camp of the other burghers on the upper slopes of the mountain, alongside the Caledon River. The men from Bloemfontein rode towards it, constantly looking upwards for signs of the enemy.

President Brand welcomed the new volunteers to the camp. He was a well-built man with a flowing beard, which he fondly caressed. As he spoke to the men, he swept the back of his hand over his long, thick moustache. He had a booming voice and did not take kindly to people smoking a pipe in his presence. Looking directly at one volunteer, he reprimanded him saying, "Where there is a *rokie*, there is a small fire, but where Brand is, then sparks fly!"

The men surrounding the President laughed heartily, as the culprit snuffed out his pipe. He slipped it into his pocket. President Brand rallied the council of war. He allocated three divisions to the Boer leaders. Commander Cornelius de Villiers was to take the north, General Fick the central area and general Louw Wepener the southern side of the mountain. Wepener requested a group of at least one dozen scouts to assist him. Volunteers streamed into the General's tent, wanting the honour of being under his command during the assault. Young men from as far afield as Harrismith, Smithfield, Bethlehem, Philippolis, Bethulie and Bloemfontein were selected from amongst the volunteers, Sam Daniel amongst them.

"*Jy, Engelsman, bly naby my*," said Wepener, pointing at Sam, "you stay with me!"

After selection, the group of scouts and young burghers who counted themselves amongst the lucky *Spreeus* camped around their own fire that night. Jacob sat next to Sam on a log next to the bonfire. The encamped boers remembered the merciless drought of Lesotho in the summer of 1862. Faced with the horror of famine, thousands of Basotho had gone into the Orange Free State in search of food. Initially, they had stuck to hunting, but in their desperation, many began ransacking boer homesteads and shooting anyone who opposed them. This conflict had been brewing for a while.

"Moshoeshoe is not a lion, Sam. He is a jackal. He is cunning and we must be wary of him," said Jacob. "If he were like a lion, he would have been easier to kill. Being a jackal, he is devious and tires his enemy out with his cunning strategies."

Included in the commando were some men of the Barolong who lived and worked on Boer farms, as well as Fingos, bringing the ranks to some three thousand strong.

The scouts celebrated Sam's birthday with a swig of brandy each. They were told not to be too merry, as they needed to be ready at any given time for the command to attack. Sam looked up at the clear, cloudless starry sky, putting all thoughts of home firmly out of his mind.

Most of the following day was spent with the commanding generals rallying their troops. Nearly two thousand men were moved into various positions on the slopes of the mountain, each group prepared for the call to attack against the mountain stronghold of Moshoeshoe. The waiting was getting to them. It was freezing cold. In the morning, white patches of frost lay on the ground and in the evenings, as the sun set over the horizon, the winter chill crept into the burghers' bones.

On the morning of 15 August, Wepener watched as the warm orange glow of the morning sun rose in the east and he saw how dejected the *Spreeus* were. When it seemed that the wait would never end, the leaders agreed on the plan of attack. One thousand men would storm the mountain. However, at that stage less than half that number were prepared to follow the command. The men were dissatisfied with the way things progressed and becoming restless.

General Wepener leant up against a rock and looked out over the open plains, filling his pipe. He was known for his fighting prowess as the *Swartmanhaarleeu*, the black-maned lion. General Fick had no idea what to do next and was agitated. Wepener waited, calmly smoking his pipe when a messenger arrived. "Sir, you are to march one thousand men and two cannons around the mountain. The attack has been called off, by order of General Fick," he said.

"Does Fick think this is Jericho and we look like the *blerry* Israelites?" Wepener replied.

The wheel of a cannon was firmly wedged in a narrow ditch. The *Spreeus* could not move it. While they pushed and heaved the cannon, some of the burghers made fires and boiled kettles of water for coffee. To Wepener, it looked more like a Sunday picnic than a military assault.

General Wepener instructed some of his scouts to rest. A few stood watch most of the night. Through his field glasses, he combed the overhang of the mountain and wrote a few notes in his book. He spotted what was undoubtedly the widest of the passes through the dolomite cliffs. It looked more accessible than the path they had considered using and seemed well worn. He guessed that the Basotho warriors were hidden on the ledges, looking down at these foolish Boers and laughing amongst themselves.

As he put down his field glasses and took a swig of water, a messenger rode up in haste and handed him another note from Fick. The scribbled message insisted that the Boers attack today, because if they did not, the Fingo and the Barolong would abandon them and refuse to support them again.

"As if I didn't know this," said Wepener, "send Fick to me at once!" he hollered.

When General Fick arrived, Wepener showed him the vantage point and reiterated it was the best place from which to attack.

"Well. What are you waiting for? I command you to storm this mountain!" shouted an angry Fick.

"I will need back-up and reinforcements," replied Wepener, "the troops must be at the ready."

"I will see to that. Good luck, Wepener."

Wepener's six hundred strong commando prepared for battle.

"We are going to attack the mountain above the mission station in three groups. Commander Bester takes the left flank. Commander David Venter, right flank. I will go up the middle with my men. As soon as we capture a few of their men, the rest will retreat in fear. Once we break through the pass and reach the top of the mountain, no one will bother us."

"Hoorah!" the men shouted in unison.

General Wepener raised his arm to silence them. "May God go with you," he said, as he swung his arm around and pointed in the direction of the Night Mountain stronghold.

The plan was to ride hard until they reached the first ledge and then dismount and proceed on foot. "This is a good day to storm the mountain," thought Sam bravely, unaware of the danger that lay ahead. Despite the beauty of the morning, he had knots in his stomach.

Adrenalin coursed through him as his body prepared for battle. He looked around at the other men, mostly older than he was, and saw only steely determination on their faces. He sat proudly in the saddle astride Champion II, tightly clutching his father's rifle.

The *Spreeus* and the other men focused on the charge ahead. Their goal was to break through the Khubelo Pass and seize the mountain fortress. The order to proceed was followed by the sound of horses' hooves trampling the dry grass and rocky terrain. The men rode in silence, their weapons held across their laps in anticipation of an ambush from the Basotho warriors.

"This is madness," Sam thought, staring up at the imposing mountain.

The sun had risen high in the sky and brightly lit up the side of the mountain. In the eerie quiet, the squeaking of his stirrup straps against the leather of his saddle seemed loud to Sam. Funny, he had never noticed it before.

In single file the men carefully negotiated the steep slopes of the narrow pass. As they reached the first ledge, the Basotho warriors started firing. Bullets whistled through the air, ricocheting off the rocks around them. From below, the Boers fired their cannons, but most of the cannonballs hit the higher cliffs or went wide. Amid the cacophony of screams and gunfire, Sam fired a shot wildly into the air, gripping Champion II tightly as the horse shied. Horses reared in fright and Sam saw Andrews tumble to the ground.

When he reached the safety of the ledge, Sam dismounted and scrambled for cover, grazing his knees and elbows in the process. He looked back and saw about a hundred horsemen further down the mountain spread out like tentacles.

To the left of the ravine the slopes were crawling with Basotho warriors, firing at their attackers. Others hurled rocks from the cliffs above. To his right, Sam saw a wounded Commander Venter writhing in pain. He crawled as close to Louw Wepener as he could and they pushed forward to the second ledge. The sound of the wounded and dying was frightening. For the first time, the general hesitated, but he refused to retreat. The Free State frontiersman sent a runner to Fick to find out whether reinforcements were on their way, letting his men rest under the shelter of the ledge. They fired off shots every now and then to keep the Basotho on their toes. Half an hour passed without word from Fick.

"We press on," said Wepener, splitting the group into three once again.

Pieter Wessels and thirty men took the left flank and Pansegrouw, with thirty men, the right. The remaining men stuck with Wepener and charged forward. Sweat dripped from the men and Sam felt the heat of the midday sun on his back. He wiped his brow and kept his eyes on Wepener. Jacob Stolz sweating profusely, was right beside him.

The Basotho warriors watched them coming and started ululating and raining rocks down on them. Then they started firing their weapons. There was no turning back for the *Spreeus* now. Wepener, Wessels and Pansegrouw returned fire and the enemy peeled back when shots were fired. When they peered over the second ledge, they were so near that Sam could almost make eye contact with his opponents. He ducked as an assegai flew past his head. A scout stumbled and fell beside him. A Basotho warrior tumbled off the ledge and rolled screaming down the steep slope.

Wepener reached the protection of the second ledge and clung, catlike, to the cliff face. He motioned the others to join him quickly as he lifted his pistol above his head and emptied the magazine. About fifteen men huddled beneath the ledge.

"The Black-Maned Lion is in the pass! The Black-Maned Lion is in the pass!"

The word spread like wildfire from warrior to warrior, until it reached the old chief's ears. Moshoeshoe began to panic as it was the first time the enemy had broken through and reached that close to the plateau of the mountain fortress. The exhausted burghers rested to catch their breath, reload their weapons and regroup. Then the few remaining *Spreeus* scrambled up towards the third ledge. Only one ledge stood between the men and the summit of the Night Mountain.

Victory was in sight!

The Basutho were trapped under fire from three sides. They had never encountered such a determined enemy. The noise of the gunfire was overwhelming and at such close range, the strong smell of burning gunpowder filled the air. Bullets flew in all directions and shards of shrapnel flew off the sandstone rocks.

Wepener scanned the path ahead, looking back at the scouts following him. They were in a critical situation and more than one man stared wildly back at him, looking for reassurance. Avoiding Sam's blue-eyed stare, Wepener resolutely turned to face the enemy. There was no going back. He stood firm. Then, beckoning his men forward, he exposed himself to the enemy. This time, the Basotho rifleman did not miss. Wepener was thrown backwards by a direct hit to the chest. Reeling back against a rock, he mumbled, "*Ek kan nie verder nie*," clutching his rifle in a death grip.

His head fell limp as he took his last, gasping, breath. The Black-Maned Lion was dead! Emboldened, the Basotho warriors peered over the precipice at the lifeless body of the slain boer leader. Some armed with guns, others with spears, charged at the stunned group of scouts. Adam Raubenheimer took a direct hit and fell a few yards away. Sam aimed carefully and fired, the loud report ringing in his ears. Through the puff of smoke he saw his target topple over the rocky edge, the top of his comrade's head was blown away. In the suffocating chaos, the Basotho warriors descended the rocky slope, screaming menacingly with upraised arms. As the late afternoon sun sank towards the horizon, the few remaining *Spreeus* huddled together uncertainly, sweat pouring from their brows. Fear coursed through their veins.

Sam reloaded. A warrior came ominously close and he realized how inadequate his hideout was. Sam had time to register that the man was about his age. He was lean and muscular, with a body that gleamed with a mixture of sweat and animal fat in the glow of the fading sunlight. Sam aimed and fired and saw the young man's eyes widen as the bullet hit him in the solar plexus, crashing him to the ground. Sam watched him flounder helplessly, blood pouring from the gaping wound and bubbling from his mouth. Numbed, the frightened youngster saw the bodies of bloodied comrades and enemy alike, scattered around him.

More Basotho poured from the top of the mountain, shouting triumphantly and wielding clubs and spears. Sam heard Jacob cry out and turned to see his friend collapse from the bullet that struck him. The mortally wounded volunteer resembled the enemy Sam had slain with his gasping breath. His blood bubbled up as it escaped through his mouth. Sampson looked around helplessly for support, but found none.

Astonished, Sam was forcefully knocked off his feet by a solid lump of black-muscled flesh. He felt a stabbing pain in his chest as he hit the rocky ground. His attacker had him by the throat and Sam fought free of the man's fierce grip. He scrambled up and staggered back, gasping for breath. He saw his blood dripping down his body and onto his leather boots. Gasping for breath, with a punctured lung and crushed windpipe, he fell to his knees and reached for his gun. As his attacker lunged towards him a second time. Sam fired at point-blank range. The warrior fell backwards, his stomach ripped open by the bullet, blood and bowels spilling out onto the stony ground. The world plunged into darkness.

Barely conscious, Sam found himself gathered into the safe arms of his fellow comrade, Peacock, as the sounds and shapes of battle receded into emptiness. His last thoughts were of his family.

"Tell my mother … goodbye …"

The news of his son's death in the battle at Khabelo Pass crippled Frederick Daniel. Normally a man of great composure, he hung his head and turned away from his good friend, President Jan Brand, and his brother-in-law, Thomas Webster, whilst the men delivered the tragic news. A few yards from them, he collapsed to his knees, retching at the thought of Sam's dying moments.

News of the battle and Sam's death was reported on 20 August 1865 in the edition of *The Friend.*

> Sampson Daniel, eldest son of Mr F. Daniel, one of the most respected citizens of this town has been shot dead on the same

> occasion ... the loss of young Daniel, a youth of but 19 years, who had grown up amongst us, and who had left us but little more than two weeks previously full of life and spirit, and who had been shot down mortally wounded while gallantly assisting to scale the side of the mountain among the foremost of the attacking column. Young Daniel had only just joined from Bloemfontein, and was much liked by his comrades for his quiet, unassuming manner. When receiving his death wound, he fell into the arms of Peacock, and turning his eyes on him, tried to speak, but with the effort died.

Lydia Daniel was devastated by the news of her son's death. In her grief, she turned young Sam's bedroom into a shrine in his memory and forbade entry. She kept all his possessions, including his rifle, his saddle and the bloodstained shirt in which he had died. She asked her father-in-law, Sampson Daniel, to make a gold locket with Sam's name picked out against a black enamel background. She placed a curl of his hair inside and wore it close to her heart for the rest of her days.

For Frederick, life continued, but the death of his first-born son plagued him and weighed heavily on his shoulders. It all seemed so pointless and life lost its meaning for the businessman.

When peace was declared with Moshoeshoe and the people of his mountain kingdom, Thomas Webster was honoured with an appointment as Commandant of the conquered territory. The government awarded him with Table Top, a farm in the district of Boshof, about seventy-four miles from Bloemfontein, in acknowledgement of his bravery and services. In peacetime, Thomas Webster became the first white man to summit Thaba Bosigo, sometime after Louw Wepener and Sampson James Daniel's deaths.

On his way to the top, and in memory of Sampson James Daniel, he stopped to erect a small wooden cross at the spot where his wife's nephew had fallen in battle.

CHAPTER 29

STORM CLOUDS

Bloemfontein 1867

The Daniel patriarch gently tapped the empty glass twice with his knife. Ting, ting! Taking his wife Amelia's hand, he looked around at the others seated around the large dining table on the patio and his grandchildren playing in the yard. Family and friends were celebrating at Haartebees Hoek, where his youngest son Charles had built his new house and a large stone cattle-dipping tank.

"We have decided to attend the 1820 Settler Jubilee," Sampson said as a matter of fact. A deathly silence fell as the noisy banter died down.

"It is to be held in Grahamstown on 25 May 1870. Our old acquaintance, Henry Dugmore, will be the guest speaker. You remember him, Frederick?" Sampson turned to his eldest son, "Dugmore was a child when we all came out on the *Sir George Osborn.* He has been asked to share the journey and the story of the British Settlers to South Africa. Why don't you come with us, son?"

"I can't, Papa," Frederick sighed, "There is too much going on for me to leave things to my partner, Hyman and my boys. What are your plans?"

"Thomas Webster and Eleanor are coming through from Boshof to collect supplies. We plan to leave early in the New Year, as it will take a couple of months to get to Grahamstown. I have written to Sophia and she has agreed that we will stay with her and her husband, Edward

Turvey, for as long as we need to."

Everyone was quiet as they absorbed the news and thought of what a long and arduous journey to Grahamstown it would be for the old couple. It was Charles who finally broke the silence.

"Thomas is a reliable and capable man. Trustworthy. You and Mother will be in good hands. But the trip will be harsh and it could be dangerous, Papa. Are you sure you are both up to it?"

Sampson skirted the question of his own strength and health. He and Amelia had an overwhelming desire to see their other children one more time, and it was too late to have second thoughts about the journey. "Our minds are made up, Charles. Your mother and I want to see our other grandchildren and meet up with old settler friends."

Frederick was tempted to leave Bloemfontein with his parents and make the trek back to the Eastern Frontier. It would bring back memories of the old days when he was just a boy and the family moved to Uitenhage. It was during those happy, carefree days in Uitenhage that he had met and married Lydia Urry. Where they had made so many plans for their future. It was the place his deceased son, Sam had been born. Sam had been a mere toddler when they left Uitenhage. The thoughts triggered the intense pain of losing his eldest son. Noticing his brother's sadness, Charles stood and motioned to him, "Walk with me, Frederick. I want to show you the new cattle dipping tank."

The two brothers excused themselves and walked away from the noise and festivity at the main homestead, in the direction of the stone tank. Frederick was not really that interested, as he had never been much of a farmer. He preferred being behind his desk in the comfort of his study at his large, stylish home in Bloemfontein. But he welcomed the opportunity to move away from the group. He admired his younger brother's enthusiasm, and the way Charles had tenaciously pursued his own dream of farming. In a few short years he had proved himself an excellent farmer, increasing his herds of cattle and had large flocks of Merino sheep.

Frederick Daniel was a director of the first bank in Bloemfontein. He, along with other leaders, put in £30 000 to create shares to start the first bank in South Africa, which was eventually to become the Standard Bank of the future. Frederick Daniel was an astute business owner, but the death of his son took a terrible toll on his health.

His brother's jovial mood and lighthearted spirit never failed to cheer Frederick up. They were completely different in character. There was a fifteen years' age difference. Their looks, too were different. Frederick was dark and sallow-skinned like their French mother, while Charles was fair with vivid blue eyes, like his Irish father. Charles' hair had turned silver-white while he was in his early twenties and this gave him an air of distinction.

An old family friend, Pieter Theron, joined the two brothers on their walk to the dipping tank. Charles indicated the new borehole he had installed near the homestead, which ensured a good supply of water all year round.

All of a sudden, Pieter drew in a deep breath and forcefully pushed Frederick away from himself, as he leapt backwards.

"Here, *my maat! Versigtig! Slang! Blerry Slang!* Pofadder!" Pieter yelled, pointing out the snake in their path.

Pieter shivered, looking like a wet dog shaking water off its body. The largest puff adder any of the three men had ever seen was well camouflaged and lay almost hidden amongst the tufts of grass, its body partially covered in a layer of rich, red soil. Thankfully, the snake was lethargic, fat from a recent meal. It lay motionless halfway across the path. The only movement came from its blue forked tongue, showing it was alive and potentially deadly.

Charles poked at it with a long twig from a tree and its enormous head lifted and swayed slightly. "Don't annoy it, Charlie," said Pieter, "that *blerry* snake gives me the *grils*," he said, shivering again.

The two brothers laughed at him nervously, thankful that the reptile was having a lazy day basking in the sun, and that Frederick had not stepped on the snake. The outcome could have been extremely different.

Frederick was deeply saddened when his parents left Bloemfontein in May of 1868, not sure he would see them again. His depression deepened. His mother, Amelia, looked frail on the day of their departure. When they said their goodbyes, she had held onto Frederick for longer than usual before allowing him to help her up onto the wagon. He firmly shook hands with his father. He would miss the old man's wisdom and advice.

After his parents' departure for the Eastern Cape, Frederick Daniel's health deteriorated rapidly. He not only seemed to have lost all enthusiasm for life, but began to make errors in judgement in his business transactions. It was out of character for this man to throw caution to the wind.

An acquaintance named Allison made an appointment to see Frederick at his home in Bloemfontein a while after his parents' departure with Thomas Webster and Eleanor. Lydia made the uninvited visitor some tea and butter biscuits, but disliked him on sight. Something about him made her feel very uncomfortable.

After pleasantries had been exchanged, Allison went straight to the point. Knowing Frederick's good standing in the community, Allison requested him to sign as a co-trustee on a deceased estate. The man was always rather shady in Frederick's opinion, but, as a man of integrity, Frederick assumed the same of his visitor.

Lydia stood just outside the closed parlour door and listened to the two men talking. She did not like what she overheard. As soon as Allison left, Lydia hurried to the study.

"Frederick, I don't trust that man," she said, "There is something about him that makes me think he is up to no good. I urge you to send him to another business associate of yours. Just tell him you are not available to co-sign anything."

"Oh, my dear woman!" snapped Frederick impatiently, "don't be so paranoid. Leave the business of this family to me. You should not have been eavesdropping!" Lydia was taken aback by his violent outburst.

"Please, Frederick," she implored, "trust me on this. It is just something I sense. Something is not right."

"Dear God, woman! You are tired and emotional! Take the children. Go and spend some time at the Floradale house. It will do you good," Frederick responded irritably with a dismissive wave of his hand.

Shocked and hurt by this unusual outburst, Lydia gave up the argument. Frederick's behavior had become increasingly erratic since Sam was killed, so much so that she felt she hardly knew him anymore. The next day she would leave for Floradale, but she was not happy about it.

With a heavy heart, Lydia packed up the children and the servants and rode the few miles out of town to their other home in Floradale. Her children were excited, as they loved roaming about on the farm, milking the cows and collecting chicken eggs. There were horses for them to ride and their dogs ran wild, barking their welcomes at visitors. The older boys, Fred, Horatio, Dick and little brother Hector loved being on the farm because they got the chance to practice their shooting skills, even though their mother hated guns after the death of their older brother. The sight of the large homestead and the beautiful gardens always lifted Lydia's spirits and she put thoughts of her husband and his business dealings to the back of her mind.

Two days later, after breakfast, the children headed out to hunt duiker and guinea fowl. Lydia, grateful for some time alone, sat beneath a large tree out of earshot of the house. Reading her Bible, she gently held the gold locket that hung from her neck, but instead of thinking of Sam, her thoughts turned to Frederick. "Oh, God," she whispered, "please help Frederick make the right decisions!" As the prayer left her lips, she felt a sense of deep foreboding. Something was wrong, she knew it!

Lydia leapt out of her chair and ran across the garden to the house, calling to her servants to prepare the buggy. She was going back to Bloemfontein and she was going right away.

She reached the house in town in record time, hot and sweaty from the fast-paced ride. A lone horse was tethered to the hitching post outside the building and she recognised it as Allison's.

Barely taking the time to remove her riding bonnet, she fobbed off the servants who tried to offer her refreshments and barged into

Frederick's study. Startled by the intrusion, her husband looked up to see his wife's worried face. The attention of his guest, Allison, was fixed on the paperwork before him. Frederick finished signing the document, saying, "Lydia! What is the meaning of this?"

"Frederick, dear … forgive me," said Lydia, out of breath, "I have given this business proposition of Mr Allison's a great deal of thought and prayer and I believe it would be foolish of you to enter into such an agreement. Surely Mr Allison can find another man of substance in town to sign as co-trustee. You do not know the deceased or his family and you are barely acquainted with Mr Allison himself."

Lydia looked at Allison with disdain, her eyes dark and her body trembling with emotion. Allison, who had been appointed as the First Trustee and Executor of the said deceased estate, looked triumphantly at the stricken woman. "Don't fret yourself, Mrs Daniel. Your husband has just completed the signing of all the documentation. It is only a matter of form. The law requires one other man of substance sign as co-trustee in the handling of this particular estate and your husband, Mr Daniel, has kindly obliged."

"You can change your mind, Frederick. Please, please reconsider," she implored.

"Too late, my dear. My signature is on the document and, as you know full well, I am a man of my word. I trust that Mr Allison is also one."

Allison clutched the signed documents, smiling contemptuously. Lydia had returned too late to change Frederick's mind and could not shake the uncomfortable feeling that more unpleasant things were to come. She moved to Frederick's side as Allison took his leave. Before Lydia could say anything else, Frederick blurted out,

"Mother Amelia died two days ago in Rouxville."

Lydia watched helplessly as her husband put his head in his hands and wept.

CHAPTER 30

THE PROSPECT OF DIAMONDS

In 1871, Frederick Daniel and his family visited Johannes Nicholas De Beer, owner of the farm Vooruitzicht in the Kimberley district.

"Frederick, I have a proposition for you," Johannes said, "I am growing tired of these prospectors coming onto my land and asking for permission to start digging for diamonds. They have this crazy notion that there are vast quantities of the mineral here on my land."

"But what if they are right and they do find diamonds here?" replied Frederick.

"I am tired of living here away from the town. I want to sit on my stoep and smoke my pipe in peace," De Beer laughed. He continued, "What about trading farms? You are young enough and have the energy and the business acumen to deal with potential prospectors. How about I swop Vooruitzicht for your farm, Floradale? It might be good to move Lydia away from all the memories of Sam."

The early evening air was still as Frederick looked out over the dry Vooruitzicht lands. Despite its harshness, he felt at peace here. Perhaps change would be good, he thought. Leaning across his saddle, he extended his right hand,

"De Beer, you have yourself a deal."

De Beer smiled, knowing that Daniel's handshake and his word sealed the deal. He looked forward to ridding himself of the gnawing demands of the diamond diggers coming onto his property.

"I'll need a little time to sort out some paperwork in Bloemfontein, but once that is done, we can complete the deal."

The two men rode back to De Beer's humble homestead and sat up well into the early hours of the morning, talking of business, family, hunting, prospectors, politics and the future in Africa over brandy and cigars.

Over the course of the next year, Allison, being the main executor of the deceased estate that Frederick had earlier signed as co-trustee, began squandering the fortune of the estate. There was little that Frederick could do to prevent this. His hands were tied and Allison's slimy slyness began to worry Frederick greatly.

As the heirs came of age and demanded their shares of the estate, Frederick was forced to sell off some of his own properties to cover their inheritance. It broke Lydia's heart to watch her husband losing his hard-earned money because of another man's dishonesty and greed. Frederick was forced to take a bond on Floradale in order to keep the property.

He entered into an agreement with Lydia's nephew, Hyman, who would run his businesses on his behalf until he was able to finalise the suretyship on the deceased estate.

Hyman took over the running of Frederick's affairs, which included the general dealer, bakery and flourmill. Unfortunately, he was young and reckless, and lacked business acumen. He played ducks and drakes with the businesses and they began to lose profitability. Frederick was too depressed and demotivated to care. He had lost his lust for life after Sam died, and this was compounded by the more recent death of his mother. He constantly berated himself for his poor judgment of Allison. To compound the issues, the currency of the day lost its value. In order to pay their workers, Frederick and Hyman minted their own coins, each good for two shillings – the amount imprinted on the coins – which could be exchanged for goods in their shops. These coins became known as "goodfors".

Hyman eventually also took advantage and swindled Frederick. Their partnership soured.

A few months later Johannes de Beer rode into town on business and, as always, arranged to stay with his friends, Frederick and Lydia. He normally enjoyed their kind hospitality and the vibrant energy from this well to do Bloemfontein family. This time was different. He arrived to find a subdued and solemn household.

"Join me in my study, Johannes," Frederick said, sending a servant for snifters of brandy. As was tradition when the two friends got together, they lit cigars, but neither man spoke for a long while. It was Johannes who broke the silence.

"What is it, my Irish friend?" asked a concerned De Beer.

"I have been swindled, Johannes … and the young man who I appointed to take over the business affairs on my behalf, has failed me dismally."

The swarthy Dutch farmer raised his eyebrows in surprise.

"What! You, Frederick? Never!"

"Yes, I am afraid to say, taken by a con artist called Allison. He led me to believe that he was a man of his word. I agreed to sign as a co-trustee in a deceased estate. I had never even met the deceased. Lydia warned me, but I did not listen. I have lost almost everything as I have had to pay out the heirs to the estate because that bastard Allison has squandered the funds and assets out of the trust."

"That is bad news, *swaar*!" said De Beer. "Never mind, you can make your money back at Vooruitzicht. The diamond diggers are still going crazy there!" he laughed, trying to lighten the heaviness of the situation, "and they are discovering more of the rare stones every day."

"I can't take you up on the offer, Johannes," replied a despondent Frederick. "I had to take a bond on Floradale in order to pay out the first heir. The bondholder will not release me to trade farms with you."

"What a shame, my good man," said De Beer, clearly disappointed at not being able to move to the beautiful Floradale farm in exchange for his land near Kimberley.

"I have just been offered an amount of 6000 pounds in sovereigns for Vooruitzicht by a syndicate who want to buy me out. I told them you have the right of first refusal. You and I had a gentleman's agreement, Frederick. I am a man of my word, just as you are."

"Sell to them, Johannes. The bondholder will not budge. He will not exchange the security on Floradale for Vooruitzicht. Thank you for your offer and your faith in me, but this damned co-trusteeship has broken me."

The once-confident Frederick looked down at the floor, his shoulders rounded by the weight of his financial burdens. He was tired and worn-out.

Frederick's friend left the next morning after breakfast. The mood was subdued but jovial. Frederick and Lydia wished Johannes well on the sale of his farm Vooruitzicht to the newcomer investor to the area named Cecil John Rhodes.

After his friend's departure, Frederick went to the quiet refuge of his study and removed a large bag of minted brass coins from his safe. He turned one of the coins over between his fingers and studied the embossed lettering on each side of it. On the outer edge on one side were the words BLOEMFONTEIN ORANJE VRY STAAT and the emblem of the Orange Sovereignty. On the flip side were the names DANIEL & HYMAN and the words GOED VOOR and 2/=.

He ran his fingers through the coins in the bag one last time. He smiled wryly at his vision for the coins and local currency to replace the Rix Dollars. His minted coins, which his father Sampson had helped him to design, were rejected by the British government at the time. He had been willing to try anything legal in those days and had been an ambitious man. Although he was not yet fifty-six years old, his body and mind felt frail and old. He knelt down and lifted one of the wooden floorboards, revealing a hole beneath his rosewood desk. He tied a knot in the bag and deposited the coins there. He replaced the carpet, concealing the trapdoor and he put the coins out of his mind.

In October 1871, Cecil John Rhodes headed for his newly acquired land and the diamond fields of Kimberley. He supervised the working of the claim at Vooruitzicht and successfully speculated. The company, De Beers Diamonds derived its name from brothers, Johannes Nicholas de Beer and Diederik Arnoldus de Beer, on whose farm the diamonds were discovered, near the confluence of the Orange River and the Vaal Rivers. The brothers were not able to protect the farm from the ensuing diamond rush and sold it to Cecil John Rhodes for £6300.

CHAPTER 31

SETTLER JUBILEE GRAHAMSTOWN 1820 – 1870

"We must take root and grow – or die where we stand!"

Henry Dugmore

25 May 1870

Albany Hall, Grahamstown, Eastern Cape, South Africa

"T'is fifty years since!"

The rich, clear voice of the well-respected Reverend Henry Dugmore reverberated over the heads of the capacity crowd of 1820 Settlers and their descendants. His mop of once unruly red hair was now neatly cropped and silver-white with age. His large forehead had surprisingly few wrinkles for his sixty years. His fluffy white beard looked as if it was stuck on with cotton wool. He scanned the large hall with his kind, deep set eyes from beneath his bushy silver eyebrows, looking for familiar faces. His neatly pressed, faded brown corduroy trousers and knee-length dark velvet jacket hung loosely on his medium frame. Highly polished, well-worn leather shoes completed his outfit for the occasion. He stood flicking through his handwritten notes, waiting for the townsfolk and visitors to settle down.

Invitations had been sent out for this auspicious occasion and notices placed in the Grahamstown Journal for this the colourful gathering of people at the Albany Hall. All were awaiting the respected Methodist minister's long anticipated 1820 Settler Jubilee address.

A natural storyteller by nature, Dugmore had been unanimously chosen to speak. His task: to celebrate fifty years since the arrival of over 4000 British settlers on the shores of South Africa and to honour those who had bravely left the comforts of Britain, Ireland and Scotland to seek a new life and fortune on foreign soil. He was there to remind those remaining descendants of the highs and lows, tragedies and triumphs experienced by their parents and grandparents in helping to establish the British Colony.

Among the original settlers in the audience were some who were frail and old, while others, who were children when they arrived, were hale and hearty. The younger settlers had adapted easily to their new life in Africa, remembering little of their lives in the countries of their birth. It had not been that easy for many of the pioneering parents, though, and only one original head of a settler party was present, William Cock of Port Alfred. Still living at the time, Sampson O'Malia Daniel, was not present at this auspicious occasion.

Henry Dugmore raised his chin. Although his eyesight was starting to fail, he spotted Reuben Ayliff, the Mayor of Grahamstown and Robert Godlonton, of the Eastern Province Press, among those now seated. Dugmore's brothers, William and John, were also present. Old Jeremiah Goldswain proudly stood up when Dugmore read out his name declaring, "This is he!"

Seated amongst those in the front row were fifty-nine-year-old Edward Mortimer Turvey and his attractive wife Sophia (nee Daniel). Despite being completely blind in one eye and partially blind in the other, Sophia was still a beautiful woman. Many men had secretly admired her over the years, not only because of her exquisite features, but also because of her warm and kind disposition. The community knew Sophia as a woman with a generous nature and a good brain. She was well-educated and she was a woman with ambition. Her doting husband, Edward, had not been privileged to receive an education, but he had grown up as a man of the soil and the outdoors. He was honest and hardworking.

They had both been settler children aged nine and seven, aboard the *Sir George Osborn*, along with Henry Dugmore who had been nine at the time. Dugmore's family had formed part of Gardner's party on board the ship. Edward Ford Turvey (Edward Mortimer's father) was initially head of the Turvey party before Peter Daniel took over. The Mills party formed the third party on the ship of just over one hundred passengers. Edward Ford Turvey and his wife, Julia (nee Daniel) had passed away more than twenty-five years before these celebrations.

Sophia's parents were 1820 Settlers under the Turvey Party. Her father, Irish-born Sampson O'Malia Daniel, aged thirty-five at the time of departure and his French-born wife, Amelia (nee D'Egville), had booked their passage on the *Sir George Osborn* from Gravesend near London with their family and almost 4000 other Settler hopefuls. Daringly (or foolishly) the couple chose to leave behind the comfortable life they had known in England – four young children in tow and one on the way. They pledged their faith in God, loyalty to one another, trust in the promises of the British Government and sailed off to unknown Africa.

"I wish Papa was here," whispered Sophia to her younger sister, Isabella. Both women were sad that neither parent had made it to the Settler Jubilee celebrations.

Their mother died two years earlier in Rouxville on the journey to Grahamstown. Sophia understood from father's letters that he had been too heartbroken and frail to continue the journey without his wife.

The speaker, Henry Dugmore scanning the hall from his position at the podium, acknowledged the handsome Turvey couple. He nodded in their direction with a broad smile. Eddie, as he was affectionately known, tipped his tawny blond head courteously in reply, affectionately taking Sophia's white gloved hand in his. Sophia smiled and shifted in her seat on the wooden bench in anticipation of Henry's reminiscences. She caught the eye of her younger sister, Isabella Bradfield. She winked and Isabella smiled in return. The sisters were proud to be representing the Daniel family on this auspicious occasion. Africa was the only land Isabella had ever known.

Sophia closed her eyes to listen. She wanted to breathe in the memories and experiences of her family's arrival in South Africa. To recall some of her own early childhood memories of growing up in the country of her parents' choice.

Childhood memories of the three-month sea adventure aboard the *Sir George Osborn* flashed vividly through her mind. Never once as youngsters had the children given thought to the formidable difficulties which lay ahead in Africa, neither could they have foreseen the hardships, tragedies and trials that the beckoning continent would bring.

Dugmore cleared his throat and the hall fell silent.

"Descendants of the pioneers and settlers of 1820, we are looking back over the span of half a century! Few and feeble are the genuine fathers and mothers of the Albany settlement who still linger among us; yet even of these are some with us in this Jubilee gathering. Men and women who headed their families from the home beyond the waters; who have lived in this sunny clime to see their children's children, even down to the fourth generation. These are they who really bore the burden and heat of the day in the work of colonising South-Eastern Africa, for their anxieties on behalf of their offspring doubles their care and toil."

He looked up from his notes over the sea of attentive listeners, male and female, old and young.

"And now those children stand themselves grey headed and almost patriarchal, the link between the old country and the land of their adoption, born in the one, naturalised in the other. It is for the information of their children that I would on this occasion call up some reminiscences, and hold up to their view a few of memory's pictures of what their father's fathers, and their mother's mothers did and bore in the old time."

Members of the audience shuffled in their seats. Some of them had lost parents and siblings in the very early days of the settlement to disease, drowning, snakebites or, worse still, Xhosa raids and wars. The painful memories of those times wormed their way to the forefront of the listeners' minds as Reverend Dugmore spoke.

"...but little more than fifty years ago, when the few surviving hoary-headed fathers of the Albany settlement were yet dwellers in the dear old land, the word Africa was suggestive of little but waterless wilds, burning suns, the death-wind of the desert and the slave trade. In many minds there was no distinction between south-east and west coasts, and their differences, physical, climatic, or social, hardly known. But despite the appalling conditions, which is often associated with the unknown, and the gloomy pictures drawn by those who would fain have detained them, there was courage enough in the breasts of these pioneers, and of their life companions, to brave the dangers, real or imaginary, of a voyage to and a settlement on, the shores of South Africa, although that was the point remotest of all from the land of their birth. Some 4000 British Settlers sailed from the island home of their fathers, in the year 1820, to found the Anglo-African community that now exists in the Eastern Province of the Cape Colony. It is hardly to be supposed that a child of nine years old could share the sympathy of the full feelings of those who were rending the ties of home and kindred and launching the boat of life upon an unknown sea. Nevertheless, the picture of the last parting, which I myself beheld, has never faded from my memory. It has rather become more vivid with the passing of years, as growing faculties enabled me to appreciate what I remembered better – the last wish and blessing of neighbours and friends, mingling hopes and fears for us – the last clasp of brothers' hands – the last falling upon sisters' necks by those who were never to look into one another's eyes again.

"I see them still. The faint hope of one day returning to visit once more the old home was never realised by those who then ventured to give utterance to it. Every one of them lies in an African grave!"

Henry's words struck a raw chord in Sophia Turvey's heart. She was overwhelmed with an intense sadness. She missed her parents. She leaned her head against her husband's strong shoulder. Hot, involuntary tears rolled down her cheeks and onto the lapel of his collared jacket. In her hand, she clutched a letter written in a shaky ink script, which she had received from her old father dated in May, two years previously.

In it, her father explained the circumstances of her mother's death in Rouxville in May 1868. There had been no medical assistance for the seventy-seven year old Amelia, who died in Thomas Webster's tent.

At the thought, Sophia was heartbroken.

Edward comforted her and discreetly wiped the tears from her face, patiently waiting for his wife to compose herself. The speaker's words became a distant muffled hum, as Sophia became lost in her own memories.

Only three of Sampson and Amelia's children attended the jubilee. Sophia's sister, Isabella, who had been born at sea in 1820 sat with her husband Edmund Bradfield, her other sister, Luisa, and her husband, George Thom.

Their sibling, Amelia had died two years previously in Bloemfontein, leaving a daughter, Emely, and husband, Henry Morell. Eleanor and her husband lived in Boshof near Kimberley. Her two brothers, Frederick and Charles resided in Bloemfontein. Eliza was unable to attend with husband John Crooks, neither could their sister, Albertijne, who was married to John Riggs.

Stifled sobs could be heard around the packed hall as other people dealt with their own memories of departed loved ones.

"Sampson Daniel?" Dugmore's voice boomed in astonishment across the crowded hall.

The packed room fell silent. Sampson O'Malia Daniel, an original applicant of the 1820 British Settler scheme, stood at the doorway of the hall. He stood proud, leaning on his ivory-handled walking stick. He wore his signature rabbit-fur hat and a neat cravat. The polished chain from his gold pocket-watch hung neatly from his tailored jacket pocket.

On either side of him stood his daughter, Eleanor, and son-in-law, Thomas Webster.

All heads in the audience turned to see who Dugmore was looking at.

"Papa! Papa!" gasped Sophia, wiping away her tears as she ran to the back of the hall.

"You're HOME!"

1820 SETTLER OFFICIAL PASSENGER LIST OF SIR GEORGE OSBORN

Number of Passengers 115 (w = wife c = child)

LIST OF GARDNER'S PARTY

ABBOTT William 39. File Maker
BAILISS Benjamin. 24. Coach Harness Bucklemaker
DUDLEY Edmund 26. Ironmonger
DUDLEY John. 36. Toolmaker. w Sarah 24. c Matilda 8. Francis1. Sarah (born at Sea)
DUGMORE Isaac 34. Clerk. w Maria 36. c Henry 9. Ann 7 William 6. Louisa 4. Caroline 2. John (born at sea)
GARDNER Edward 31.Plater. Mary 31. c Hezekiah 8. James 5. Elizabeth 5 (died at sea)
HARE Mary 42
ROE Robert 30. Carpenter
SEAL William 21. Plater
WILLIAMS Sarah 30
WRIGHT John Cecil 22. Coach Painter

LIST OF MILLS PARTY

CARTER James 34. Blacksmith and farrier. w Sophia 33. C James 2
CURTIS John 27. Sawyer. w Esther 28
FISHER Charles 22. Bricklayer. w Harriet 18
HANES William 26. Farmer
HILLS Charles 38. Gardner. w Elizabeth 45. c James 15. Jane 14. Elizabeth 10. Charles 8. Henry 6
JACKSON Robert 22. Farmer
MILLS Daniel 60. Farmer. w Martha 40. c Martha 16, Harriet 14, Daniel 10. Maria 8. James Dawkins 3. Caroline 1
POTTER William 29. Carpenter. w Hannah 27. c Mary 10. Ann 6
SAMPSON Robert 22. Labourer

LIST OF TURVEY'S PARTY

BURGIS John 38. Farm manager. w Ellen (died at sea). c John 10. William 8. Mary 6. Francis 4. Josiah 2. Eliza 1
CARTWRIGHT Robert 39. Carpenter. w Mary 36
DANIEL John 19. Jeweller
DANIEL Peter Clarke 44. Jeweller. w Eliza 38. c Peter 15. Isabella 14. Thomas 9. Sampson 7. Eliza 4.Ann 2. Frederick 1
DANIEL Sampson 32. Jeweller. w Mary 27. c Sophia 6. Eliza 5. Amelia 3. Robert 1. Isabella (born at sea)
HOLLAND Henry 26. Gem Cutter
KEEVEY John Martin 28. Gardener. w Mary 27. c Matthew 10. Francis 7. Ann 1. Mary (born at sea)
KEMP John 35. Sawyer. w Mary 34. c Nancy 15. John 14. Sophia 11. Thomas 9. James 6.William 4. Ann
MITCHLEY Ann 31
MULLIGAN John 35. Navigator. w Mary 26
PENNELL Thomas 17. Farmer
TURVEY Edward 39. Drawing Master. w Julia 39. c Mary 14. Eliza 11. Edward 9. Louisa 8. George 6
TURVEY John 82. Farmer
WILLY Thomas 25. Carpenter
WRIGHT Benjamin 17. (Stepson of Edward Turvey)
WRIGHT William 24. Ironmonger w. Rosa 24. c Martha 3. William 1. (Stepson of Edward Ford Turvey) Sally 14 (servant)

Author's note: Intensive research into the Daniel family records confirms that Frederick William Daniel was indeed the son of Sampson O'Malia and Amelia Margarith Daniel. However, on the *Sir George Osborn* ship's register of passengers, his nephew, Robert Daniel, is incorrectly listed as their son. Robert Daniel was in fact the son of Peter Clarke Daniel.